DUALITY

DUALITY

A Nick Ross Novel

D. M. LOCKWOOD

ISBN: 0692792430
ISBN 13: 9780692792438

Prologue

Mavis

She loved going to midnight Mass. There was something about entering the church in the middle of the night that felt almost trancelike. The smell of incense, the soft light of flickering candles, the quiet echoes that resonated softly from the movement of shadows, all brought her peace and a sense of relief from the harsh realities of life.

She was raised Southern Baptist but had become enamored with the Catholic Church when her transition took place. It was a priest who had counseled her and helped her come to terms with her way of life.

She'd felt tonight's Mass particularly important and had wanted to talk to Father Geraghty but he was not there. It was her only night off and she welcomed the blue jeans, loose-fitting blouse and sandals she wore, a world away from the tight-fitting sequined costumes she paraded on stage at the Follies.

She'd laughed when she first received the letter telling her she would die on a particular day. It had made reference to a biblical quote that declared people of her kind should be put to death for their sins.

"Crazy fucker," she'd thought and had thrown it in the trash. But now the day had come, and she wasn't so sure. Her tech-savvy boyfriend had taken the letter seriously and kept warning her, trying to get her to go to the police. He had even made her a special necklace to wear that could record conversations. She wore it to keep him happy but couldn't resist making silly comments into it just to drive him crazy. As far as going to the cops, that was a joke.

She lit a candle, left Mass and headed to the nearly deserted parking lot. She noticed a white van parked next to her old Honda but no one was around. Looking down in her purse to search for her keys was the last thing she remembered. A sharp blow to the back of her head sent her tumbling forward.

⨙

A searing pain slices deep behind her eyes and the bitter, oily taste of the rag stuffed in her mouth makes bile rise in the back of her throat as she wakes up. She's cold, naked and roughly bound with braided rope to a large wooden chair, hands tied firmly behind her back, and ankles secured to the chair legs. With her head throbbing and a sick feeling in her stomach, she struggles to look around the small bedroom in what seems to be a cabin. There's a musty smell she can't identify coming from the floor in front of her where stains in the wood run for several feet then stop. Even though the windows are boarded up, a faint fragrance of pine lingers throughout the room from the rough cut timber.

He enters the room carrying several knives and an axe. He slowly walks past her, his eyes staring down at the small table a few feet away. With precision, he sets down his weapons in surgical fashion. She tries to scream and violently thrusts her body back and forth in an effort to get free, her eyes bulging, her breathe short, her face turning red. As the terrifying nightmare besieges her, she begins to shake, her dark skin glistening with sweat. He stands tall before her wearing a long, silver robe, his black hair slicked back hiding the faint beginnings of gray, his chiseled face emotionless.

The letter wasn't some joke. It was real. And the monster of this nightmare is standing right in front of her with a knife in his hand. He stares into her eyes as he raises both of his arms up toward the heavens.

"All these things I do, I do in the name of God. He is my only master and I follow his will by carrying out his laws. Therefore you must know: If a man lies with a man, as he lies with a woman, both of them have committed an abomination: they shall surely be put to death: their blood shall be upon them."

She screams a muffled scream that no one can hear, the sound only resonating in her mind. She struggles to bounce the chair away as he turns toward her with the razor-sharp stiletto. Slowly, he makes an incision and she blacks out.

Within minutes both of her breast implants have been carved from her body and thrown on the floor in front of her. When she regains consciousness she looks down at her chest and tries to scream but can only feel her heart pounding in her ears. Her eyes sting as tears run down her cheeks, she tries desperately to break free.

He steps up to her again and reaches down between her legs. She pulls her legs together but the rope is too tight. In one swift motion he slices off the last of her identity and tosses it on the floor.

Blood runs down her legs and pools at her feet as the horror overcomes her. She's trembling so hard the panic she feels makes her gasp for breath as she stares at her mutilated body. When she looks up, he's gone. Trying to move is pointless, and her thoughts of the inevitable paralyze her with fear. She prays death will come soon and begins to lose consciousness again when she hears him walk up behind her.

"In the name of the Father, the Son and the Holy Spirit, I am here to carry out your commandments, Lord."

He grabs her short, curly hair yanking her head back with one hand as the other grips the stiletto and stabs it deeply into her neck just below the left ear. The blood begins to run down her chest covering the necklace and rendering it useless. He slowly slices her throat until he hits a main artery. Blood spurts out several feet in front of her as he draws the knife slowly across to the bottom of her other ear. The gushing red tide has turned into a stream. She gasps and shakes violently as the blood pours down her body, pooling on the floor. Her eyes roll as her head drops to her chest, breathless she collapses lifeless and still.

He casually walks to the table, picks up the axe and turns back to her. He unties her arms and places the right one back on the chair, looks up and shouts: "For the next chosen one, my Lord." The axe wields through the air directed downward on to her right arm, severing her hand at the wrist.

A few days later the body will be found at a landfill just outside Vegas.

CHAPTER 1

Happy Halloween

It's three in the morning and I can smell the cheap whiskey as I sit at the end of the bar in some Vegas dive. It's well off the Strip on the west side of town, a favorite watering hole where many of the late night show biz crowd go to get away from the selfie-crazed tourists.

I knew when I walked into this joint I was going back in time. Dusty, faded, black and white photos of Frank, Sammy and Dean, each enjoying life with a cigarette in one hand and a cocktail in the other, are the first things you see when you walk through the door.

The place looks like it could have been a favorite hangout for the Rat Pack in its heyday but then most of the old bars in Vegas do. All it takes is tobacco-stained paint, tarnished lights and years of neglect or maybe indifference to look like an old Hollywood movie set.

The bartenders are all male. Most of them look like ex-linebackers with flat-top hair cuts, thick necks, and squared-off shoulders. They all sport the same sleazy black pants, starched and stained white dress shirts, flimsy bow-ties and over-sized vests with the bottom button undone.

The temperature in this place borders on freezing, a common practice in many bars since it makes women's nipples get hard. Good business strategy if you ask me.

Since I walked in I've already heard two Sinatra songs, "New York, New York" and "The Way You Look Tonight", one of my all-time favorites. Dean Martin's, "Ain't That a Kick in the Head" is on now. I could listen to this music all night.

The showgirls are starting to filter in after their last performances of the evening but the way they move it's hard to tell if the performance is really over. Their long strides, wispy hand motions and deliberate turns of the head accompany quick requests for cocktails.

I'm here to meet one of these ladies who claims she needs my services. We'll see about that. I've gotten mixed up with some of these showgirls in the past and it never ends well. Maybe I'm a slow learner when it comes to women or maybe it's just my run of bad luck with them lately. I don't know.

I order tonic water with a twist so it looks like I'm drinking. I can't risk another DUI. As I look down the dimly lit bar I see a beautiful woman walking toward me. She seems to sway from side to side like she's being carried by the wind. As she nears I see a gorgeous blonde, tall and slender, with classic high cheek bones and deep-set almond eyes blue as the sky. She doesn't move like the others, she has a more determined and sultry air about her that says, "Give me what I want." She must be the woman I'm here to meet. At least I hope so.

"Are you Nick Ross?" she says as she lights one of those long, skinny cigarettes Vegas women seem to favor.

"That's me. You must be, Roxy Lynn. Pull up a seat. Can I get you a drink?"

"Thank you, but no." She sits down, puts her purse on the bar and crosses her long, shapely legs showing just the right amount of thigh.

I should probably make some small talk and get to know her better but it's the other side of three in the morning and I'm beat, ready for the rack. So I stick to business.

"What can I do for you, Miss Lynn?"

"I need a good P.I. and I'm told you're one of the best."

From the corner of my eye I see two men enter the bar and sit down a few tables away. Being observant is crucial in my line of work and these guys look suspicious. They're scanning the room but haven't ordered drinks just sitting quietly looking like soldiers straight out of *The Godfather.*

"Thanks, Miss Lynn. What exactly can I help you with?"

"I need you to find out who wants to kill me."

"And why do you think someone wants to kill you?"

"Here, read this," she says handing me a slip of paper. "I found it in my dressing room last night when my act was over."

As I look at the note I'm also a bit curious about Miss Lynn's body language. On the one hand, she's clearly scared and very nervous. On the other hand, she seems a bit sturdier than most women in receipt of a death threat would be. She also seems a little impatient and keeps moving around in her chair while playing with a strand of her hair.

I need to find out more, whether this is a real threat or not.

"This note says you're going to die on October 31. That's Halloween. Could just be a prank."

"No, no I'm positive it's not," she says leaning towards me slightly to make her point.

"How's that?" I ask trying not to be too obvious as I glance over my shoulder at the two guys. Still there, still suspicious.

"My friend Mavis Rodgers got a similar note a month ago and now she's disappeared."

"Mavis who?"

"Rogers, Mavis Rodgers. You know her?"

"Uh, no, no I don't. Sounds like you should go to the police."

"I can't go to the police, Mr. Ross. I have a few problems with my past."

"Look, Miss Lynn, I don't really work as a bodyguard if that's what you're looking for."

"No, no I'm not. I've already taken care of that," pointing toward the two men who'd caught my attention a few minutes ago. Mystery solved, I think to myself as I turn my full attention back to Roxy.

"I've been told there are others besides Mavis. I want you to find out who's doing this before it's too late for me or anyone else. And please, call me Roxy."

"OK, Roxy. I'll look into it but I need you to be completely honest with me."

"I understand," she says taking one last drag from her ciga-rette. "Would you please walk me to my car?"

We stand and start walking towards the door with Roxy's two protectors following close behind. When we get to the car her driver opens the door and I watch her get in. Showgirls, al-ways performing. She extends her hand and I lean forward to take it. "Thank you, Nick," she says with a firm handshake.

"The 31st is only ten days from now, Roxy, so we don't have much time. Be at my office tomorrow at three and we'll start piecing this together. And bring a list of friends and enemies, especially the enemies."

"Will do. See you tomorrow, Nick."

Driving home I'm having second thoughts about taking the case. My instincts keep telling me something isn't right, or maybe it's just that name from the past: Mavis Rodgers.

▲

The next morning I walk down to Ronnie's Bistro for my usual breakfast. Ronnie's is a popular little hole in the wall run by Jasper Watts and his partner Rick. It's frequented by the wannabe entertainment crowd as well as a lot of the local LGBT community. Jasper's a tough little compact guy who stands about five feet two but acts like he's six five. I like the place because the people-watching is superb and the cof-fee is strong, black and hot, the best in town. I also get a lot of good info from Jasper who seems to know everybody in Vegas.

"Hey, Jasper, how goes it?"

"Good morning, Nick, or should I say good afternoon? Looks like somebody had a late night."

"Yeah, it's the business I'm in. Say, you happen to know a showgirl named Roxy Lynn?"

"Roxy, oh sure I know her. She's gorgeous, though the term showgirl might not be accurate."

"What do you mean?"

"Let's just say Miss Lynn doesn't have all the right parts required to be a showgirl."

"You mean…"

"Yep, she's a he."

CHAPTER 2

DIRTY LAUNDRY

I arrive at my office around two-thirty. Alice, my secretary, is on the phone ordering shoes or something. She gives me a little wave and hands me my messages, all without looking up.

"Nice to see you too, Alice. Don't let me disturb you."

I grab a cup of stale coffee and sit down at my desk. I think about the pint of Jim Beam in the lower left hand drawer but decide to pass for now and take it black.

I see Roxy enter and Alice is kind enough to put her shoe purchase on hold while she brings her over to my office.

"Good afternoon, Mr. Ross. I trust you slept well?"

"Have a seat, Roxy, and please call me Nick. The last person to call me Mr. was a judge and that didn't go well."

Roxy sits down and looks up at me with a wry grin. "So, Nick, have you figured it out yet?"

"Figured what out?"

"You're staring at me looking for clues. Does she have an Adam's apple, is there a trace of facial hair, any tone in her voice? But you're not coming up with anything are you?"

I don't say a word. I just keep looking at Roxy.

"So how did you figure it out?"

"A friend of mine knows who you are and he told me. I was surprised to say the least."

"Ah, I see. So, you OK with it?"

"Of course I am. I wouldn't have taken the case if I wasn't. You're my client. I work for you. It's not my job to judge you, I'm here to help you."

"OK, Nick, where do we start?"

"How about a little history lesson. You tell me what you've been up to for the last ten years."

For the next hour I listen as Roxy tells me everything including her transition from Raymond Tisdale to Roxy Lynn. She's very thorough except for one thing.

"That's a lot of good info, Roxy, but you still haven't told me what's in your past that's keeping you from going to the police."

"No, I haven't and I'm not going to. All you need to know is it could land me in jail. If I tell you we'd both be in trouble. Don't worry, Nick, I didn't kill anybody. I just don't want to wind up in a real life episode of 'Orange is the New Black'."

"Guess I can live with that for now but it doesn't mean we won't revisit it in the future. In the meantime I'll start doing some background checks on your enemies list but you should get prepared to disappear for a while if need be."

"I don't want to run, Nick. I've been running all my life."

"Let's hope you don't have to, we'll see. Just take one step at a time, OK? Here's my cell number. Check in with me every day."

After Roxy leaves I'm not far behind. When I walk by Alice's desk she's off the phone but now she's doing her nails.

"Any messages, Alice?"

"Oh yeah, your parole officer called and said he'll see you at the meeting."

"He's not my parole officer, Alice, he's my sponsor."

"Whatever, he sounds like a parole officer."

"Don't know how I could live without you, Alice. See ya later."

Part of my probation requirement for the DUI that lucky me got, is attending AA meetings every week for the next six months. It requires me to get a sponsor who will sign my card every week and verify my sobriety as best he can. In return for this I get a temporary license that allows me to drive when I'm working, which is any time I want.

At my first meeting I was somewhat perplexed by the nature of the group and how things were run. Nobody said their last name and every time someone spoke the first words out of their mouth were: "I'm an alcoholic." And then there was this whole thing about God as you understand Him. One guy said that a tree in his yard was God. Then a woman stood up and said her dog was God. Really? That dog spelled backward thing? All I knew was I had to find a sponsor to get my card signed.

Walter Pickles was my choice. A stout man in his seventies with pure white hair and rosy cheeks that set off his alabaster skin. He seemed to have a perpetual smile on his face and when he laughed his whole body would bounce up, down and sideways at the same time. Walter is what they call in AA an old timer. Having been sober some 25 years he's seen many a drunk come and go.

So here I am at my second meeting. I look around the room searching for Walter when I see him waving at me from a corner table.

"Hello, Nick, come over here and sit by me."

"Hi, Walter, how's it goin'?"

"I'm fine, Nick, how about you? Did you read about the first step in the Big Book I gave you at the last meeting?"

"Well to be honest with you, no, I haven't got around to it yet."

"That's fine. This meeting is a first step meeting so you'll hear from others how they were powerless over alcohol and how their lives became unmanageable."

"Great, Walt, hey could you please sign my card?"

After finishing her last gig of the night Roxy walks back to her dressing room where she finds a large bouquet of red roses.

"Oh my, looks like I have a secret admirer." She plucks the card from the vase holding the roses and opens it. It reads, "Nine days left."

CHAPTER 3

DEVILS AND DEMONS

Every Sunday I drive over to Henderson to see my old man. Fifteen years ago he and my mother moved there from New York. She loved the idea of a planned retirement community but my old man hated it. A retired detective from the NYPD, he still misses the Big Apple. The energy of the "city that never sleeps" is a hard thing to forget, especially when you move to a elderly neighborhood that seems to languish in continuous naps.

Since my mom passed three years ago Pop has started to get involved in some of the community's planned activities but still bristles when I bring them up. I'm the only family he has left so he's committed to living out his life here.

"Those things are going to kill you, Pop."

"Well, something's gonna do it, might as well enjoy myself." He takes another drag from his Marlboro Light, a concession he made five years ago when he stopped smoking unfiltered Camels.

"So, Pop, I'm working on a case that has some resemblance to the David Berkowitz case you worked on back in the 70's."

"Oh yeah, 'Son of Sam'. One crazy son of a bitch. Thought he was possessed by demons but in reality he just hated women, especially his mother."

"Why do you think he started killing?"

Pop shrugs. "He got off on it."

"So what was he like?"

"You want the list?" He takes a drag from his cigarette and looks up exhaling slowly.

I wait for the smoke to clear then utter a simple, "Sure."

"Abandoned by his mother, multiple foster families, abused, then finally adopted but didn't fit in. A loner, a bully, anti-social, aggressive, unattractive, depressed, and oh yeah, he had sex once in his life and managed to get the clap."

"OK, I get it. So is there any common thread with serial killers?"

"Well, yes and no. They may have some of the traits I just rattled off but then lots of people do and they don't become killers. That's what makes them so hard to catch." He flicks the ashes off his cigarette into a Vegas-themed tray beside him and takes another drag. This isn't going to be easy.

▲

On my way back into town I decide to take a detour on the chance I might run into some old friends.

Lyle Carson and Mitch Sutton are watching the game at O'Connell's Pub, a watering hole where lots of Vegas cops hang out. Even though I left the force five years ago I still stop by to swap stories, place some bets and down a few cold ones when I can.

Lyle is your stereotypical detective for every crime novel ever written. He's been divorced three times. Has a daughter who won't talk to him. Always in debt from gambling too much and lives in a one bedroom apartment that has pizza boxes piled to the ceiling. Maybe that's why Lyle perpetually smells like pepperoni.

Mitch, on the other hand, has been married for 33 years, has a son and a daughter who admire him and a wife who adores him.

"Hey, Nick, where ya been? Haven't seen ya for a while."

"Just been takin' it easy, Mitch. Layin' low."

"Oh yeah that's right, the DUI. Sorry man, I tried to fix it but these days it's easier to get a murder charge dropped than a DUI."

Lyle raises his glass and tips it towards me. "Well, if it ain't the super sleuth. Where you been, Dick Tracy?"

"Hey, Lyle, how you doin'?"

"Good as anybody could that has to hang out with Mitch all the time."

"Right, Lyle, like you're some prize. So, Nick, you want a drink?"

"Sure, tonic with a twist."

"Wow, bet that packs a wallop, you on the wagon or just goin' sweet on us?"

"Fuck you, Lyle. Don't suppose you guys got any info on a Mavis Rodgers, the showgirl that's missing?"

"Oh, the tranny that got the letter. We can't do much until there's a body, right now she's just a missing person, but Mitch here thinks she may be linked to the murders in Reno a few months ago."

"Let me know if you come up with anything, would ya?"

Lyle leans in and with his right hand rubs his earlobe between his thumb and forefinger, a Lyle habit from way back. "You got yourself involved in this, Nick?"

"Let's just say I'm looking into some things and leave it at that for now."

▲

Roxy looks in the mirror, takes off her make-up and ties her hair up in a bun. With the make-up gone from her face the transformation begins. From her dresser drawer she takes out the tight-fitting elastic straps she uses to flatten out her breasts and slips them on. Blue jeans, ball cap, a T-shirt and flip-flops complete the transition back to Raymond Tisdale.

She hasn't driven in years, and the borrowed car is unfamiliar, but the drive out to the desert is mesmerizing. As the air gets cleaner, the stars grow brighter and the mountains become looming shadows emerging in the distance. Roxy pulls on to a side road where the sign directs her to a large tent. "Come and worship" it says. "We are Brothers and Sisters of the Original Church of God, in Jesus' Name, with the Reverend Wesley Kootz."

She enters the tent just as the music is starting. A quartet of black gospel singers dressed in long purple robes take the stage and begin to sway as they belt out Jesus' and Hallelujah's in harmony. A spotlight follows Wesley Kootz as he walks onto the stage dressed in a white sequined jumpsuit and a dark blue cape with a large gold cross spread across it. It's an outfit that would make Elvis proud. The congregation cheers and shouts "Praise the Lord!"

"Welcome brothers and sisters, glory be to God!" The Reverend raises his arms and takes command of the stage mesmerizing his followers with his deep baritone voice. The crowd erupts with a joyful roar that crescendos into a jubilant "Hallelujah!"

"Behold the scriptures of brother's Luke and Mark. And these signs shall follow them that believe. In my name shall they cast out devils they shall speak with new tongues. Take up the serpent and if they drink any deadly thing it shall not hurt them. They shall lay hands on the sick and they shall recover. Can I get a Hallelujah?" Kootz commands.

The tent roars back with "Hallelujah" and "Praise be to Jesus!" Kootz moves to the center of the stage where a hand-woven basket stands. He removes the lid reaches in and pulls out a four-foot rattlesnake. He grabs the snake with both hands, raises it over his head and says: "Behold the devil and cast him out."

The roar in the tent escalates as people throw their hands in the air and dance in the aisles as Roxy moves toward the front row.

▲

My phone buzzes and I see it's my new client. The text on my cell reads: *Checking in like you said. Looking into something Mavis told me about. Back tomorrow to fill you in.*

I'm sure glad to know Roxy took me seriously when I told her to stay in touch but who the hell's the detective here?

The next morning I'm having coffee at Ronnie's when my phone rings, it's Lyle.

"Nick, we got a note last night about Mavis. It said: 'If you're still looking for Mavis you can find her where the rest of the trash is.' He signed it *Leviticus 20:13*. They found her this morning in the Apex landfill just outside of town. I'm heading there now."

"Thanks, Lyle, talk to you later." Shit, this isn't a game anymore we've got a killer in town and Roxy has a real threat.

I put my phone down as Jasper is walking up with my breakfast.

"You OK, Nick? You look a little peaked," Jasper says as he sets the plate down.

"They found Mavis Rodgers' body in the landfill outside of town this morning, Jasper."

"Oh no, poor girl. That damn place has more dead bodies than Forest Lawn."

"Hey, Jasper, you know the Bible?

"Oh hell yeah, my old man was a Holy Roller. He made us memorize dozens of verses, why?"

"Are you familiar with Leviticus 20:13?"

"Yes, sir. Especially that one, it goes like this: 'If a man lies with a man as one lies with a woman, both of them have done what is detestable. They must be put to death; their blood will be on their own heads.' "

CHAPTER 4

REUNION AT THE APEX

A few hours later I decide to drive out to the Apex landfill hoping to find out from Lyle how Mavis met her demise. In all my years in Vegas I can't say I've ever had the pleasure of visiting the city's landfill. I'm told it's one of the largest in the world. At 200 feet deep and 300 acres wide it looks like some kind of a development project where you would expect to see houses popping up anytime, but the 105 degree heat creates such a stench it quickly reminds you it's a landfill.

I pull into the entrance and talk to the officer in charge. He recognizes me and lets me through. I drive as far as I can and then get out and walk to the crime scene where Lyle and Captain Tucker are talking to one of the employees who found Mavis. Tucker is my old boss. A 50-something, never-been-married, mother-worshipping asshole who lives for his job.

"Lyle, can I talk to you a minute?"

Tucker and Lyle both turn toward me and Tucker takes a step forward.

"What do you think you're doing here, Ross? This is police business, get the hell out of here."

Lyle steps in between Tucker and me, putting out his hands.

"Take it easy, Tuck. Nick's got some info that might be helpful to us."

"Well, keep him away from the crime scene and keep him away from me, got it?"

"Yeah, yeah, Tuck. I got it."

"What the hell crawled up his ass?" I ask Lyle as we walk away.

"You know what it's about Nick, same old shit he's never let go of from five years ago."

"He's an asshole, that's history. So what ya' got here, Lyle?"

"It's pretty bad. Who ever did this is one sick son of a bitch."

"How bad?"

"Her throat's been slit from ear to ear, her breasts have been removed and her right hand's been severed."

"Damn, Lyle…"

"Oh, that's not all. Her dick was cut off and stuffed down her throat. That doesn't sound right does it?" Lyle scratches his head and grimaces.

"Jesus, what a sick bastard. You think this is some sort of a revenge killing?"

"No, it's almost surgical. The person who did this knew what they were doing. Ballistics is combing through everything but I'll bet it's going to be a waste of time. I highly doubt she was killed here."

"Hang on, Lyle, I got a call. Roxy, where the hell have you been?"

"Sorry, Nick, there was something I had to check out."

"Check out? I'm the detective, remember?"

"Look I think I may be on to something, can we meet later?"

"My office, four o'clock."

I get to my office a few minutes before four and see Alice is deep into her Facebook page.

"Any messages for me, Alice?"

"Yeah, your parole officer called again about another meeting and that reporter from the Sun called."

"You mean Kate Simon?"

"Yeah, that's her."

Kate and I go back about five years. She was just getting started with the Sun as a cub reporter when my partner was murdered. Despite the department's pledge to find his killer, no one has ever been charged.

Kate is the only person I know who hasn't given up on solving the case besides me. And she never will since my partner was Kate's brother.

At first Kate blamed me for her brother Mark's death as did several of the detectives in my division. It's only been in the last year that she's realized I couldn't have helped him and that has led us to become friends, close friends.

"Could I speak with Kate Simon, please?"

"Simon here, how can I help you?"

"Kate, it's Nick, Alice said you called. What's up?"

"So you decided to call me back."

"Sorry, I know it's been awhile."

"I'm getting ready to break a big story and it's going to make some people very unhappy."

"OK, I'm listening."

"Well it seems the Reno Police Department has been sitting on the fact there have been four murders of transgender women up there in the past several months. All have the same M.O. and all were sent a letter telling them they would be killed."

"So you're saying there's a serial killer on the loose."

"That's right and you know what, they're not that good for tourism."

"So where do I come in?"

"I had a lead on a possible murder this morning. An employee from Apex called me and told me about a body that was found in the landfill. He said it was one of those shemales he'd seen down on the strip. I drove out to the landfill to check on the story but the cops wouldn't let me in. I did happen to see you leaving though."

"Oh, really?" Here it comes.

"C'mon, Nick, the cops won't tell me what's going on but you know something don't you."

"So what are you doing for dinner tonight?"

"And now you're hitting on me? Damn it, Nick, tell me what you know."

"Meet me at Ronnie's around seven. Gotta'go, I have an appointment."

As Roxy enters the office Alice glances up and asks how she can help him. Still dressed as Raymond, Alice doesn't realize its Roxy.

"Would you tell Mr. Ross that Roxy Lynn is here for our appointment?"

"I'm sorry. Roxy Lynn? You're the same person who was here the other day?" Alice looks confused and doesn't know quite what to say.

"Yes, dear, I just don't have my make-up on today."

Roxy enters my office as I spin around in my chair to greet her.

"Roxy, oh. . . you're not in…. I mean, should I call you Raymond?"

"Is this too confusing for you, Nick? Sorry I didn't have time to change."

"No, no, have a seat. I need to tell you something." I hate delivering bad news but I have no choice.

"This doesn't sound good."

"No, it's not. They found Mavis' body this morning in the landfill."

"Damn, damn, damn! Why do people do shit like this?" Roxy shakes her head and drops it to her chest.

"There're a lot of sickos out there, Roxy. Sorry, I know she was your friend."

"What did he do to her? What did that son of a bitch do to her?" Roxy takes a deep breath and shakes her head again, bending over elbows on her knees.

"I know you're angry, Roxy, but details won't make it any better. I promise if anything is made public you'll hear about it first. Can I get you something, water, coffee, bourbon?"

"No, I'm all right, let's just go on." She takes another deep breath and sits up straight.

"So tell me what you found out."

"Well, I remember Mavis telling me she was seeing a guy named Bobby. She met him in Reno a few months ago when she was visiting a friend. He was traveling with some revival group led by that infamous snake handler, Wesley Kootz.

"Who the hell is Wesley Kootz?"

"He's that preacher who led the fight to outlaw homosexuality in Kentucky."

"What the hell is a gay guy doing with a bunch like that?" This is getting weird.

"He ran their audio and lighting for them and, believe me, they had no idea he was gay. Bobby's 250 pounds of solid muscle and once was drafted by the Rams. Anyhow, the show moved down to Laughlin from Reno a couple months ago and that's when he and Mavis started seeing a lot of each other."

"How long after that did Mavis go missing?"

"Just recently. Maybe a few days."

"Have you talked to Bobby since then?"

"That's where I went yesterday. I drove out to the revival hoping I would get a chance to talk to him."

"And?" I can tell by the look on her face it's not good news.

"He's gone and nobody would tell me anything."

"Seems like a good idea for me to pay Reverend Kootz a visit," I say to Roxy but I'm thinking, something's not right.

The whole thing smells bad. I need to see this Kootz guy face to face.

Just then Roxy's phone buzzes, she has a text: *Eight days left, enjoy your week.*

CHAPTER 5

Crazier Than a Koot Owl

After Roxy leaves I gather up my things to head out but first I stop by Alice's desk.

"Hey Alice, could you get some of those little Hershey Kisses and put them in a bowl over on the coffee table. I've been craving sweets lately, especially chocolate."

"That's cause you're not drinking anymore. Your body wants sugar."

"Gee, thanks. So when did you become the medical expert?"

"Let's just say there are certain things I know." Alice rolls her eyes at me and smiles.

"Good night, Alice. I'm going to a meeting and then having dinner with Kate. Forward my emails to me, OK?"

"Oh, you going to one of those AAA meetings?"

"Yeah, Alice, I'm going to an Alcoholics Anonymous Automobile Club meeting, see ya."

⚑

I walk into the room right before the meeting is ready to start. There are probably 15 people sitting around several large tables. Coffee seems to be the drink of choice. I spot my sponsor Walter Pickles over by the back wall and wave at him. He waves back motioning me to join him.

The chairperson calls the meeting to order. "Would everyone please stand."

Everyone gets up and after a moment of silence the recital of the Serenity Prayer follows. The chair then asks if there are any newcomers here tonight. He quickly qualifies that by explaining the definition of a newcomer as anyone with less than 30 days sobriety.

I reluctantly raise my hand and he asks me to introduce myself.

"Hi, my name is Nick and I, uh, well, I'm here because the court ordered me to."

Everyone in the room responds with a "Hi, Nick, welcome!" I'm really kind of shocked, thinking what I said might not be acceptable, but no one seems to care.

And so it goes from person to person, each telling their story or talking about whatever is on their mind. I listen but quite frankly can't connect with some of the things that are being said and the whole God thing is a little overwhelming. It's not that I'm an atheist or anything, I'm just not big on organized religion and that's what a lot of this feels like. One thing I do find amazing is everyone's ability to laugh at themselves and some of the stupid shit they've done.

Then it's my sponsor Walter Pickles' turn to speak. I'm sitting next him so I can get my card signed but I also feel comfortable around him which is more than I can say for some of the others.

"Hi, my name is Walter and I'm an alcoholic. I'd like to say a few words about my higher power."

"Hi, Walter," the group responds in unison.

Now I'm wondering if old Walt has the power to read my mind, or if this is just a coincidence, but I find myself actually interested in what he has to say.

"When I came into AA it wasn't because I wanted to or because I had found God. Nope, I just wanted to survive and knew I had no choice other than death. I hated God and all I thought He stood for. The way I see it, religion has killed more people on this planet than anything man has ever invented. So I knew I would need to find some sort of higher power I could relate to. First, it was my sponsor, then it was the meetings. Eventually I began to see 'the God' in everyone, even the ones who couldn't bring themselves to believe. For me it was about acceptance. That was the key to my higher power."

The chairperson stands and thanks Walter for his contribution. "Would everyone please rise and join hands together in the Lord's Prayer?" he says.

I stand and join in. I'm less reluctant than before but holding hands with other guys is a little strange.

⋏

When I get to Ronnie's, Kate is already there talking to Jasper. I walk to the table and give her a hug before I sit down. She hugs me back which I take as a good sign.

"Well, I see you got here early. Has she been pumping you for information, Jasper?"

"She's been trying but I told her she'd have to talk to you first. So we've just been talking about hair styles. And oh, by the way, Kate, love yours."

"Hair styles? Yeah, OK." I'm wondering how anybody could talk about hairstyles for more than 30 seconds.

"Can I get you anything to drink, Nick?"

"I'll take a tonic with a twist."

"Comin' right up," says Jasper as he turns and heads for the bar.

"Wow, you're taking this abstinence thing seriously aren't you?"

"I don't have much choice at this point, Kate." That's what comes out of my mouth but what I really want to say is, "Bring me a Scotch rocks".

"We always have a choice, Nick. It's just that some of our choices are better than others."

"You sound a little judgmental. Am I talking to the reporter or my friend?"

"Both. So what do you have on the dead woman in the landfill?" Kate fiddles with her pen as she pulls out a notepad.

"If I tell you and you print it they're going to know you got it from me."

"No they won't. I'll quote a source from Apex who wishes to remain anonymous."

"Well, it looks like whoever did the murders in Reno is now in Vegas. A transgender named Mavis Rodgers was murdered and dumped at the landfill a few days ago. She had body parts surgically removed like the others up in Reno. She also got the same letter telling her exactly when she was going to be murdered."

"So that makes five and the damn cops and the FBI haven't released anything to the public yet. The FBI's involved, aren't they?"

"They are now. Lyle called me and said he talked to a station chief who was really pissed off that they were just now finding out about the Reno murders. Somebody's ass is in big trouble."

"Well, they're going to find out a lot more when my story breaks tomorrow."

"Look, there's something else, Kate, but you can't use it yet.

"All right. What is it?"

"A note was sent to the cops telling them where they could find Mavis's body. It was signed with a bible quote, Leviticus 20:13."

"What's that?"

"It's essentially an anti-gay biblical rant about men lying with men and how they should be put to death. Jasper can quote it exactly if you want to hear it."

"So what do we have here, Nick? A serial killer who can perform surgery, is a homophobic fundamentalist and can kill you even though you know exactly when it's going to happen?"

"Yep, that's about it. After dinner I'm driving out to Laughlin to follow up on a lead. You want to come along?"

"What sort of lead?" Kate looks at me quizzically not quite sure if she wants in.

"Mavis had a boyfriend named Bobby who works for a pay-for-pray preacher named Wesley Kootz. He's got a nice little revival business set up in the desert outside of Laughlin. It seems

Bobby has gone missing since the murder and I'd like to ask the Reverend Kootz a few questions."

"Yeah, sure, I'll go."

There's something about the desert at night that's absolutely magical. Away from the city lights the stars put on a show that make Vegas pale in comparison. As the moon rises in the evening sky, the stars color the landscape in hues of purple and red. I want to reach out and touch them like I'm in some kind of fairy tale but then the wonder of the immense, never-ending darkness hits me and suddenly I feel very small.

I want the top down but Kate doesn't. She wins. One of my passions in life is classic cars. They're all I've ever owned. Right now my ride is a red '66 T-Bird with the iconic wire wheels. There's something about this kind of car that just makes me feel comfortable. Maybe because it stems from a time when things were simpler or maybe I want to be different than the BMW and Mercedes crowd. All I know is my T-Bird has tons more character than the plastic look-alikes on the road today.

We don't talk much on the drive out. Kate seems unusually quiet like something is on her mind. She also looks a little pale like she might be getting sick.

"Kate, are you feeling OK? You look a little pale."

"Oh no, I'm fine. Sometimes I get a little carsick that's all."

I put on some music so we can relax and enjoy the ride. We're both jazz fans so Miles, Brubeck and Ray Brown serenade us under starry skies.

As we approach the turn-off for the traveling God-and-Serpent show I can see the tent lit up down the road in the distance. It looks just like the big top at a circus.

"Look, Kate, I think we need to have a little plan here. Reverend Kootz may not be all that amiable to seeing a private eye asking questions about one of his employees. How about you saying the paper is thinking about running an article on the show so you'd like to interview him."

"Oh, so that's why you asked me along." Kate gets a little hissy and looks down her nose at me.

"No, but it does give me a better shot at snooping around."

"So what role are you playing? An assistant or my idiot brother?"

"Real funny, Simon. I'll grab my camera equipment out of the trunk and be your photographer." I want to pinch her cute little butt and kiss her but I'd probably get slapped.

We make our way to the tent entrance where a very large man stops us and asks what our business is. Kate flashes her press credentials and tells him she'd like to interview Reverend Kootz. He looks us over then tells us to wait until he comes back.

"Don't worry, Nick, we'll get in, a guy like Kootz never turns down the opportunity for publicity."

The large man is walking back toward us when he stops and waves his hand for us to come in. We follow him through the back of the tent to a luxury coach that looks fit for a rock star. "Wait here," he says over his shoulder as he climbs up into the coach. Within minutes the door flies back open and the

Reverend Wesley Kootz appears at the top of the stairs in full costume looking like the consummate Elvis impersonator.

"Come in. Come in, brother and sister. Welcome, I'm Wesley Kootz and you are?"

"I'm Kate Simon reporter for the *Las Vegas Sun* and this is my photographer Nick."

"Welcome Kate and Nick, have a seat. What can I do for you?"

"I'd like to ask a few questions about you and your show while my photographer takes some pictures. Would that be all right?"

"Certainly, feel free." Kootz is beaming at the chance for publicity.

I snap a few shots of Kootz then excuse myself to go back out and take some shots of the tent while Kate begins her interview. They're just breaking down some of the equipment from the last show as I make my way over to the sound engineer.

"Hey, how's it going? I'm Nick. My paper is doing a piece on your show."

"Oh hi. I'm Jack, can I help you?"

"Big tent. About how many people do you get in here a night?"

"Place holds up to 300 though they tell me they get more on a good night."

"How long you been with the show?"

"Just started a few days ago, they needed somebody right away when the other guy up and quit on them."

"Quit, huh? Did you get to meet the guy first?"

"Nah, he was already gone when I got here. Funny thing though, he left most of his equipment behind. That's a real strange thing for an engineer to do." I make a note of that last comment.

Walking around to the stage I snap a few more shots when a young Hispanic boy who had been sweeping up approaches me.

"You find Bobby? You here cause I call?" The kid seems excited and nervous at the same time.

"I don't know what you're talking about, I'm a photographer." I figure playing dumb is the best thing to do right now. And I'm quite good at it.

"I call police tell them Bobby missing. They say no, I need to prove. I tell them Bobby don't leave like this he my friend. They say no."

"So you think something happened to him?"

"It not right here, I know. Bobby don't leave like this. He not afraid of nothing. I know, he my friend. You help find Bobby, yes?" The poor kid is now practically pleading with me.

"Look," I say to him, "take this card, put it in your pocket and tomorrow call the number on it. A friend of mine will help you."

"Yes, but they find out it me that call, I get big trouble here."

"I'll talk to my friend. Nobody will find out about you."

As I make my way back to the coach I can hear Kootz rambling on about the last days and how this country is being besieged by the devil and his disciples. As I walk in I can tell Kate is ready to get the hell out of here.

"I think I got all we need, Reverend. I'll let you know if the paper decides to run the article. You got everything Nick?" Kate's walking out as she's talking.

"I'm good."

"Well, God bless you, my dear. May he shine his light on you and keep you safe in your travels. Praise be to Jesus."

In the car on the way back I can hardly stop Kate from talking. She tells me about the interview and what Kootz had to say about everything from our government to gay marriage.

"I tell you this guy is crazy as a loon. Did you see his right hand? He lost two fingers from snake bites. Maybe I really should do a piece on him."

"Well, I think I found out what I need to know. Bobby left in a hurry, like he was running from something or somebody." As the words come out of my mouth I notice a change in Kate's demeanor.

Kate goes quiet for a few minutes, just looking out the window. Suddenly she turns, looks at me and says, "I'm pregnant."

"What? You're what? Do you know whose it…". Before the words even leave my mouth I realize what a stupid and insensitive question that is.

"Do I know whose it is? Well, let's see, I was in San Francisco a few months ago, maybe it's one of the '49ers. I'd have to check their roster. Do I know whose it is? You asshole, it's yours."

I'm stunned. I don't know what to say but I know that anything I do say will probably be the wrong thing.

"Jesus, Kate, I'm sorry. It's just that we were only together that one time."

"You mean the time we both got drunk and hopped in the sack with each other then you didn't talk to me for a week? Or return my phone calls or texts? And when I finally hear from you, you give me that crap about just wanting to be friends? That time?"

I knew I'd say the wrong thing. I try again.

"I'm sorry. I really liked you and it scared the hell out of me. I've had a very hard time with relationships since my wife died. I was afraid I'd hurt you."

"Well, guess what? You did. I don't know what to do, Nick. I wasn't going to tell you, it just came out."

CHAPTER 6

EMILY

The ride back to Vegas is quiet but very tense. My mind is flooded with thoughts, one question after another, questions that can't be answered. I wonder if Kate is feeling the same way so I try to say something to her but the words just won't come out. When we finally arrive at her apartment I pull over and turn off the engine.

We both turn to face each other wondering who will be the first to break the silence. Kate wins.

"Look, don't worry about it," she says. "I'll handle it. It's not your problem."

"Kate, c'mon. Don't do this to yourself. We can work it out OK? I just need some time."

"We all need time, don't we? The thing is, for most of us there's never enough." Kate turns away brushing a tear from her cheek.

"Look, Kate, let me call you tomorrow. We can get together and talk. There are things I need to tell you about me and my wife Emily."

▲

On my way home I try to think about Kate. Try to get my mind wrapped around what is happening, but all I can think about is Emily.

It seems like every time I start to get close to a woman thoughts of Emily come rushing back into my life. Her touch, her smell, the way she moved still haunt me, whispering memories of a love I can never forget. And each time that happens I do what I always do, I replay our life together from beginning to end. I loved our life together.

The first time we met I was working security part-time at one of the casinos while attending the police academy. She was working as a waitress in the casino's cafe and bar. I'll never forget when I saw her. I walked into the cafe and sat down to grab a quick bite. When I looked up from the menu there she was. She had a sparkle-in-her-eye kind of smile, beautiful dark brown eyes and warm olive skin. She also had great tits and an out-of-this-world ass.

"Can I get you something to drink, sir?" she asked, brushing back a loose strand of her swept back hair.

Her smile mesmerized me. It was tough not to just keep staring at her. I was hooked.

"Sir, can I get you something to drink?" Her tone the slightest bit annoyed this time, but understandably so.

"Oh, yeah. Sorry. I'll have coffee, please."

"Sure, I'll be right back." There was that smile again.

I watched her walk away feeling like I'd been struck by lighting. I knew in that moment I wanted to get to know her. Had to get to know her. She just might be the one.

I spent the next two weeks going to the cafe every day just to see her, exchange a few words. I'm not sure a 13 year old, acne-faced kid could have been more awkward. I eventually kicked my courage into high gear and asked her out. When I finally did she said, "You know I was just going to ask you the same thing. Glad you beat me to it."

We began dating and learning about each other. She had just finished college and was starting her first job as a kindergarten teacher in the fall. Her face lit up every time she talked about teaching little kids.

She soon found out I was a cop which she was a little cool to at first. But after getting to know me, and my family's long history of serving our community by working in law enforcement, she was fine with it. My father and his father before him had both been cops which soon made her proud that I was carrying on the family tradition.

Six months later, on a cool December evening just outside Red Rocks, I asked her to marry me. She said yes, flashed that great smile of hers and once again said: "You know, I was just going to ask you the same thing. Glad you beat me to it."

I asked her if she wanted a big wedding or a small intimate one.

"C'mon let's go find a wedding chapel, this is Vegas remember?" she said.

Two hours later we were married and on our honeymoon.

The next two years were the happiest years of my life. I didn't think it could get any better until one day she came to me, looked me straight in the eye and said, "We're going to have a baby."

She was so happy. I think all she ever really wanted was to be a mother. I thought she was beautiful before but, as trite as it sounds, she now had this glow about her that only comes to a woman with child.

Seven months later on a warm April morning, we were lying in bed talking about our plans for the day. I remember the conversation word for word.

"I'm taking my car in for service this morning before I go to my doctor's appointment," she said as she rubbed her hands over her gorgeous, swollen belly.

"Do you need a ride? You want me to go to the doctor's with you?" I know I sounded like a blithering idiot but the closer she got to delivering the more nervous I became. She, on the other hand, was as calm as can be.

"No, I'm fine. This is just a routine check-up, everything's good. And the dealer is giving me a loaner for the day. But don't forget we have dinner at your parents' tonight."

"How could I forget? My mom's so excited about this baby it's all she ever talks about. Now why don't you roll over here and let me feel him kick."

"You don't know for sure it's a him. Maybe it's a her."

"Nothin' but boys in the Ross clan, Emily, so I'm pretty confident."

➤

Later that day my partner and I were on patrol when we got a call about a gang related shooting. The hotter it gets in Vegas the more they shoot things up. We arrived at the scene just before the ambulance.

The two cars were side by side, their engines still running with smoke coming from the car on the left. We jumped out and ran towards them. I took the car on the right. As I got closer I could see a woman trying to help who ever was inside. Her hands were blood-soaked red.

"What happened here?" I asked as I approached her.

Her voice trembled and her hands shook as she tried to speak. "A drive-by, this poor woman just happened to be getting into her car and got hit by a stray bullet. Is help coming?"

I moved closer as she leaned in to help the woman. "The medics are just pulling up now. How is she?"

"She's not breathing, but I can still feel the baby's heartbeat."

"Baby? *Get out of the way*!" I screamed pulling her back out of the car. "Let me in there! Oh my God no! Emily! Emily! No, this can't be."

I felt someone tugging on me, pulling me backward, but could hear nothing but my own screams. Finally the medics pulled me out and launched into action on my wife and our baby. I stood in shock as they pulled her from the car, placed her on the stretcher and raced to the ambulance. I heard one of them say, "The other guy is dead."

"You go," my partner called out. "We'll find this perp, he won't get away."

Then in a moment of clarity I turned to him and sobbed with a conviction in my voice I never knew was in me. "When you do, bring him to me so I can look him in the face and tell him if he ever gets out of jail he'll be a dead man."

Time stopped. I waited at the hospital for what seemed forever, pacing, sweating, barely able to breathe. Finally the ER doctor came in to get me. We walked down the hallway, my fear and apprehension growing with every step. He stopped, turned and looked me straight in the eyes as he firmly placed his hand on my shoulder.

"I'm sorry, Mr. Ross. Your wife didn't make it. We tried our very best to revive her but she was too far gone. I know this is of little comfort but she didn't suffer."

I fell against the wall pounding my fist into what seemed a godless reality.

"The baby, what about the baby, is it OK?"

"It was too late to save the baby. I'm so very sorry." The doctor hung his head, removed his hand from my shoulder and turned away. I had never felt so alone.

I dropped to my knees and began screaming, holding my head in my hands trying to keep it from exploding. After a few minutes my screams became sobs and between them I managed a hoarse whisper. "Was it a boy or a girl?"

"It was a boy."

A week later I finally managed to read the report my partner filed. It seems a young black man named Terrence White pulled up next to Emily in his red Caddy with rap music blaring. Emily had just picked up her dry cleaning and was getting in her car when another car pulled up next to Terrence and opened fire. One of the bullets went through his car and into Emily's. Now when I hear rap music I want to scream.

At the funeral I thought I saw the woman who was at the scene trying to help Emily. I wanted to thank her but never got the chance or truly made the effort. Grief is a paralyzing emotion.

The police report said the witness was standing at the bus stop when the cars pulled up. She'd managed to get the license number of the shooter but was afraid of forgetting it so wrote it on the window of Emily's car with the blood on her hand. Three hours later the police made the arrest. The bastard got a life sentence and is now locked up. I tried hard to get the D.A. to go for the death penalty but didn't succeed. If the son of a bitch ever gets out, I will kill him.

I tried to contact the woman at the scene several times but each time I tried all I could think of were her hands soaked with the blood of my wife and just couldn't do it.

I've never forgotten her though. The report stated her name was John Reynolds, a.k.a. Mavis Rodgers.

It's been 15 years now but sometimes I still wake up in the middle of the night dripping sweat, screaming Emily's name. The blood curdling images race through my mind like it's happening all over again.

I lie in bed trying to remember and trying to forget. Love versus pain, but remembering love is not the same as living it, so the pain usually wins.

Before I go back to sleep I always say a prayer for my wife, Emily Madson Ross, and my son, Dylan Delaney Ross. May you rest in peace.

CHAPTER 7

SLEIGHT OF HAND

On the way to my office this morning thoughts cascade through my mind like rapids on a river. I'm confused and frustrated. I can't think straight. My mind won't shut off its endless obsession with "what if's" while my emotions surge from one strange feeling to the next. Where is this going? My heart still lives in the past with deep-felt memories of Emily but my mind is telling me to let go. For God's sake, Kate is pregnant with our child.

When I snap back to reality I find myself behind one of the slowest morons I've ever seen on the road. OK, now these are feelings I understand: anger and rage. Why do these people always get in the fast lane? Now there are two of them, no three. If just once I did what I wanted really wanted to do I'd start laying on my horn at them and not stop. However, I may be pissed off but I'm not an idiot so I hold my temper and just belt out expletives that can only be heard by me.

I catch an opening and blow by four cars on their right, making sure to glance over at each one with a look of disgust as I pass by. Would so love to flip them off, but once again I manage to control myself.

Arriving at my office I see that someone has taken my parking place. It's not that I actually have my name on it or anything, but it's where I'm used to parking and we're all creatures of habit. I manage to squeeze into another place that's in the sun and will bake my car like a pig roasting on a spit.

I walk up the stairs to my office and am surprised to find the door still locked. Hmm, no Alice. Well, it is 9:15 so maybe she's taking her first break of the day. After all, she starts at 9. Luckily I remembered my key so I go in, make some coffee and sit down at my computer. I'm reading the headlines of Kate's breaking story when my cell rings, it's Lyle.

"Hey, Lyle, what's up?"

"Just calling to let you know I ran those cell phone numbers for you but nothing came back. They're all throwaways."

"Yeah, that's what I figured but you never know."

"So, Nick, when you going to tell me what this is all about?"

"Soon, Lyle, real soon."

Just then Alice comes sauntering into the office, doing a balancing act with two cups of coffee and a shoulder bag, her ample store-bought breasts stabilizing every step.

"Sorry I'm late. The drive-thru at Starbucks was backed up into the street."

"You know, Alice, we do have a coffee machine here, it wouldn't kill you to use it once in a while."

"Actually it might, I've tasted the swill that thing makes."

"Never mind, did you manage to get the research done I asked for yesterday?"

"Sure did. Got a full background on Wesley Kootz, but the other two didn't have much except for a few misdemeanors and bad credit scores. I'll bring it all into you as soon as I set my coffee down and turn on my computer."

After strategically placing the Starbucks on her desk and turning on the computer, she takes the reports, makes sure they are properly aligned and attaches a clip at the top of each. Then she arranges the flowers in the vase on her desk, pulls out the Hershey Kisses and replenishes the bowl in the waiting room.

⏶

Roxy Lynn is just waking up when she hears the knock at her door. "UPS" a voice calls out, as the foot steps fade down the stairs.

"That better be my new shoes. It's about time," she says as she opens the door and reaches for the package. She squints against the strong Vegas morning sun as she steps back inside, tears open the box and folds back the tissue.

"*Ahhhh, ahhhh,*" she screams. "Oh my God!"

She drops the box and stumbles backward shaking and sobbing. Minutes pass. She finally forces herself to open her eyes and stare at the contents. She gags and covers her mouth. Inside the box is a severed hand and rolled up in the fingers is a slip of paper that Roxy pulls free.

"Mavis just wanted to wave bye-bye," it reads.

Roxy drops the note and frantically grabs her cell phone off the table.

"Nick! Nick! You've got to catch this sick son of a bitch. He cut off her hand, Nick. He cut off Mavis' hand!"

⚔

"Alice, Roxy Lynn is on her way in and she's very upset, please be nice and try to show a little sympathy towards her, OK?"

"Well, of course I will. Just tell me which one of her is going to show up." Alice glances up from her computer just long enough to toss me her classic smirk.

⚔

Detectives Lyle Carson and Mitch Sutton are sitting in a meeting with Captain Tucker waiting for what they pretty much know is coming. Tucker has been feeling the heat from higher-ups to get a viable suspect to pin the murders on.

"So, what have you boys come up with on the Mavis Rodgers' case?" Tucker says leaning back in his chair and clasping his hands behind his head.

"Not much, Captain. We just got the results back from the crime lab and they're no help."

"Look," he says pounding both fists on his desk. "I just had my ass reamed out by the Mayor who wants the FBI to get involved. We need results and we need them now, damn it. What about the boyfriend?"

"We've got an APB out on him but there's no trail. It's like he just disappeared," says Mitch."

"Son of a bitch, find him and pin this on him. We can't have it looking like there's a serial killer loose in this town. And I expect the two of you to understand the consequences if you don't. Am I clear?"

"Yes, sir, we'll find him," says Lyle.

Captain Tucker stands, looks straight up like he's praying to the heavens, then walks out of the room leaving a somewhat stunned pair of detectives.

"Well, that was worse than usual. What the hell got into him?" Lyle says as he loosens his tie.

"I don't know but I wish he'd go back to that task force in Reno and stay there. It was nice not having him around the last six months."

"Mitch, why don't you drive up to Laughlin and see if you can find out more about the boyfriend. Talk to Kootz and his band of snake herders. Make them sweat a little. I'm going to go have a talk with Nick. He knows something he's not telling us."

⚔

Roxy walks into the office carrying a shoebox under her arm. Alice eyes her up and down spotting every change that was made to transform Raymond Tisdale back to Roxy Lynn.

"Well, good morning, Miss Lynn, how are you today?"

"Been better, Alice, is Nick in?"

"Yes he is. Can I get you something? Coffee, a soft drink or some water?"

"No thanks, just Nick."

"Ooh, new shoes?" Alice says eyeing the box Roxy is carrying. I just love Nordstrom's shoe department, ever shop there?"

"Uh, yes, sometimes. . .Alice, I really need to see Nick right away."

"Ok, sure. . .but I'd just love a peek at those shoes first."

Exasperated, Roxy walks over to Alice's desk and opens the box. Alice peeks in and jumps back screaming, tossing one of her Starbucks halfway across the room.

I run out of my office to see what's going on.

"What the hell is going on out here?"

"I was just showing Alice my present from Nordstrom's, you know, the one that son of a bitch sent me."

"Jesus, Roxy. Really? Come on back to my office."

⚔

"Look, Roxy, this is hard evidence, we need to get the cops involved."

"No, Nick! I told you I can't."

The frustration level is building in my gut. I'm losing patience and getting angry. I slap my hands hard on the desk as Roxy pulls back in the chair. Shit, not cool to lose it with clients.

"Look, I'm sorry, Roxy, but I need answers and I need them now or I really have to go to the cops. My ass is probably already in trouble. Tell me why we can't get the police involved."

"All right, all right, I'll tell you. I grew up in L.A., Inglewood to be exact. Never knew my real father but had an asshole of a stepfather. Does this sound like your typical sob story so far?"

"Just go on, Roxy."

"My mother cleaned houses in Redondo Beach while my stepfather collected disability and mostly drank all day. I had a half-brother who was a gangbanger trying to live up to his old man's heritage as one of the founding members of the 18th Street Gang. Seems his father thought it a rite of passage for his son to carry on the tradition."

"Were you involved?"

"How many blue-eyed white boys do you think they accept, Nick? It happened a long time ago. We were just stupid kids trying to get by. My brother and one of his buddies were working at a Bob's Big Boy over on the south side. He'd get a job long enough to file a Work Comp claim and then move on to the next mark. I get a call one day from my brother asking me to come pick him up from work. When I get there, him and his buddy jump in the car and ask me if I'll take them by the bank so they can cash their checks.

"So I'm sitting there in the parking lot at the bank waiting for them when they both come running out, guns in one hand and money in the other. There's a 300-pound security guard chasing them while trying to pull his gun out of his holster. Just as he squeezes through the front door out into the parking lot, my brother's friend stops, turns, and shoots him. Then they both jump in the car screaming at me to hit it."

"So you did and became an accessory."

"Yeah, I did. What choice did I have? You think the cops would have believed I was innocent?"

"So then what?"

"I waited at a friend's place for a few days to see if maybe they'd gotten away with it, while my brother and his stupid friend got high and gambled most of the money away. I see on the news a week later one of those grainy stop-and-start videos recorded at the bank they robbed. Of course neither of them bothered to hide their identity, so a rival gang member gave them up to get the reward money the bank offered."

"And then what did you do?"

"I ran. Never looked back, never regretted it. I got a new life and a new identity that no one would look for."

"What happened to your brother and his friend?"

"My brother's buddy made it to Mexico, last I heard he's dealin' drugs for one of the cartels down there. My brother got nailed by the cops after he stole a car and was pulled over for runnin' a red light. He was a real brain-trust."

"So he's doing time?"

"You might say that. He got 25-to-life for the robbery but they dropped the attempted murder charge when he gave me up. At least that was what I was told. Six months after he got sent up a rival gang member stuck a shiv in his neck and killed him."

"So, you really don't know if the cops are after you or not."

"No, and I'm not going to find out. I can't do jail, Nick. People like me don't last long in there. I can't and I won't."

"Look, Roxy, let me find out if there's still an outstanding warrant. Maybe you're running from nothing."

"And what if there is, Nick, what would you do? Turn me in? Wouldn't you become an accessory harboring a fugitive if you don't?"

"Anything I do will be strictly confidential, you have to trust me."

"That's not something I'm good at, Nick."

My phone rings. It's Alice letting me know that Detective Carson is here to see me.

"Here's your chance, Roxy. Lyle's a good guy, I trust him and if you don't act soon you'll be in real trouble."

Roxy gets up shoves the shoebox onto my desk and turns to walk out.

"I need time to think, Nick. I just can't do this now. I have to go."

I watch Roxy as she walks out of my office and through the reception area, her pace quicker and tense, more like a man than her usual sexy sway. She looks down as she passes by Lyle and shoves the door hard as she exits. Alice takes in the entire scene.

"Have a nice day, Miss Lynn, and oh, by the way, loved the shoes, hon."

After Roxy leaves Alice turns to Lyle whose eyes are still following Roxy out the door.

"Isn't she gorgeous? You should have Nick introduce you to her. You just never know how life can surprise you," Alice says with a sigh.

"I'm still holding out for you, Alice."

"Told you before, Lyle, you're not my type."

"Yeah, well what is your type?"

"Old guys with a lot of money and no family, you can go in now."

Lyle walks into my office in a slow, deliberate manner, scanning the walls that display my family history, generations of law officers.

"So, Lyle, what brings you by? I wasn't expecting you."

"I was in the neighborhood so thought I'd stop by and check in with you. See if there's anything new goin' on. By the way, who's the blonde?"

"She's not your type, trust me."

"I get it. Keepin' her for yourself. I understand. What's in the box? New shoes?" Lyle asks with more than a twinge of skepticism.

"Oh, yeah, I'm taking them back. Let me put them away."

"Somethin' kinda smells in here."

"Yeah, I got to get the cleaning people back up here. So Lyle, what's on your mind?"

"Nicky, Nicky, Nicky, you're holdin' back something. You know more about the Mavis Rodgers' case than you're telling us. You don't want to withhold evidence, buddy. It'll get you in big trouble."

"Look, Lyle, I appreciate the concern if that's what you want to call it, but there's nothing I can tell you right now. What about you? Got any leads on the boyfriend?"

"We have an APB out on him and Mitch is up there questioning those sideshow clowns but there isn't much to go on."

"Tell Mitch to talk to the kid that sweeps up, he was good friends with Bobby."

"Oh, so you've been up there snoopin' around?"

"You know Kate and I went up there and you know why."

"Yeah, I know about Mavis and what happened to your wife, that's why I'm giving you the benefit of the doubt. Gotta tell you though, if Captain Tucker gets wind of anything you're toast."

"Something is wrong with that asshole, Lyle, just can't put my finger on it."

"Yeah, maybe. I don't know, Nick, but he likes the boyfriend for these murders and wants him bad. Looks like Bobby was in Reno when the others got it and there's some evidence that he knew them all. Then he comes down here and Mavis gets it? And now he's disappeared? You got to admit that looks pretty bad."

"It just looks a little too convenient to me, Lyle. Something's not right about the way he disappeared, and that whole bible verse thing doesn't add up. I'd take a closer look at Wesley Kootz if I were you."

"I'll keep that in mind, Nick. Now remember what I told you. You get something, you call me, got it?"

"Yeah, Lyle, I got it."

CHAPTER 8

Dear Diary

Just one more, *just one more, then I must stop. I must wait for guidance while doing the Lord's work. I will carry out his plan. They must suffer and die for their sins. Man can not lie with another man. It's unnatural, ugly and unholy. I will punish one more then wait for the Lord's guidance.*

God is all-powerful and he instills that power in me to carry out his work. His wisdom runs through my veins, I am a piece of God.

Only he is my true Father, not the sinner who brought me into being. He rots in hell and justice is served.

In five days the man who calls himself a woman will meet the true Maker and learn the everlasting gospel of Jesus Christ our Lord and savior.

Amen.

CHAPTER 9

You Can't Handle the Truth

It's late morning and the breakfast crowd has come and gone at Ronnie's. Jasper Watts is taking a well-deserved break from the schmoozing he performs so adeptly with his clientele. Sipping his coffee, he reaches for the morning paper lying on the bar. The headline reads: "Serial Killer Loose in Vegas?". The byline is Kate Simon.

The article goes on to describe the death of Mavis Rodgers, a well-known local drag queen, and raises the possibility that the serial killer who struck in Reno could be linked to her murder.

"What do you think, Jasper? Is it Pulitzer worthy?"

Jasper looks up to see Kate standing in front of him. She looks tired like she hasn't slept, but seems all pumped up about the story breaking.

"Kate, what a pleasant surprise, I was just reading your article. Great job, girl, bet you've stirred up a hornet's nest with this."

"Yeah, looks that way. At least I hope so. I had to get out of the office for a while. The phones are ringing off the hook."

Kate looks away for a moment then back at Jasper.

"Kate, what's wrong?" he says noticing that her eyes are now rimmed with tears. "Are you OK?"

"I need to talk, Jasper," she says taking a deep breath.

"I need to ask you about Nick."

"Oh, I see. Thought that might be it."

"You've known Nick a long time. Do you think he's is capable of loving someone after what happened?"

"I don't know, he really had his heart ripped out when he lost his wife."

"Yes, I know but that was a long time ago."

"Look, Kate, for some people it's always like it was yesterday. The pain never goes away and they never love again. For others it actually makes them stronger, able to connect and love even more deeply."

"So which one do you think Nick is?"

"I honestly don't know. I'd like to think he's the latter but I just don't know."

"I asked my brother once how Nick lost his wife, but he wouldn't tell me. He just said it was a horrible tragedy. Do you know how she died?"

"That's something you need to ask Nick. It wouldn't be right for me to say, especially now."

"OK, Jasper. I get it," Kate sighs. "I researched everything I could find but nothing ever came up on her except a simple obituary. I know there's a lot more to the story but maybe you're right. I'll ask him tonight, he's coming over for dinner."

It's an unforgiving day in the desert outside of Laughlin. The sun is boring down on the desolate landscape with a merciless tenacity.

Wesley Kootz sits in his air-conditioned land yacht watching the latest episode of the "151 Club". He often tunes in for inspiration from the TV preachers he secretly envies.

Detective Mitch Sutton sees the sign and turns on to the dirt road leading to the tent of, "The Original Church of God in Jesus' Name". As he heads down the road he passes a pickup truck heading the other direction. A quick glance through the rising cloud of dust reveals a large man wearing a cowboy hat behind the wheel with a younger Hispanic male in the passenger seat. As the vehicles pass each other, the young man turns his head to look at the detective till he is out of sight. Mitch catches a glimpse of him and thinks he sees a certain anguish on the kid's face. Or maybe it's just the goddamn heat getting to him.

The detective pulls up to the tent and waits a minute for the trailing cloud of dust to settle. When he opens his door he's met by a large man with arms inked up in an intricate pattern of demons and angels.

"Something I can help you with, mister?" he says, clearly not laying out the welcome mat.

"Yes, I'd like to see Wesley Kootz."

"You mean the *Reverend* Kootz?" he says scowling. "He ain't seein' nobody today. He's gettin' ready for the show tonight. Y'all come back another time ya' hear?"

"Yeah, I hear. Tell you what, you go tell Mr. Kootz that detective Mitch Sutton with the Las Vegas Police Department is here and would like to speak to him."

"Oh, why didn't ya' say so?" he says suddenly a bit more cordial. "Wait here a minute. I'll be right back."

The large man lumbers back into the tent and disappears. A full five minutes pass before he reemerges from a side entrance and waves the detective to come forward.

"Reverend Kootz says he can give you a few minutes, follow me."

The door to the high-end motorhome is open as the detective is shown in and asked to have a seat. A few minutes later Wesley Kootz walks out from the bedroom wearing a floor-length robe sequined in gold with dark green and deep maroon lapels.

"Welcome detective, Sutton. Welcome and God bless. How can I help you?"

"Well, you can start by answering a few questions about Bobby Westbrook."

"Oh yes, dear Bobby. Our sound and lighting engineer. God bless that young man. Don't know what got into him. He just up and disappeared one day."

"He didn't give you any notice or tell anyone he was leaving?"

"Not to my knowledge. No, sir."

"Do you know the last person he might have talked to?"

"I really couldn't tell you, Detective. I try not to get personally involved in my employees' private lives. Is Bobby in some kind of trouble?"

"We'd just like to talk to him, he's what you call a person of interest right now. Do you know if anyone heard from him since he left?"

"Not that I know of, but you'd have to ask them that question. Now if that's all, Detective, I do have a show to get ready for."

"That's all for now. Oh, there is one more thing. Who's the young Hispanic boy who works for you?"

Kootz narrows his eyes as if to help him recall. "I think his name is Juan, or Julio, I'm not sure. Ask Max on your way out he'll know."

"I'll do that and if you happen to hear anything from Bobby you be sure to let us know. Here's my card."

"Yes, yes, I certainly will. Now Max will show you out. God bless."

As they're walking back to the car, Mitch starts to question Max about Bobby.

"So, Max, what can you tell me about Bobby Westbrook?"

"Not much. Always thought he was a little strange. If I didn't know he'd been a pro football player, I'd a thought maybe he was a fag but those boys ain't like that."

"What do you mean?"

"Well, it's like the few times he went out drinkin' with us he never seemed to care much about the ladies. But then one night I see this woman show up at the revival and him and her are all over each other."

"Do you remember what this woman looked like?"

"She was black, tall and lean, good lookin' in a rough sorta way."

"Did you happen to get her name?"

"Think I heard him say it one time. Something like, Mabel or, Marge."

"Could it have been Mavis?"

"Yeah, coulda been Mavis."

"Thanks, Max. Just one more thing, who's the young Hispanic kid that works here?"

"Oh you mean, Julio."

"Yeah. I hear he's good friends with Bobby. Is he around? I'd like to speak to him."

"He just left with Frank to pick up supplies. Probably won't be back for awhile. Frank likes to visit the local cathouse whenever he goes to town."

"For a religious group you boys seem pretty open-minded about booze and sex."

"We're just good ole' boys tryin' to make a buck. If we didn't sin we wouldn't need savin'," Max says with a deep chuckle and showing off a couple of gold-capped teeth.

"Well, you tell Julio I want to talk to him. I'll be back real soon. In the meantime if you hear anything about Bobby give me a call. Here's my card."

Mitch gets in his car and rolls down the window, pointing at Max. "You take care, now, ya hear."

While Max watches Mitch drive away he gets a call on his walkie-talkie.

"Yeah, boss, whata ya want?"

"Come back, now! I need to talk to you."

Max can tell the Reverend is upset and hurries back to the RV.

"As soon as Frank gets back you bring Julio to me. I want to talk to him. We need to make sure he doesn't go talkin' to the cops. I wanna make it clear he'll be deported if he says anything."

"Got it, boss, will do."

A

"Hello? Hello? Is someone there?"

"Roxy?"

"This is Roxy, who's this?"

"Roxy, it's Bobby. Bobby Westbrook."

"Bobby, it's you?"

"Yeah, Roxy, it's me."

"Oh my God, where are you? Everyone is looking for you. Are you OK?"

"I'm good but the cops think I did it, don't they?"

"Well yeah, Bobby, what the hell? Why did you run?"

"I have my reasons."

"They better be damn good ones. Where are you?"

"I'm in L.A. and I need a favor."

"Look, Bobby, I don't know if I can help. I'm in some trouble myself."

"C'mon, Roxy, please. You want to find out who killed Mavis, don't you?"

"What do you want me to do?"

"I need you to go see a friend of mine, his name is Eddie. He runs the Boom Boom Room in south Vegas. You know the place?"

"Yeah, I sure do, then what?"

"Eddie will have a package for you. Once you've picked it up wait to hear from me."

▲

When I left the office I had every intention of going straight to Kate's apartment. She's making dinner and wants to have the "talk" tonight. I'm quite sure the talk will include questions about my deceased wife and how she died.

But I don't quite make it to Kate's. Instead I find myself sitting at the bar in O'Connell's pub.

"Give me a seltzer with a twist, Jimmy, would you please?"

"Still on the wagon, eh? Comin' right up, Nick."

Just then I see the Captain walk in. He spots me at the bar but doesn't bother to acknowledge me. That's just fine since I don't like the prick anyway.

The place is starting to fill up. It's the sixth game of the World Series and St. Louis is leading Boston three games to two, meaning the Cards can wrap it up with a win tonight.

I don't really follow baseball that much during the season but when it comes time for the playoffs and the Series, I'm a diehard fan. I've had a few favorite teams over the years but the Cardinals are at the top of the list.

As they are introducing the lineups Lyle comes through the front door announcing himself by shouting, "I'll take Boston in seven." He makes his way to the bar and pulls up the stool next to me.

"Hey, Jimmy, get me a Jack and Coke, would ya?"

"Comin' right up, buddy."

"Well, I sure didn't think I'd see you here, Nick. You going to watch the game?"

"Nah, just the first inning or two. I'm meeting Kate for dinner."

"Jesus, Nick, this is the World Series we're talkin' about, doesn't she know that? You two can have dinner anytime. Call her up and reschedule."

"Can't do it, Lyle, this is important."

Lyle runs his finger around the rim of his Jack and Coke and lifts it up to his mouth. He gives me a look of disapproval. "Ain't no dinner important enough to miss a Series game between the Cards and the Sox."

"Really, Lyle? That's the kind of thinking that made wife number three leave you."

"Kiss my ass, Nicky."

"Hey, Lyle, what's Captain Tucker doing here? I didn't think he drank."

"I don't know. Why don't I call him over and see if he wants to join us. Hey, Tuck, c'mon over and join us."

"Shit, Lyle, what are you doing? Shut up. I don't want him over here."

"Oh, c'mon, Nicky, you boys need to kiss and make up."

"Fuck you, Lyle."

As Captain Tucker makes his way over to where we're sitting, I can see on his face the same old look of disdain he has for me.

"Hey, Lyle, how goes it? I just stopped by to watch the game," Tucker says blatantly ignoring me.

"Pull up a stool, Tuck, and join us. Can I get you a drink?"

"Sure, I'll have a beer."

"Hey, Jimmy, the Captain here wants a beer. Bring him a Stella."

"Comin' right up, Lyle."

"So, Tuck, who do you like, the Cards or the Sox?"

"I gotta go with the Sox they got more power in their lineup."

"Yeah, that's what I think too, but ole Nick here likes the Cards. Ain't that right, Nick?"

"Yep, that's right. The Cards have better pitching and that's what wins games."

"Well, we'll just see about that, won't we?" Tucker says staring at the TV above the bar.

A few minutes pass then Lyle gets up and heads for the men's room. Tucker sets his beer down and turns toward me. I can feel him staring at me but I don't turn my head. Two can play at this game.

"So I see you're still hanging out with cops, hey Nick? Make you feel like more of a man?"

"Not really. Most of 'em I know became cops to compensate for their little dicks. Is that your problem too, Tucker?"

"Why you little. . . !"

Tucker lunges at me and tries to throw a punch. I jump to the side and shove him into the bar head first. He spins and comes at me again but a returning Lyle steps in and holds him back.

"I'm going to kick your ass, Ross. You'll get what you deserve."

"Let him go, Lyle. Let's finish this once and for all."

"Jesus, Nick. Are you nuts?"

Tucker backs off from Lyle and straightens himself up. Then he points a finger at me as his face grows beet red.

"This ain't over, Ross. Mark my words you're going to pay, I'll see to it." Then he turns, shoulders his way through the crowd and leaves.

Kate is feverishly getting things ready for dinner when her phone rings.

"Kate, it's Barry."

"Hey, Barry, what's my editor calling me about now?"

"We just got info that the FBI is going to hold a news conference regarding the Mavis Rodgers case. Word is they are going to confirm it was a serial killing."

"Holy shit. When are they going public with it?"

"They're down at the Courthouse now. We need you down there right away."

"Oh no, not now, I can't."

"Kate, this is your story, you have to go. What could be more important than this right now?"

"It's complicated, Barry."

"Look, I need you there. You don't want me to give it to someone else, do you?"

"Shit. OK, OK, I'll get down there right away."

Kate hangs up the phone, turns off the oven and blows out the candles on the table. As she grabs her bag she pulls out her cell and calls Nick. No answer.

"Damn it, Nick, answer your phone."

"I'm out of here, Lyle, heading for Kate's. I guess I should thank you for stepping in but next time let me finish it."

"You know, Nicky, you might want to think about just walking away from it. It takes a bigger man to do that sometimes than it does to fight."

"Maybe, Lyle, maybe. I'll think about it. See you later."

On the way to Kate's I think about what Lyle said but there's this underlying anger in me that I can't let go of. God knows I want to, just don't know how.

I get to Kate's at seven on the dot, right on time. I ring her apartment once, twice, three times but there's no answer. What the hell? I thought this was supposed to be so important to her and now she's not even here?

I reach for my phone to call her but it's not in my back pocket. Damn. It must have fallen out in the scuffle with Tucker. Guess I'll have to go back to O'Connell's and look for it. Man, could I use a drink.

CHAPTER 10

Step One

wake up mid-afternoon staring at the tuck-and-roll upholstery in the backseat of my T-Bird feeling as if I'm being baked alive. The top's down and my clothes are soaked with sweat. One eye only wants to open a sliver and the other is sealed shut. I try to move but I am, as they say, dazed and confused. I finally manage to get an arm underneath my chest and push myself up in the seat. What the hell happened?

For a brief moment I think I'm really not feeling that bad for whatever stupid decisions I must have made the night before. But as my other eye begins to unglue itself and open, my head begins to spin and my stomach lunges toward my throat. I throw myself over the side of the car, hanging halfway to the ground. I want to purge the poison from my body but it won't come out. I just hang there limp. Then my head starts spinning again and I feel a jolt to my gut like my body is imploding. I start heaving and I can't stop. I keep it up until nothing is coming up but I still can't stop.

Finally, I'm able to pull myself back up into the car. I see something odd in the front seat for a moment just before everything goes dark and I pass out, collapsing back down into the seat.

$$\blacktriangle$$

"Damn it, Nick, why aren't you answering your phone?" Roxy kicks back in her chair flipping her hair over her left shoulder and tossing her cell on the table. She gets up from the chair and paces back and forth from her kitchen to her living room, talking out loud to herself trying to calm her nerves. "I have to pick up that package at the Boom but I sure don't want to go by myself. Can't take the bodyguards, they can't know about it. Oh screw it, I'll just go." Finally, she goes out to the front porch to have a smoke and talk to Tony and Gus.

"Tony, you and Gus can take the night off. I'm going to visit some friends so I'll be fine. See you tomorrow."

"OK, Miss Lynn, be safe. We'll see you in the morning."

After the bodyguards leave, Roxy gets herself ready and calls a cab. She hasn't been to the Boom Boom Room in years, even though it was there where she got her start. She hasn't seen Fast Eddie in years either. Not since their break-up when she caught him with two other "showgirls" in the back office. They don't call him Fast Eddie for nothing.

Roxy sees the cab arrive and walks out toward the street, glancing over both shoulders. Just a little precaution to make sure she is not being followed. She gets in and eyes the driver. Another cabby refugee from some part of the world she's never heard of.

"The Boom Boom Room on South 89th. You know the place?"

"Oh yez, mum, I do."

"Good, there's an extra twenty in it if you make sure no one is following us." Roxy leans back in the seat and looks out the window wondering just what she's getting herself into. She looks up at the rearview mirror and sees the driver's dark and mysterious eyes.

"Oh yez, mum, I take care of that. You not to worry."

He deftly maneuvers the cab through the heavy traffic on the boulevard, turning and dodging with skilled precision right through the heart of town. Roxy is impressed.

"Excuse me, sir, what's your name?"

"Saleem."

"Hi, Saleem, my name is Roxy. When you get to the club, pull around to the back entrance please."

"Oh yez, Mizz Roxy, no problem."

When they get to the club Roxy sees the place doesn't look much different than it used to. The same weathered exterior in need of paint and Boom Boom Room spelled out in now-dull neon lights. Some of the regulars are standing out front smoking E-cigarettes filled with questionable contents. Saleem pulls the cab around to the back and Roxy starts to get out.

"Oh, let me get dat for you, mum."

"Thank you, Saleem. I'm not going to be too long, can you wait for me?"

"Yez, mum, no problem. I be here for your return."

Roxy gets out of the limo looks around and takes a deep breath. She throws her shoulders back and walks toward the entrance. When she enters the club she's suddenly taken by the sights, sounds and smells that bring back old memories. The dim yellow lights throughout the bar and the blacked-out walls help seclude patrons seated at tables where all sorts of intimate transactions take place.

In contrast, the stage is lit as brightly as a fourth of July finale to draw attention to the Boom's stable of showgirls working their talents for the appreciative clientele.

Roxy makes her way through the sexually eclectic, happy hour crowd to a room behind the bar where Fast Eddie's office is. Towering in front of the door to the office is Jake Malone. Jake stands six foot six, weighs in at 300 pounds and has a neck the size of a tree stump. He still wears his hair flat-top fashion at a level two-inches. Jake is Fast Eddie's bodyguard, enforcer and occasional chauffeur. Before Roxy can say anything, Jake spots her and throws his arms up in the air.

"Roxy! Is that you? It's been too long, girl. Come here and give me a hug."

Jake takes Roxy in his huge arms and spins her around several times.

"Good to see you too, Jake, it has been awhile. How have you been?"

"I'm fine, girl, and you look great. What brings you back to this side of town?"

"I need to see Fast Eddie. Is he in?"

"Yeah, he's got somebody in his office right now but he shouldn't be too long. Can I get you a drink?"

"Sure, why not. A gin and tonic would be nice. Thanks."

Roxy peruses the room for old acquaintances as she waits for Jake. A lot of memories come back to her as she thinks about the good, the bad, the illegal and the sad. The door to Fast Eddie's office swings open and out struts a showgirl brushing back her hair and straightening her blouse. Fast Eddie follows right behind and gives her a pat on the butt sending her back into the crowd. Roxy steps forward and Eddie's face widens with a broad cap-toothed smile.

"Oh my god, Roxy! I can't believe it. You came back."

"Hey, Eddie, still up to your old tricks I see. Were you interviewing her?"

"Oh come on, Roxy, you know me, I was just havin' some fun. It doesn't mean anything. You're the only one I've ever loved." Eddie wraps his arms around Roxy and squeezes her tight. Roxy smiles and pulls back, wagging her finger at him.

"If I had a dollar for every time you've used that line, Eddie, I'd own Vegas.

"Here's your drink, Miss Lynn," Jake roars as he lumbers back from the bar. "Isn't it good to see her, Eddie? It's been too long."

"It is, Jake, it is. So what brings you back, darlin'? Is this a social visit?"

"Business, Eddie. Serious business. We need to talk."

▲

When I wake up again the sun is going down. I push myself up off the backseat and try to get my bearings. I know I'm somewhere in the desert and it's starting to get dark. Purple-grey shadows are setting in giving the landscape an eerie and lonely feel. I just keep wondering what the hell happened? For the life of me I can't remember. I rest my head on the seat, close my eyes and try again but I still have no memory of anything after leaving O'Connell's. Now I'm on a dirt road in the middle of nowhere with no sign of life as far as I can see. All I know is, according to the setting sun I must be heading west through the desert.

I do remember losing my phone and going back to O'Connell's to look for it. I struggle to lift my head and now see it's laying on the console. I reach for it and find it's dead, of course. The downside of driving a classic car is there's no way to charge your phone, especially when your cigarette lighter doesn't work.

I decide to just turn this thing around and head east. There has to be a road or a town within a few miles. I turn the key and the engine cranks but the motor won't turn over. I glance at the few simple gauges. Fuel. Shit, I'm out of gas. I can't fucking believe this. I don't remember anything, must have had a complete black-out and just kept driving till the car stopped. Or maybe somebody slipped me a mickey.

Now I'm in the middle of nowhere, dehydrated from the booze and with no water. It's starting to get dark and the temperature is dropping fast. I weigh my options: spend the night in the car and head out on foot tomorrow morning in the heat, or start out tonight and try to get as far as I can while the sun's down. I decide it's better to start now. After all, I've been sleeping most of day.

The desert is lit up by a full moon casting shadows over its terrain, hauntingly beautiful but cold and uninviting. Despite my throbbing head I walk at a good pace eyeing no sign of life. It's quiet out here, too quiet for my liking. Occasionally I hear the howl of a coyote which gives me chills and sets my mind conjuring up thoughts of whatever else this godforsaken place may have in store. I imagine a nest of rattlesnakes lurking behind the next rock or perhaps more of those boisterous coyotes surrounding me and eyeing me as dinner.

Like a beacon, the moon stares down on me and this sea of sand from an ocean long gone. After walking for a couple of hours, my body starts to rebel. Deep chills make my body tremble and I feel short of breath. I keep going. More miles go by and though my heart is racing I can hardly stay awake. I'm getting confused. Maybe I should try to take a short cut across the desert and leave the road.

I lose my balance, stumble over a rock and fall to my knees. I look up at the stars, every beat of my heart seemingly getting louder and louder. It suddenly crosses my mind that I might not make it out of here alive. I try to get up but I'm too dizzy to stand and immediately start to fall. Just before I hit the ground I catch a glimpse of light far off down the road.

▲

"So, Roxy, you're here on business? Sure this ain't just some excuse to see me again?"

"Jesus, Eddie, if your ego was any bigger you'd have to park it in a hangar."

"Well, you just look so damn good and you're bringin' back old memories. You know the kind," Eddie says as he winks and raises an eyebrow, his patented come-on look.

Roxy sits back and rolls her eyes, gives Eddie a smile, then shakes her head, as if to say, "Let's get back to business."

"I'm here to pick up a package that Bobby Westbrook sent you."

"No, no, no, girl, you don't want to get involved in that, it's all trouble."

"You're right, I don't, but I said I would because of Mavis. I need to find out who killed her."

"Shit, Roxy, let the cops do that. Don't get yourself involved."

"I have to, Eddie."

"Why?"

"Because I'm next."

▲

"Nicky, wake up, you all right? Wake up, Nicky." Lyle picks me up off the ground and shakes me.

"What? Where am I? Who's there?" My eyes roll as I look up, still in a daze.

"You're in the middle of the fuckin' desert for God's sake. It's me, Lyle."

"Lyle? *Jeez*. . .what happened? How the hell did you find me?"

"Yeah, it's me and we gotta get you to a hospital. I think you have hypothermia."

"No, no, is Kate all right? I have to see her. Is Roxy alive? Did he kill her? I need Pickles."

"Pickles? What the hell are you talking about? You're delirious. I gotta get you into the car where you can warm up. There's a survival kit in the trunk with water and blankets, I'll grab it."

Once in the car with the heater and the blankets I start to come around and begin to guzzle the water.

"Easy, Nick, not so fast, you'll make yourself sick. Here, eat this power bar. You need something in your stomach, slowly though." Lyle tears the wrapper off the power bar, reaches over and hands it to me as he shakes his head.

As I look up I see my face in the rearview mirror. I'm red as a beat and my lips are blistered. My eyes are bloodshot and my hair's matted with sand and sweat.

"Shit, Lyle, what the hell happened to me? Where am I? Thought I was dead."

"I don't know what happened to you, but you're in the middle of the fucking desert and you weren't far from being dead. Good thing there's a full moon or I'd a run right over you."

"How the hell did you find me?"

"Well, after Alice called the third time and told me you hadn't shown up for any appointments or called in I thought I'd better look into it. I called your wireless carrier and had them do a trace on the last coordinates before your cell gave out. I plugged those into my GPS and here I am."

"If you ever hear me say how much I hate technology, slug me." I lean back, take a deep breath and rub my eyes.

"Amen to that." Lyle puts the car in gear and we start to take off and then he looks over at me.

"Are you starting to feel any better?"

"Yeah, a little chilled but better." I pull the blanket around me a little tighter.

"I still think you need to go to the hospital." Lyle points his finger at me in a fatherly manner.

"Can't, I need to get back. I have to talk to Kate."

"Kate can wait. I'm worried about you. And how about explaining your other two comments."

"What comments? What do you mean?" I try to play dumb but Lyle's having none of it.

"Like, some crap about needing Pickles and asking if Roxy's still alive? Did he kill her?"

"Shit. OK, Pickles is Walter Pickles, my AA sponsor. I'm sure you can understand why I might need him right now. I don't know about that other thing, I was probably dreaming or delirious." I'm never a good liar but right now I'm really bad.

"Nicky, don't be lying' to me. It'll get you in big trouble."

"I can't talk about it, Lyle." I turn away and look out the window hoping to end this line of questioning.

"Who wants to kill Roxy? Does this have anything to do with the Mavis Rodgers' case?"

"Dammit. Come on, Lyle."

"Holy shit. Roxy's a tranny? She is, isn't she?"

🡇

"Are you tellin' me that serial killer nut job is after you, Roxy?"

Eddie sits up grabs the back of his neck with one hand and pours himself a Scotch with the other.

"That's what I'm telling you, Eddie." Roxy rolls the ice around in her drink and takes a good swig, staring at the floor.

"Damn, what are you doin' about it? He'll kill you."

"I've got a P.I. working on it. At least I did." Roxy rolls her eyes and heaves a big sigh.

"You need to go to the cops."

"You *know* I can't do that, Eddie."

"Oh, right, I forgot. How about I have Jake watch over you for awhile?"

"Thanks, but I already have two bodyguards."

"Maybe you should get out of town. Here, take the keys to my cabin up in the mountains. Nobody will find you there." Eddie tosses the keys on to the desk in front of Roxy.

"Thanks, that's very kind. I'll let you know. Now how about the package?"

"Oh yeah, it's here in my desk." Eddie reaches into his lower drawer, pulls out a small package and tosses it at Roxy. "Here ya go."

"You didn't open it?" Roxy says, somewhat surprised.

"Nah, plausible deniability. Can't be involved if I don't know what it is. Besides I don't even know Bobby that well. He's a friend of Jake's. They played ball together in college."

Roxy takes the package, tears the paper off and opens the small box.

"I don't get it. It's just a necklace. What the hell does it have to do with any of this?"

"Guess you'll have to wait and hear from Bobby," Eddie says casually as he takes a drink of his Scotch.

"That better happen soon. I'm running out of time." Roxy downs her drink, sets it on Eddie's desk and stands up.

"Thanks, Eddie. See ya around," she says as she waves and walks out the door.

CHAPTER 11

DEAR DIARY

To my Holy Savior who guides and protects me, watch over me as I do thy bidding. Help me to show poor miserable sinners the error of their ways so they may repent and be saved.

May I exact God's revenge on those who would break His laws. I will bring the Man/Woman to justice and make him pay with his life for defying the will of God. Only then will his soul be cleansed of the evil within.

So it is told. Thy will be done.

CHAPTER 12

A Higher Power

As the sun begins to bake the landscape we head back to Vegas. The car is filled with an uncomfortable quiet that can only be eliminated by the truth, and that's not going to happen. I fake sleep so I don't have to talk, but Lyle knows I'm hiding something. When we stop to drop off the keys to my T-Bird at the local sheriff's department, I get up and walk around a bit.

"I'll have a couple of the deputies get your car and bring it down to Vegas tomorrow. You can pick it up at the station house, but give them some time. Maybe around three or so."

"Thanks, Lyle, I appreciate it."

"No problem. You ready to talk to me, Nick?" Lyle puts his hands on his hips and cocks his head to the side waiting for my reply.

"Give me a few minutes, I need to think. Can I use your phone?"

"Be my guest."

I'm thinking about Kate and Roxy and how I let them down when they needed me the most. It's not like me. It confuses me. I think about Walter Pickles and what he said at the last meeting about being powerless over alcohol and how it can make your life unmanageable. I'm also thinking about that higher power he talked about and how I might be dead right now if not for that possibility.

I don't know. Facing change can be a scary proposition. Most people don't handle it very well and I'm probably one of them. One thing I do know, I have to call Kate and apologize.

"Nick!" Kate answers on the first ring.

"Hi, Kate."

"Where the hell have you been? I've been calling and texting you since yesterday." I can tell she's as much pissed off at me as concerned. I don't blame her.

"I know. I'm sorry. I had a slip."

"Sounds like more than a slip, you scared the hell out of me. Did you get my message?" Well, maybe she is more concerned than pissed, thank God.

"No, my phone's dead. I haven't gotten anything."

"I left you a message that I had to go to a press conference the FBI was holding about the Mavis Rodgers' case. Now they're saying it's part of a serial killing spree that started in Reno."

"Did they give you any credit for breaking the story?"

"As a matter of fact they did, but I couldn't have done it without you." Now she's sounding much better.

"I need to see you, Kate, but there's some business I have to take care of first."

"But, Nick. . ."

"It's important, Kate, someone's life may depend on it."

After I finish talking to Kate, I call Alice to let her know I'm on my way to the office. She reads me the riot act. It's like I'm answering to my mother or worse. After a solid two minutes of being told how inconsiderate and immature I've been, Alice finally returns to being my secretary and says how relieved she is to hear from me. Her remarks duly noted, I ask her to contact Roxy and see if she can come by the office for a meeting.

The rest of the trip with Lyle is quiet but tense. He knows I'm not telling him everything but respects me enough to believe there must be a good reason why.

When I finally arrive back at my apartment, I shower and shave which makes me feel like a new man, or at least human. Looking at myself in the mirror though is not as easy. Guilt and shame look back at me with a newfound vengeance. I call a cab and head for my office.

"Hi, Alice, it's Roxy. Got your message about wanting me to come by the office to see Nick. What's going on? Is he working for me or not? I've called him at least a dozen times but he hasn't called me back."

"Right. . .well, uh, he's had a bit of trouble, Roxy, but nothing that. . .look, I'd better let him explain. Don't worry, he's fine. Can you come by today?"

"OK, Alice, I'll be in around eleven. Gotta go, I have another call coming in."

⟟

The October morning air is crisp, cool and dry. Vegas does have seasons but only the people who live here believe that. Roxy stands on her balcony looking out at the city that took her in and helped give her a new life. Her hands are wrapped around her favorite coffee mug, the UCLA emblem beginning to fade along with her past dreams. She looks at the number coming in on her cell but doesn't recognize it.

"Hello."

"Roxy, it's Bobby. Did you pick up the package?"

"Good morning, Bobby. Yes, I got it. A necklace? It's not my style, sweetheart, and I really don't understand. But then there's a lot I don't understand right now."

"Yeah, I know. It's a special necklace, Roxy. There's a recording device in it and it may very well have the voice of the person who killed Mavis on it."

Roxy lets out a deep sigh, walks back into her kitchen and sits down.

"That damn thing has a tape recorder in it? Bobby it's too early for this shit."

"Now hang on, Roxy. I bought that necklace then modified it by adding a recording chip. That way I could track Mavis and listen to any conversations she may have had with psychos who wanted to hurt her. By the way, I'm a sound engineer not a jewelry designer."

"I know, I know, Bobby. That was actually pretty clever. So how the hell did you get the necklace back from the cops?"

"After Mavis' mother picked up her belongings from the police station I contacted her and asked her if I could have the necklace to remember Mavis by and had her send it to Fast Eddie. The cops had no idea about the recording device."

"OK, so what do you want *me* to do with it?" Fear, irritation and a dose of doubt resonate through Roxy's voice.

"I need you to come to L.A. and bring me the necklace so I can record the voices off the chip. But first I need you to go get Julio away from Wesley Kootz and bring him with you."

"What? For God's sake, Bobby, who the hell is Julio?" Roxy reaches for the coffee pot and begins to worry about the day ahead.

⚜

"Good morning. Nick Ross Detective Agency, how may I help you?" Alice rolls her chair back from her desk and reaches for her Starbuck's latte, her second one of the morning. As I walk through the door I hear her taking the incoming call.

"No thanks, we're not in the market for any reverse mortgage consultations today, everyone here is independently wealthy. Have a nice day." She takes another swig of her coffee and swivels back to her desk. It's the little things she does, like her expert customer service, that remind me how could I not love Alice.

"Good morning, Alice. I wish you would have called me to tell me how rich I am. I wouldn't have come to work today. Maybe never."

"Well, good morning to you too. Feeling better today, are we?" I know sarcasm when I hear it and it's one of Alice's strong suits.

"Jury's out. Thanks for asking. Would you mind making me a pot of real coffee, please? Any word back from Roxy?"

"Yes, she called just a few minutes ago. Said she'd be here by eleven. She's pissed you haven't returned her calls. And she's worried. Mostly worried."

"Got it. As soon as the coffee's ready could you bring me a cup? Guess I need my messages and reports too. Please." I'm thinking how much my head still hurts and hoping Alice will lighten up on me.

"Actually they're already on your desk waiting for you. You do have a little catching up to do." Ah, more sarcasm. Pile it on.

As I walk back to my office I suddenly have a feeling of dread come over me. A nagging thought starts rolling around in my brain that I've screwed something up causing a great deal of harm to someone I love. It's not something I can grasp as a specific truth, just a panicky sickening feeling that something bad is going to happen. I had the same feeling the day Emily was killed.

I spend the next two hours alternating between getting caught up on work and trying to think of anything I might have done that could have been harmful. Eventually I pick up the phone and call my sponsor Walter Pickles. No answer, so I leave a somewhat cryptic message about what's going on and ask if he has time to meet later in the day.

Just before eleven o'clock Roxy enters the office, slinging her shoulder bag over her halter top. The high-heel clogs she's wearing makes her tower over Alice. As Roxy walks up to her desk, Alice looks up and raises her hand in the air, forefinger out, as she takes the phone from her ear.

"Hang on a sec, honey, I have a client. Hello, Miss Lynn, you're looking fab, love that top. How are you?"

"I'm good, Alice, how are you?" Roxy tosses her hair back, a nervous habit but sexy.

"Just couldn't be better, hon. Nick's in his office you can just go on back."

When Roxy walks in, she rouses me out of my apocalyptic stupor which makes me glad to see her. She gives me the once-over, obviously looking for any physical damage, then pulls up a chair in front of me and gives me a piercing look. My headache's back with a vengeance.

"I apologize, Roxy. I screwed up. I'm sorry. It will never happen again."

"I don't know what to say, Nick. I needed you to be there for me and you weren't. I was scared to death. All I could think of was the killer came after you." Roxy eases up slightly on her glare, takes her death-grip off the chair arms and leans back a bit.

"There's no excuse for what I did. I hope you can forgive me."

"I'll think about it and let you know. While you were off on your little 'leave of absence' things have gotten more complicated. A lot more complicated. I heard from Bobby."

I really want to say something about the leave of absence remark but decide it's not worth it. "Bobby Westbrook?"

"Can you believe it? Surprised the hell out of me too. He asked me to pick up a package, said it contained something that might help identify the killer."

"OK, so where's this package we have to pick up and what the hell's in it?"

I can't quite read Roxy's face. Her anger with me seems to have dissipated, replaced by a sort of Mona Lisa smile. Or maybe my brain's still in recovery mode. Roxy leans forward in her chair and dangles the necklace around her neck.

"I'm wearing it, it's this necklace," says Roxy. "Ta-da."

"OK, you're losing me now. What do you mean?" I really need more coffee.

"Mavis always loved jewelry, the big chunky stuff, ya know. Most girls do, but me, not so much."

Roxy glances down at her chest and the intricately woven coils of silver and copper artfully twisted around a dozen, thumbnail-size, vintage turquoise stones, a thick, hammered silver cross hanging from the center. A talisman piece for sure. The proportions? Hell, I don't know.

"When Mavis started getting death threats Bobby rigged up this necklace with a chip in it so he could monitor Mavis when she wasn't with him." Roxy rubs her fingers back and forth over the cross as she talks.

"Great idea. So what happened?"

"He's not sure. He thinks she got too far out of range and he couldn't pick up the signal, but he says the device should have kept recording."

"So the killer's voice may be on the chip?" I say that out loud but I'm thinking solving this murder spree won't be that easy.

"Exactly, Nick. It could prove Bobby's innocence."

"Look, Roxy, why don't we just take it to the cops and let them listen to it. They have more resources."

"I asked Bobby that. He told me that in order to read the chip you have to know the code and only he knows it. He thinks this is his only chance to clear himself. And there's more. He wants me to bring some kid named Julio to him from Wesley Kootz's revival. Now why would I want to do that?"

"I met Julio. Bobby promised him he would get him away from Kootz. I know I'm going to regret this, but I'm all in. I'm going with you. We need to leave as soon as possible."

"Oh Nick, thank you. You are now officially forgiven."

"Shit, I don't have a car until tomorrow."

"No problem, I ran into a great cabby who says he can be my driver anytime I need him."

"That's probably a good idea. That way no one can trace us, no trail. I have a few things I need to do before we leave. Why don't you pick me up at three and we'll go get Julio while Kootz is in the middle of his performance. Then on to L.A., I hope."

▲

After Roxy leaves I throw a few things together I might need for the trip and lock-up my office.

"Alice, I'm going to be out of town for a few days. I'll check in but you won't be able to reach me on my cell. I don't want any traces."

"You're not going on another bender, are you?"

"Thanks a lot, Alice. Give me a break, would you? No, I'm going to be in L.A. with Roxy, but that's confidential."

"Oh my, I mean I had no idea. . .you two?" Alice looks up, her eyes as big as saucers.

"For Christ's sake, Alice, it's not like that. Do me a favor and put your talents to work finding some connections between any of the cops that worked the killings in Reno and the victims."

"Will do, boss. Hang on a sec, I have a call coming in. Ross Detective Agency, may I help you? It's your parole officer Walter Pickles. You want to talk to him?"

"How many times do I have to tell you. . .never mind. Just tell him I'll see him at the meeting. I'm headed to Ronnie's to meet Kate."

Captain Tucker is sitting in his office going over the latest briefings from the FBI and his own detectives when his outside line rings.

"This is Captain Sam Tucker LVPD. How can I help you?"

"Hey, Tuck, it's Eddie Cologne. How's it goin'?"

"Ah, Fast Eddie, to what do I owe this honor?" The last time Tucker saw Eddie he was in a lineup accused of pimping teenage girls. The charge was mysteriously dropped a day later after Eddie ratted out a low-level Mafia enforcer.

"I may have something for you, Tuck."

"What do you want, Eddie? You don't give anything away for free." Tucker stands up and walks to his office door, points to his phone, looks at Lyle and mouths the words, "Trace this."

"You're lookin' for Bobby Westbrook, right?"

"Yeah, Eddie. Us, the FBI and half the country, why?"

"I might have somethin' for you if we can make a deal."

"Oh here it comes. What kind a deal, Eddie?"

"You know the Fed's got me on some porn charges. Underage crap, that kind a thing. And you guys are still lookin' at chargin' me with runnin' prostitutes out a my club. Which you know is bullshit."

"Yeah, so what?"

"So I give you Bobby Westbrook and you make it all go away." Eddie's voice is getting nervous, he's talking fast like he's afraid Tucker won't buy the deal.

"Why don't I just haul your ass in here and make you talk?"

"Because you'll never be able to find me, that's why. I'm layin' low. Things are happening fast, Tucker. If you want to make the deal there's not much time."

"I'll see what I can do. Have you an answer by three."

▲

When I walk into Ronnie's Jasper is sitting at the end of the bar on the phone with his boyfriend Rick. He's tapping his fingers on the bar and his round face is getting red with anger.

"So when are you coming back?. . .Oh really? Well that's nice, you take as much time as you need. I'm sure it's just lovely in Laguna Beach." I love it when Jasper's sarcastic, he's so good at it. Even better than Alice.

Jasper nods and motions for me to sit down.

"Yes, of course, you just need some time for reflecting, to get your head together. I'm quite sure none of those bronzed boys on the beach are involved. Call me when you get your shit together, Rick. Good-bye!"

"Hey Jasper, how's it going?"

"Hello, Nicholas. Did you hear all of that? He's such an asshole, don't know why I put up with him. Damn relationships are such a hassle. Think I'll go back to one-night stands."

"Maybe you love him, Jasper."

"Oh God, don't use the L word, Nick, please. It makes me shudder. Love is for teenagers and delusional housewives."

"Jasper, I'm meeting Kate here shortly. We're going to have a little talk. Know what I mean? How about a nice quiet table in the back?"

"Oh dear, you poor boy. I know what you're in for. Don't worry, I'll take care of it. No one will bother you. *Promise.*"

Jasper puts me at a table looking out over the street but on its own little balcony with a private entrance. As the waitress brings me coffee, I see Kate about halfway down the block headed this way. She must be on the phone since one arm is swinging and the other is glued to her ear. Maybe she's practicing to take a swing at me.

I'm feeling as nervous and jittery as a schoolboy about to ask his first girlfriend to go steady. Kate then walks through the door with Jasper by her side.

"Well, look who I found walking down the street, Nick. You two behave now."

Kate's looking a little nervous herself, so I walk over and give her a big hug. She responds but in a very subdued manner, stepping back toward the chair. I can't tell if she's pissed or relieved.

"OK. . .so what exactly happened?" Kate says taking the seat nearest the railing. Me? I'm in the hot seat, deservedly so.

"I screwed up, made a mistake and I'm sorry. Do you want me to explain?"

"Yes, I do. I think that might be a good place to start."

I take a breathe and think about all that has happened while I look into Kate's eyes. Her beautiful blue eyes look back at me and my heart skips a beat. Then I begin to explain.

"I was at O'Connell's with Lyle, we were watching the ball-game. I wasn't drinking. Then Lyle saw Captain Tucker and invited him to join us. Well, you know how Tucker and I get along. He started giving me shit, one thing led to another and punches got thrown. Then I left for your place and our dinner. When I got there you were gone, which really upset me."

"Well, why didn't you answer your phone? I left you a message about the press conference." Kate shakes her head and raises her arms in a "what the hell" gesture.

"When I reached for my phone it was gone. I thought maybe it had fallen out during the fight, so I went back to O'Connell's to look for it. It wasn't there either and that's when I had a drink. I don't know why, I just did. I only wanted one but I'm not sure what happened. I don't remember anything between finishing the first drink and waking up the next day out in the desert in the middle of nowhere. I swear, it's like I was drugged or something. I found the phone in-between my seat and the console in my car, but it was dead. So I couldn't call until Lyle found me. Luckily found me."

"You could have been killed or died out there, Nick." Her tone is softening but only slightly.

"I know, Kate. I'm sorry but there was something I found out that made it worthwhile."

"About the case?" she asks, still pissed-off but her attitude now all-business.

"No, I found out something about myself. And you," I say leaning towards her across the table, arms extended, hands open. "When Lyle found me, the first thought I had was of you. That's when I realized I love you, Kate. I haven't let myself feel anything for such a long time I'd forgotten what it's like, but you woke me up. You helped me love again."

Kate sits back in her chair and I see a tear roll down her cheek. "Damn it, Nick, you made me so angry when I didn't hear from you, and then I got so scared when I thought something had happened to you." She pauses and brushes away the lone tear. "I was truly worried about you. I couldn't sleep, you're all I thought about. And that's when I knew. I'm in love with you too, Nick. So now what?" Kate reaches across the table and puts her hands in mine.

"We're going to take one day at a time," I say, certain I've never felt relief and gratitude like this before. "We both have some things to work out, but we'll work on them together. It'll be OK. We'll be OK. I promise."

Kate smiles, squeezes my hands and softly asks, "Will you tell me about her, Nick, will you tell me about Emily?"

I look up at the sky and try to push away as I take a breath, hoping the sickening feeling in my gut will go away. "Don't run, Nick," I tell myself. "Not this time." I look Kate straight in the eyes. "Yes, yes, you do need to know." I fight off the ache in my voice and begin to tell Kate about Emily.

Kate studies my face and listens intently, only asking brief questions about what Emily was like. I tell her about our time together and all the plans we'd made. I talk about how much we loved each other and our excitement about the baby that was on the way.

Then I get to the day Emily was killed and I go silent for awhile.

"Nick, are you all right?"

"Yeah, I'm OK. . .Just give me a minute."

I begin to explain to Kate about the day Emily and the baby were killed. How my partner and I had answered the call and were the first on the scene. I tell her about seeing Mavis Rodgers bent over trying to help the driver in the car, blood all over her hands. I try to describe my shock and terror as I reached the car and suddenly realized it was Emily lying there. I tell her how I screamed for the medics to help as they pulled her from the car and wheeled her to the ambulance.

Kate listens quietly as I talk about the agony I felt waiting in the emergency room for what seemed forever, not able to let myself think about our unborn child. Praying, begging, pleading with God to save Kate and our baby. And I tell her about how the doctor led me into the hallway with his hand on my shoulder and told me that my wife and son were both dead.

Kate sits across from me staring out toward the street, tears running down her cheeks. "Oh my God, Nick, I'm so sorry. Why wasn't this in the papers?"

"I had them withhold her name for our family's sake. She was just a Jane Doe."

I look out at the street and sit in silence for several seconds feeling the intense pain of that loss once again. Then I turn to Kate. "Remember the old adage 'What doesn't kill you makes you stronger'. Well, it's bullshit, some things can keep killing you everyday and you don't even know it. But I want to get on with my life, Kate. I think I'm finally ready to."

"I understand, and yes, the past can destroy your future if you let it, but Emily wouldn't want that for you, Nick."

"No, no she wouldn't."

"Now I know why you're so involved in the Mavis Rodgers' case. Finding her killer would help resolve some things."

"It's more than that, Kate. After Mavis was killed another transgender came to me and asked for help. She thinks the killer is after her now and she's running out of time."

"So are you working with the police and the FBI on this?"

"No, she has some trouble in her past and is afraid to go to the cops. That's why she came to me. There's not much more I can tell you, Kate. I don't want to get you involved."

"I'd say I'm pretty involved already and, since I'm very involved with you, let me help. Oh, and by the way, the killer has a name now. Somebody leaked the info about the bible verse. So they've named him Leviticus.

⚔

It's early afternoon and I'm on my way to meet with Walter Pickles at the Men's Club where the AA meetings are held. I'm feeling a strange yet peaceful sensation coming over me. The talk with Kate did something for me that I hadn't experienced in a long time, maybe never. That release of pent–up emotion seems to have also brought me a newfound sense of gratitude and awareness.

As I walk into the AA meeting I notice people seem to be looking at me differently. Their smiles seem genuine and their greetings honest. As I walk by a mirror in the hall I notice a relaxed smile on my face that I was not even aware of.

Walter's at the other end of the room talking to a newcomer. I glance at the dingy walls covered with battered slogans that have been there forever. I slow down to read each one for the first time. "Let Go and Let God", "Easy Does It", "Live and Let Live", "This too Shall Pass", "But for the Grace of God", "One Day at Time" and my favorite, "Poor Me, Poor Me, Pour Me Another Drink".

As I approach Walter he extends his hand. When I reach for it I feel a sense of comfort and honesty as we greet each other. It's so powerful I'm not even aware of my words. We sit down at the table and look at each other ready for the meeting to start. I can tell Walter sees something in my eyes.

"How are you doing, Nick? I got your message."

"I don't know, Walter. I'm having a very strange day."

"You do have a rather different look about you."

"What kind of a look? Do I look strange, weird, sick?"

"No, no, Nick. Nothing like that. But I have seen it before. Sometimes it's when people are having a spiritual experience."

"I have been having some really strange feelings in the last few hours. Not something I'm at all used to, but not really bad either." I look at Walter and laugh, "Am I making any sense?"

Walter slaps my shoulder as if we're old friends. "Absolutely, Nick. Remember the feeling and enjoy it while it lasts. It often signals the start of something new, a rebirth if you will."

The rest of the meeting is a blur. I listen but it all sounds like background noise. Everyone's words seem to flow through me like music. Then it's time for me to speak. I don't remember what I said or if I said anything at all. All I know is the thought that strikes me when I finally sit down. In this moment, for the first time, I admit I am powerless over alcohol and my life is unmanageable. I look at Walter and no sooner do the words leave my mouth when I feel a pure, clean, undeniable truth and something in me changes.

CHAPTER 13

"Danke Schoen"

Before I left Kate I told her about going to L.A. though I didn't explain other than to say it was business. She was somewhat skeptical or maybe curious would be a better word. Being the diligent reporter she is, a few probing questions were asked but not answered. She finally accepted the fact I had to respect a client's privacy and gave up.

Back at my apartment I throw together a duffel bag for the trip and sort through my mail which is mostly junk. There's a postcard offering a free dinner if I'll sit through a retirement planning sell-job, two credit card offers and my power bill. I do see one envelope that looks a little odd. No return address, just an ink-stamped cross in its place. My name is typed out in an Old English type of font. Kind of a *Game of Thrones* look.

I open the envelope and unfold the page:

Dear Sinner,

If you continue to help the blasphemous she-male, I will kill you. Save yourself. Step aside and let God's work be done. His justice will prevail.

—Leviticus

Now this asshole is really getting on my nerves. I take the note and carefully place it back in the envelope setting it aside on my desk. Maybe I should feel fear but I don't. In fact, I expected something like this and it only steels my resolve to find this nut job and put him away. I go to my closet, take out my .38 and throw it in the duffel.

The intercom on the wall buzzes signaling that someone is at the front gate. I push the talk button to ask who is there.

"Oh yez, Mr. Ross, this is Saleem. Miss Roxy ask I pick you up. I am driving you the next days, thank you."

"Is Roxy with you?"

"Oh no, she at the Follies to talk to a friend, we pick her up on way out the town."

"Give me a minute, Saleem, and I'll be out."

"Oh yez, Saleem wait, thank you."

I take the .38 out of the bag and place it in an ankle holster on my leg. I'm sure this guy is legit but for right now I'm not taking any chances.

As I walk through the front gate I see Saleem standing next to a black town car. He's a tall slender man with perfect posture. His dark skin shines in contrast with his coarse, grey-tinged beard. He's wearing a cream-colored turban and matching jacket with a red ascot. Aviator glasses hide his eyes giving him a mysterious aura.

"Hello, Saleem. I'm Nick Ross, nice to meet you."

"Oh yez, hello, Mr. Ross, is my pleasure to make your acquaintance. Please may I take bag for you."

"Thanks, nice car, Saleem. It looks spotless."

"Oh yez, she my pride and joy. I own her. I'm an independent livery."

As Saleem opens the car door for me, I'm thinking maybe this guy just came from a casting call. He opens the door with one arm tucked behind his back nodding so slightly for me to get in. I oblige and nod in return as I get into the car.

⚑

Captain Tucker sits in his office contemplating a call to the FBI. He doesn't like the agent in charge of the investigation of Mavis Rodgers and has had run-ins with him in the past.

In his mind Mathew McCain is a two-faced, power-grabbing politician who will step on anybody or anything to promote himself. Tucker detests McCain's hypocrisy of publicly showing off his perfect God-fearing family, while privately cavorting with who knows who and doing who knows what.

Tucker knows that ultimately he must make the call and inform the FBI about Eddie Cologne and the deal to get Bobby Westbrook, but that doesn't mean he can't give his department a few hours head start. After all, it would be quite a feather in his cap to capture Westbrook.

But first things first, he has to call Eddie and make the deal.

"Eddie, it's Captain Tucker. You ready to talk?"

"It's about time, Tucker, you're pushing it. You got me my deal?"

"I got you a deal as long as we get Westbrook. If we don't get him, then no deal."

"That's bullshit. I can't be responsible for stupid cops who can't find their asses with both hands."

"That's the deal, Eddie. Take it or leave it."

"Fine, I'll take it, but I want it in writing."

"I'll get it to you but I need the info now."

"You fuck me on this, Tucker, and I'll make sure every informer in Vegas knows. You'll never get anybody to snitch again."

"I've got no reason to screw you over, Eddie. Let's have it.

"OK, OK. . .Bobby contacted a showgirl named Roxy Lynn. She's a transgender who headlines the Follies. He had a package sent to my nightclub for her to pick up, so she could take it to him."

"And what was in the package?"

"I don't know. We didn't open it. She had to wait to hear from Bobby."

"I'm only believing part of this bullshit, Eddie."

"Yeah, well all you have to do is find Roxy and follow her to Bobby."

"Exactly how long ago did she pick the package up?"

"Last night."

"Shit, she may already be gone. I'll be in touch, Eddie. . .don't leave town."

⅄

Saleem pulls up in front of the Follies and I jump out to go find Roxy. I walk through the main entrance where posters of the Folly Girls line the hall. Roxy is predominant in most of them, clearly the star, but the dozens of others featured with her have beauty that is equally as startling. If I didn't know better I'd swear these are some of the most gorgeous women in the world.

I come across a lady in the hallway who I can tell is one of the performers and ask her if she has seen Roxy.

"Oh yeah, sweetheart, she's back in the dressing room talking to Kim So Hung. Just go through those doors, turn left and it will be down the hall on your right."

Not that I'm into it or anything, but I've heard the name Kim So Hung before. She's an Asian actor turned transgender who became a famous porn star. Once I find my way to the dressing room I see Roxy and Kim talking to each other over by the make-up tables. When I see Kim in person I now know why she became famous. Lustrous, long black hair, flawless skin, delicate features and a perfectly sculpted body. I get it.

"Hello, Roxy. Saleem's out front, we're ready to go."

Roxy smiles, grabs my arm and nods towards her friend.

"Oh, Nick, this is Kim. She's going to fill in for me while I'm gone."

"Nice to meet you, Miss Hung."

"Oh, call me Kim. Probably rolls off your tongue easier." She says with a wink and a soft, sexy tone that in itself is a showstopper.

"You bet," I say, ignoring the double entendre. "Sorry to cut this short, Roxy, but we need to get on the road."

"OK, I just need to grab my bag. So good to see you, Kim. Thanks again for filling in for me. I owe you one."

"Yes, Miss Kim, it was nice to meet you."

"And it was *certainly* nice to meet you, Nick. Maybe we'll see each other around?"

"Yeah, sure." I say as Kim gives me yet another wink that's again just a tad too suggestive to be comfortable.

As we leave the building Saleem walks up, takes Roxy's bag and puts it in the trunk.

"Where are we headed, Miss Roxy?"

"Head towards Laughlin, Saleem. I'll give you more details when we get there."

Within an hour the billboards of Vegas start to transition to the billboards of Laughlin and my education about the world of transgender continues.

⋏

After talking to Fast Eddie, Captain Tucker immediately summons Lyle and Mitch to his office.

"Guys, we just got a big break on the Mavis Rodgers' murder case. A transgender named Roxy Lynn is on her way to meet Bobby Westbrook. We need to find her fast and follow her to Bobby."

"Did you say Roxy Lynn, the star of the Follies?"

"Yeah, that's what I said, Lyle. Is she a friend of yours?" Tucker smirks.

"No, I just recently met her. She's a client of Nick Ross."

"Oh, this just keeps getting better and better. Put a tail on Ross too."

"What about the FBI?"

"I'm not worried about the FBI, Mitch. I'll deal with Agent Mathew McCain in good time, but for right now we have a head start so let's make the most of it and find Westbrook."

"Are you putting out an APB, Captain?" Mitch says looking somewhat confused.

"No, not until I contact the FBI. Grab as many uniforms as you need to start the search and check back with me in an hour."

Mitch and Lyle walk out of Tucker's office and start down the hall. Lyle looks at Mitch, rolls his eyes and shakes his head no. Mitch shrugs and walks on.

🠪

Once in the car Roxy starts to settle in. The leather seats are deep and comfortable. Saleem must use some kind of freshener because it smells like lavender in here. Lots of lavender. I crack my window a little to get some real air.

"So, Roxy, are you ready for this? Oh, and by the way, you need to keep your cell phone off. I've got a throwaway if you need to make a call."

"Guess I'm as ready as can be for a person that only has a few more days to live."

"Well, that's something that we're going to change."

"So why do I need to turn off my cell, Nick?"

"If the cops find out about us they could triangulate your cell phone signal and track us."

"But how would the cops find out about us?"

"Do you trust Fast Eddie?"

"Sure I do. . .well, I think I do. Well, actually maybe not."

"From what I know about Fast Eddie, there's nobody he cares about more than Fast Eddie, but I hope you're right."

Roxy seems to be studying my face as she's talking.

"Nick, you seem different. Your eyes look like they're smiling. Are you all right?"

"I'm fine. I have been having a rather unusual day to say the least, but in a good way. You know what I mean?"

"Yeah, I think so."

"Changing subjects, have you ever considered the possibility that Bobby really is the killer and he's just using this story about the necklace as a ploy to lure you in and kill you?"

"I've thought about it, and it does scare me, but right now what choice do I have?"

"Turn the necklace over to the cops, cut a deal and let them handle it."

"I gave Bobby my word, Nick, and besides why would he want me to get Julio if that was his motive?"

"OK, good point, but remember whoever is doing this is smart and very deceptive, a good combination for a serial killer. They make you believe what they want you to believe until you find out too late that everything is not as it seems."

"Well, I know one thing for sure," says Roxy. "I'm starving. Saleem, take the next exit where we can get something to eat, please."

"Oh yez, thank you, mum. Saleem is starving too."

We're about halfway to Laughlin before we see an exit that has something other than the truck stops with McDonald's or

Subways. Saleem finally spots a Bob's Big Boy which I feel compelled to accept though I'd been hoping for an In-N-Out burger.

The hot, dry desert air sears our skin the minute we open the car doors. The three of us squint and lower our heads as we run towards the building. Lovely weather if you're into that sandblasted look. Once inside, the AC-chilled air feels like a cold shower as I slip into a booth with Roxy and Saleem.

I look around the room, an old habit of mine, and I see several people whispering and pointing to a table in the back. I strain to see past two star-gazed elderly ladies with notepads and catch a glimpse of the object of their desire sitting at a nearby table with two others.

And there he is, Mr. Las Vegas himself. Yes, Wayne Newton. Saleem spots him at the same time and can hardly control himself.

"Oh, do you see who I see? I can't believe. It's Wayne. Must have the autograph, please may I borrow notepad?"

"Sure, Saleem, we'll wait here."

"No, Saleem too shy, not want to disturb Mr. Wayne."

"Come on, Saleem, I'll go with you." Roxy takes Saleem by the hand and leads him away.

"Oh, Miss Roxy, you do that for Saleem? Thank you, thank you."

I just sit and watch as a Middle Eastern man in a turban and a Nehru jacket, accompanied by a transgender bombshell saunter up to the Vegas icon's table. As Roxy and Saleem approach, I can see Wayne's eyes getting bigger—well, as big as they can considering. . .well, you know. Saleem bows to introduce himself as Roxy throws a hand on one hip and tilts her head to the side.

Wayne stands up and acknowledges Saleem, then reaches for Roxy's hand, taking it in his and kissing it. In my book this beats any Vegas show, great seat and the price is right.

Saleem hands his notepad to Wayne then watches intently as pen touches paper and the entertainer hands it back. I think Saleem may just cry. He bows twice, then slowly backs away nodding a thank you. Wayne gallantly gestures for Roxy to take a seat and leans in close to talk to her. Roxy smiles a devilish little grin as she turns my way and winks. She then turns to Wayne and whispers something in his ear. Clearly taken aback, Wayne smiles and raises his hands in a "no harm, no foul" gesture. Roxy and Saleem come bouncing back to our table laughing their asses off.

"Wow, Nick, you missed it. I just got hit on by Wayne Newton."

"Yeah, and how did that go?"

"Well, you saw it. He was quite surprised to say the least."

"Oh, Miss Roxy, thank you so kindly for going with Saleem."

"No problem, Saleem. Best laugh I've had in a long time."

Thirty minutes later we're sitting at our table enjoying the finest chicken fried steak, meatloaf and lasagna this little diner has to offer, when Wayne and his compatriots walk by on their way out. "Love you," Roxy and Saleem call in unison as he picks up his pace and heads straight for the parking lot. The three of us break out in the kind of laughter that brings tears to your eyes and makes you gasp for air.

Back in the car there's a new feeling of camaraderie as we get ready for our journey. Roxy opens up with small talk by asking Saleem if he has a family.

"Oh yes, mum, a wife Callista, and my lovely daughter Ariel." Saleem's love for his family comes through loud and clear.

"How nice, Saleem, how old is your daughter?"

"Ariel is 19. She is an excellent student at UCLA."

"Good for her, you must be very proud."

"Oh yez, mum. What about you, Miss Roxy, do you have love in your life?"

"Yeah, Roxy, you got a boyfriend?" I say in my best smart-ass tone.

"A boyfriend? What makes you think I'm gay, Nick?"

"Well, I just thought, I mean, uh. . ." Shit, she got me on that one. "Sorry, Roxy."

"Take it easy, Nick. Lots of people are confused about that. I'm just saying not all of us are gay. A few of us are straight and some go both ways. Yes, most are gay, but you'd be surprised how many straight guys like to go out with us. Must be some kind of fantasy you boys have. Of course, women love us too. It's their way of having a threesome without the extra person. What else you want to know, Nick?"

"That's enough for now, thanks, Roxy," I say, getting much more of an education than I bargained for.

"What about you, Nick, got a girlfriend?"

"Yes, I do. She's a reporter for the Sun."

"Is it serious?"

"Yes, well, at least it's getting that way, I think."

"OK, now we're getting somewhere. Tell us about her. What's her name?"

"Her name is Kate, Kate Simon." I can tell the interrogation has started.

"I know her, I've read her articles, she's a good writer. She's the one who broke the story about Mavis, right? Wonder where she got her info from?" Roxy smiles, rolls her eyes and looks away.

Nick glances out the window. "Can we move on now? Saleem, you're going to need to take a right at the next junction, then follow the signs to the revival."

Roxy and Saleem keep a discussion going about Wayne while I refocus on thinking about just how to get Julio away from Wesley Kootz. I'm hoping it will be relatively simple, but I have no idea what his story is or why he wants to be with the good people of the snake-handling Reverend. Or maybe he doesn't and that's the point. I know I need to avoid all the good ole boys as much as possible. We don't want any run-ins with them that might bring out the local authorities.

Ahead I can see the yellow-hued lights of the revival tent looking like an oasis in the middle of the desert. If you didn't know better you might mistake it for a three-ring circus that's wandered off course. Dozens of cars and even more pick-up trucks are parked out front. Kootz must have a full house tonight.

It's a cool evening and the wind is gusting, creating dust devils all around us. The entrances to the tent are sealed with flaps pulled taut to keep out the little tornados of blowing sand. How to get in is the problem. Once we open the flaps everyone will see us.

We pull up near the tent and I have Saleem stop while I talk to Roxy about how to pull this off.

"Roxy, we need a plan. Julio doesn't know you so I need to go in, find him and hope he remembers me. I'm going to grab my camera out of my duffle and pose as the photographer from the paper. Can you make some sort of grand entrance and create a diversion while I sneak in under the tent in back?"

Roxy beams and can't answer fast enough. "Why, of course I can. I do it all the time."

"Saleem, kill the lights but keep the engine running and point the car towards the road. We may need to make a quick getaway."

"Oh yez, no problem." Lucky for me Saleem seems nonchalant about our little adventure.

"OK, Roxy, let's go." We both jump out of the car and I give her the thumbs up. She heads for the entrance as I walk around the back to sneak in. I figure Julio will probably be backstage.

I watch as Roxy throws the flap open and struts into the tent as if the orchestra had just struck her cue. Wesley Kootz is in the middle of the stage sermonizing to his brothers and sisters, his hands raised to the sky. His cape flutters open with each gesture making him look like he has wings. He spots Roxy walking in out of the corner of his eye. Roxy seizes the moment.

"Hallelujah, brothers and sisters, glory be to God!" Roxy's voice booms through the tent. She throws her arms above her head, spreads them wide as if to welcome the heavens, then slowly parades down the aisle towards Kootz.

The crowd looks somewhat stunned not knowing what to make of her. Some think she's just part of the show and start clapping, others sit staring in silence.

"I'm here to bare witness to the miracle I have seen," she says slowly turning toward the crowd and clasping her hands together as if in prayer.

A cacophony of "Praise Be to God's" rise up from the crowd which is now fixated on Roxy. Kootz marches to the front of the stage seizing the opportunity to regain his audience's attention. He adjusts his cape, stretches his arms out in a welcoming manner and bends over toward Roxy.

"Come forward, my child. Come tell us your story. Bare witness to your brethren." "This guy is a master of pious, BS rhetoric," I mutter to myself.

Roxy steps up to the front of the stage and once again raises her arms into the air as if she is summoning God Himself. Her voice starts to tremble and her body shakes. Definitely Oscar worthy.

I'm in the tent now and can see what's going on. I wanted her to grab the spotlight but didn't plan on her stealing the show. Too late to pull her back now and I still need to find Julio.

Kootz walks over to Roxy, ceremoniously takes her hand and blesses it. His every move looks choreographed as if the cameras were rolling and a director had shouted "Action."

"Tell us your story, child," Kootz proclaims in a tone that would charm the skin off a snake.

"Oh, thank you! And God bless you, sir. Yes, yes I will." Roxy puts her hand over her heart, hangs her head for a second, then addresses the crowd. "I was a poor miserable sinner with no faith until one day God blessed me with a miracle!"

"Praise be, child! Tell us your sins, tell it!" Kootz raises his voice a level and works the crowd like the pro he is.

"I had desires and needs contrary to God's law. I lived a lie fooling myself, fed by new world beliefs and the power of Satan. Then one day, when I was in the arms of another, God suddenly spoke to me." Roxy perks up as if she's seen a vision and looks out into the crowd. Man, she knows how to play a room.

I cautiously make my way to the back of the stage as I listen to Roxy go on about her miracle. I'm beginning to wonder where the hell she's going with her story when I see Julio standing in the wings alongside Max.

I try to get his attention but strike out. I walk up closer and start shooting pictures of the stage, attempting to make myself look legit. Julio turns but doesn't seem to recognize me. Max glances at me, shrugs his shoulders and turns back around to watch what's happening on stage. I nod at Julio and point for him to move away. Finally I see a glimmer of recognition and he off moves to the side away from Max.

Max looks over at us but seems somewhat dumbfounded. He's more intrigued with what's going on out front with Roxy and Kootz than with my interest in Julio. As Julio walks up, I take his arm and whisper, "Bobby sent me."

"Bobby! *Really?* Hey, you that photographer for the newspaper woman?"

"Yes, but actually I'm a private detective and I'm here to take you to Bobby in L.A. You need to be quiet, I'll explain to you outside. Stay close and don't look around."

"Yes, L.A., that my home. I go with you, get my things, OK?"

"Do it fast, we need to hurry." I try to look professional while Julio is gone but I'm getting very nervous. Max has got to catch on that something's up pretty soon.

Roxy turns to Wesley Kootz on stage, bows her head and drops to her knees as if she were in front of the Pope himself. She holds her prayer pose just the right amount of time to keep the crowd mesmerized.

"Go on child, tell your story. Testify." Kootz moves down onto one knee.

"Yes, as I was saying, God came to me as I was in the act of fornicating with another. His message was so powerful and so real it resonated through every fiber of my being."

"Yes sister, yes, bare witness. What did the Lord say, tell it." Kootz now tries to dial up the level of excitement for the crowd.

"He said. . .he said," Roxy pauses to work the moment. "He said, 'Raymond! You're a woman, get out of that man-body and become the woman you are!' " Roxy stands up straight and scans the audience while flashing a wide smile.

The crowd goes dead silent. I can hear the wind blowing the flaps back and forth. Wesley Kootz stands in disbelief, for once speechless in the shadow of his now unwelcomed visitor. Then he erupts. I'm thinking maybe the show's over. Time to clear out.

"Blasphemy, blasphemy, you have taken God's word in vain. Sinner! *Sinner!* Repent or burn in the fires of hell!" He stomps on the stage raising a fist in the air.

The whole tent begins to boo and shout at Roxy and calling her everything from a whore to Satan himself. Kootz stomps over to the wicker basket on stage, reaches in and pulls out a rattlesnake. Grasping it with both hands and raising it above his head, he starts towards Roxy.

"Now the serpent shall be removed just as I hold him above. Repent, repent and kiss the Devil's own. Come to me, child." Roxy gives him the finger and moves away quickly, looking for the exit.

I can't see what is happening out front but from the sound of the crowd I know we have to get the hell out in a hurry. I grab Julio as he clutches his duffle bag and we hurriedly make our way out of the tent and back toward the car.

As we get close to the car I turn and see Roxy running out of the tent toward the dirt parking lot, laughing her ass off, four-inch heels slowing her down not one bit. What she doesn't know is, Max is right behind her. Before she can make it to the car he grabs her by the back of her blouse and pulls her into him.

"What are you people up to? What the hell is this? Julio, Julio, you get over here now!" Max has Roxy in a headlock dragging her back toward the tent, towering over her like a giant.

"No, let go her, leave alone!" Julio yells back at Max stomping his foot.

"You get over here, Julio, or I'll break her neck." Roxy's face is turning red as Max puts more muscle into the headlock.

I start to go for my gun but Max sees me. He yells a threatening warning.

"Put your hands in the air, don't even think about, mister, or it's the last time you see her alive."

Before I can stop him, Julio starts walking towards them. Suddenly Max falls to his knees releasing his grip on Roxy. As his face hits the dirt I can see the silhouette of Saleem standing in the shadows with a baseball bat in his hand.

"Holy shit, Saleem."

"Yez, it's Saleem," he says matter of factly. "We better go now, yez, Mr. Nick?

"Yeah, let's get the hell out of here." Still not believing this mild-mannered man just waylaid a giant.

As we drive away I see Julio looking back. I can't tell if he is sad or relieved.

"Julio, are you all right?"

"Yes, fine, will be better when back in L.A."

"Good. Well, let me introduce you to everyone. This is Roxy Lynn, and up front is our home run hitting driver, Saleem. I'm sorry, I don't know your last name, Julio."

"It's Hernandez, Julio Miguel Hernandez, nice to meet you. And thank you for my freedom."

"Glad to do it. Bobby asked us to get you, but he didn't give us a lot of details. Were you being forced to stay there?"

"I not know if I should say." Julio looks away as his voice fades, seemingly embarrassed to talk.

"How old are you, Julio?"

"Julio 15," he replies, his voice barely above a whisper.

"It's OK, Julio, you don't have to be afraid. Did you run away from home?"

"No. My family in L.A., I no runaway, they throw me out."

There's a new awkwardness in the car. No one knows quite what to say as, each of us feeling the emotion behind Julio's words and the obvious pain he's endured. Roxy gives Julio a little hug and pats his leg as she smiles at him with kindness. "You want to tell us about it? I'm a very good listener," she says.

"I don't know, well, maybe yes," Julio says, his voice slightly less timid. "My family very strict Catholic, we go church almost every day. I love it too, it make me happy but have conflict. Everywhere I hear talk about gay people be OK now. They marry, have own family, all come out and be liked for self, they good people. I think Julio is good person too. I should be honest and not hide. So tell my parents the truth. Tell them I just want to be me and I gay.

"They say no! Not in this family. God does not allow this, it break His law. They say I must change, no be gay or not welcome in family and must leave. I say no to them, can not do this any more. So I leave."

"Oh my God, you poor boy, that's terrible and so sad. Can I give you a hug?"

"Yes, Miss Roxy, thank you."

"Julio," I ask, "just how did you meet Wesley Kootz?"

"Julio on street for weeks, I scared and hungry. Then one day a man come to me. He say he got job for me if I go with him, so I go. He take me to Reno and we go to revival show. Then I see him talk with Mr. Kootz and take money from him. He come back to me and say I stay at revival, it my new job and he leave."

"Then what happened?" Roxy looks over at me and I can see the anger in her eyes.

"Things OK at first, everyone nice to Julio, then I find out why there. Mr. Kootz he like young boys. He make clear to Julio what he want or else."

"That son of a bitch, I knew something was wrong with him. What did he threaten you with?" Roxy's anger boils up. I'm thinking it's a good thing she didn't know this back in the tent when she was arm's-length from Kootz.

"Julio not in country legal, I come with family five years ago. He say he turn me in and I get sent back to Mexico with no family. He tell police I drug runner, a mule he say."

"So where does Bobby come into this, Julio?" I'm curious as to why Bobby has such concern for this young man and I'm anxious to see Julio's reaction.

"Bobby come to run sound at the revival months after Julio be there. He nice man and talk to Julio many time. He tell me one day he know I'm gay, he can tell because Bobby gay too. But he say no one can know or big trouble for him.

"So I tell Bobby why I there, about Reverend Kootz and what he done to me. Bobby get mad, want to punch him, but I say no. Then he tell me when he leave he take Julio with him but everything change and Bobby gone."

"Well, you're safe now, Julio, we'll get you to L.A. and to Bobby." Roxy pats Julio on the head leans into him and whispers in his ear. "Don't you worry, sweetheart, everything will be all right."

Back at the Vegas Detective Bureau things are heating up. Mitch and Lyle are under the gun to come up with leads so they can track down Roxy and have her followed to Bobby Westbrook. They know Captain Tucker is getting a lot of arm twisting from the higher-ups and when he's under pressure they feel the brunt of it.

"Hey, Mitch, you come up with anything on Roxy yet?"

"Nah, I went by the Follies, Roxy had been there with Nick, but they didn't tell anybody where they were going just that she'd be gone a few days. I got the surveillance tapes from security so the crime lab is going over them. How about you?"

"I went and talked to Kate about Nick. She told me he'd been there but couldn't tell her what was going on because he was working on a case. At least that's what she tells me. How about phone records, anything?"

"Shit, Lyle, I'm still going through them, not a damn thing. They both must have their cells turned off because we're not getting a trace on them."

"I don't know, Mitch, Captain Tucker is not going to be very happy if we don't come up with something, and fast."

"Well, maybe the S.O.B. should have gotten the FBI involved right away instead of grandstanding to be the hero." Mitch shakes his head and leans back in his chair, grumbling.

"You checked all the rental companies and Nick's credit cards, right?" Lyle knows the answer but asks the question anyway.

"Yeah, nothing," says Mitch, growing more frustrated.

Lyle paces back and forth across the room. "Look, they have to have a car, either rented or borrowed, because Nick's car hasn't been returned yet. Does Roxy drive?"

"I don't think so. I'll check with DMV and see if she has a license."

"Maybe she has a driver or a service she uses. Check all the phone records again Mitch, look for a car service."

CHAPTER 14

WAYNE'S WORLD

We've been on the road for an hour or so and as yet there have been no repercussions from taking Julio away from the snake-handling pedophile. Saleem has some nice jazz on the radio. Roxy and Julio are each taking a nap. The desert is unforgiving outside our climate-controlled cabin. You can see the heat rising off the pavement of the highway and disintegrating in the slipstreams of traffic. It's another three hours or so to L.A. not counting the inevitable traffic tie-ups that could add another hour to the trip.

Saleem starts to slow down and I look up ahead to see a limo on the side of the road with its flashers on.

"Shall I stop and offer assistance, Mr. Nick?"

"Sure, Saleem, good idea. This isn't a good place to sit stranded for very long."

Saleem pulls up behind the limo, puts the flashers on, walks up to the driver's door, and taps on the window. After a few exchanges and head nods from Saleem, I see the rear door of the limo open and a tall, well-dressed man step out. His hat is pulled down over his forehead so I can't see his face. As he and Saleem walk back toward our car I see a big smile on Saleem's face. I bump Roxy on the arm to wake her up.

"Hey, looks like we have company."

"What? What are you talking about?" Roxy says, yawning. "Why are we stopped?"

Saleem opens the rear door and leans in. His grin barely fits through the door.

"Please, Miss Roxy and Mr. Nick, can we give ride to Mr. Wayne?"

And there he is, Mr. Las Vegas himself. Wayne Newton steps forward, tips his hat back and smiles. "Hello again, I seem to be in a difficult place. I have a show tonight in L.A. and they can't get another car here for a few hours. Would you be so kind as to give me a ride?"

Roxy is wide awake now and I can see a devilish look in her eyes with a quirky smile that seems to indicate we're going to have a good time with this.

"Yeah, sure, Mr. Newton, I'm OK with that. How about you, Roxy? And you, Julio?"

"Why not, the more the merrier. Right, Julio?" Roxy says nudging his arm.

"Yes, Miss Roxy."

"Oh, thank you all, and please call me Wayne."

"Julio, why don't you ride up front so Roxy and I can keep Wayne company."

Saleem retrieves two, large Vuitton bags from the limo and puts them in the trunk. As soon as we're all clicked in, the awkward silence is deafening. Finally Wayne clears his throat.

"*Ahem. . .*Miss Lynn, I just want to apologize for my behavior at the restaurant. I was surprised by your admission and shocked. You are such a beautiful woman. I mean, uh, well you know what I mean. Anyhow, I didn't know how to respond. I'm sorry. I have no animosity toward the LGBT community. Some of my good friends are gay." Wayne's voice quivers just a little with his last sentence and his tone deepens.

"Well, that's nice to hear, Wayne, apology accepted. You know, I actually have some good friends who are straight. Well, at least they say they are. You never know do you?" Roxy says with a grin.

"You mentioned you're headed to L.A.," I say making a conversational detour.

"I'm the M.C. at a benefit tonight for the USO. I've been the Chairman of the USO Celebrity Circle ever since Bob Hope asked me to take over for him."

"Wow, that's fantastic. What time does it start?"

"I need to be there around seven or so for sound checks and some rehearsal. The doors open at nine."

"How long to L.A., Saleem?"

"Should be two to three hours, Mr. Nick, depend on traffic."

"Sounds like we'll get you there right on schedule, Wayne, but I'm curious, why didn't you fly to L.A.?"

"Well, my private jet is in for maintenance and I can't stand flying commercial. So it was a limo because I'm sure as hell not driving to L.A myself."

◢

"I think we may be on to something, Lyle. Looks like Roxy used a car service just this morning. I called their office but all I got was a recording. They left a cell number to contact."

"Don't call it. Have the phone company trace it and find out where the signal is, then check with the crime lab and see if they have anything on the security camera footage from the Follies. I have to go see the Captain. Let me know as soon as you get something."

Lyle heads over to the Captain's office for his meeting and an update but when he gets there Tucker isn't in yet. His secretary tells Lyle to go on in and wait. Though Lyle's been in Tucker's office many times he's never had the chance to actually look around at things.

There are no pictures of any family except one that looks as if it could be his mother. Several letters of commendation and a few diplomas hang on the walls along with a picture of Ronald Reagan and George W. Bush. On the shelves behind the Captain's desk are dozens of intricately carved wooden statues, many resembling biblical figures. The detail of the carving is amazing. Lyle is admiring the statues as Tucker comes into the room.

"What do you have, Lyle? It better be good news. And don't touch those carvings."

A startled Lyle jumps when he hears the Captain's voice, nearly falling into the shelf.

"Right, yes, sorry, Captain."

The two sit down and Lyle begins to go over the leads he's gathered, updating Tucker on the investigation. He can see that his boss isn't very happy about what he's hearing and is about to explain when his phone rings.

"Excuse me, sir, I need to take this it's Mitch," Lyle says. "Yeah, Mitch, what have you come up with? . . .Good, that's great. Thanks."

"I think we've got them, sir. We've traced the cell to a car service Roxy uses, looks like they're on the 15 headed for L.A. maybe two hours out. The video from the Follies confirms that Roxy and Nick are in the car."

"Good work, Detective. Now I'll call in the FBI. Get Mitch and meet me downstairs right away. We're flying to L.A."

⬥

Wayne shuffles his legs back and forth finally crossing them for a little extra room. He looks at Roxy, studying her for a second when a thought flashes through his mind.

"Hey, aren't you the star of the Follies in Vegas?"

"Yes I am, Wayne. Have you seen the show?"

"Uh, well no, but I've seen pictures of you around town."

"Oh, then you should come down sometime, you'd love it. I'll leave some passes for you at the box office. And don't worry, there are tons of straight people who attend all the time."

"I just might do that, thank you. So I'm curious, what takes you all to L.A. I mean, no offense, but you're a rather diverse group of friends."

"We are, aren't we, Wayne?" I say as I give Roxy a sarcastic wink. "We're just headed down to see a friend and take Julio back to his home. He's been visiting relatives in Laughlin."

Saleem's phone rings and I jump. It scares me a bit since my phone and Roxy's are both turned off. The call seems to be from his wife but it still makes me uneasy. I didn't even think about Saleem's cell being traced. He finishes his call and I tap him on his shoulder.

"Hey Saleem, could you do me a favor and turn off your cell until we get to L.A.? I've got a throwaway if you need it."

"Oh yez, Mr. Nick, no problem."

"So what's the big deal, you guys on a secret mission or something? Why do you have to keep your phones off?" Wayne says only half-laughing.

"Uh, no, Wayne, it's nothing like that. You're certainly welcome to use yours."

Wayne gives me a puzzled look, then pulls his phone out as if to make sure it's still on. Then he checks his mail and texts. He keeps fidgeting around seeming somewhat uncomfortable. He looks toward Julio in the front seat.

"So, Julio, you live in L.A.? What part?"

"South L.A., Mr. Wayne."

"Oh really? I love L.A. especially Beverly Hills. I almost bought a house there once. Say, do you know who I am, Julio?"

"No, Mr. Wayne, but you must be famous. Saleem show me your autograph he got."

"Well yes, Julio, I am. They call me Mr. Las Vegas. I've been performing there since I was fifteen, when I had my first big hit. You may have heard of it, 'Danke Shoen'?"

"No, sorry, Mr.Wayne, have not heard it."

"Well, anyhow, my brother and I were booked in Vegas for a two-night stand and we wound up staying for six months. I've won about every award there is in the music industry and have sold millions of records."

"You singer, Mr. Wayne? Must be very good. I sing too."

"Really, what kind of music do you sing?"

"Julio only allowed to sing in church or choir. Only sing hymns and religious songs."

"Well, let's hear something."

"Yeah, Julio, sing something for us," Roxy says trying to encourage him.

"Yes, OK, I sing."

The car goes quiet as Julio almost instantly seems to transform into a confident, self ordained young man and begins to sing "Ave Maria". If God had sent an angel down from heaven to serenade us he couldn't have sounded anymore amazing. Julio's soprano voice rings out crisp and clear with every note. The three of us sit in the backseat taking in every measure, dumbfounded and staring at each other, while Saleem conducts Julio with his free right hand.

When Julio finishes there's a brief moment of silence before Roxy starts clapping. Soon Wayne and I join in. "Bravo!"

"Amazing!" Wayne tries to stand at one point, then quickly remembering he's in a car, so reverts to bouncing up and down in the seat yelling, "Encore! Encore!"

Our ovation has barely subsided when I swear I see dollar signs reflected in Wayne Newton's eyes.

"Julio, you have an incredible voice. That was beautiful! Who taught you to sing?"

"My mother teach me from time I start to talk, Mr. Wayne."

"Have you ever thought about performing in public? Maybe singing more conventional music, like some old standards or even rock?"

"No, Mr. Wayne, but I could try."

"Yes, you need to and I can help. How about I set up a meeting with my record company, they're always looking for new talent."

"Julio would like that very much, Mr. Wayne. Thank you, thank you so much."

CHAPTER 15

With a Little Help from God

Kate sits on the floor in her bathroom, head hanging down waiting for the next heave to start. The morning sickness that started a few days ago has turned into morning, afternoon and evening sickness. She hasn't been out of her apartment all day. She wanted to tell Nick when he was there earlier but hesitated thinking it might upset him so much he wouldn't be able to concentrate on his case.

As she heads to the fridge to get a Coke, which seems to be the only thing that helps combat the nausea, her phone rings.

"Kate, it's Barry, why aren't you at the office?"

"Hi, Barry. Sorry but I haven't been feeling well."

"Well, you better get your shit together because your story just got picked up by the major wire services along with the big search engines. It's gone national and CNN called. They want to interview you on the nightly news."

"Oh my God, really? I'm suddenly feeling much better, be there in an hour."

A

At the airport the three detectives are getting ready to board their plane when Lyle gets a text from Lance at AT&T:

Subject's phone has been turned off. We are unable to track at this point. Will keep trying and contact you if we regain signal. Sending last coordinates.

—Lance, AT&T Exigent Requests

"Shit, we've lost them, Captain. The driver has turned off his phone."

"What? I thought we could trace phones even if they were turned off."

"Yeah, if we would have had the time to hack them and plant an app to keep the GPS running we could have."

"Don't most phones stay on partially, even in the off mode, to keep receiving info from the carrier?"

"They do, Captain, but Nick's a pretty smart guy. Chances are he bagged them or just wrapped them in aluminum foil. They won't get a signal then."

"Damn it, we're too close to blow this now. I'm getting on the phone with LAPD and the Sheriff's Department. They can find them and put a tail on until we find out where they're headed. Don't let this plane take off till I'm back, got it?"

"Got it, boss."

A

"The TV crew just arrived, Barry, where do you want them to set up?"

"Let's put them in the conference room. Kate can do the interview with Anderson and there will be a good background of the Las Vegas skyline. Speaking of which, has anybody seen Kate?"

"I saw her come in but she went straight to the restroom and hasn't come out. Wouldn't it be great if she hurled right in the middle of being interviewed by Anderson Cooper on live TV?"

"That's not very funny, Terry, especially coming from an intern."

"Sorry, Barry, I was just making a joke. You think like maybe she's pregnant or something?"

"I don't have any idea. Now why don't you go see if the film crew wants any water or soda."

Kate comes out of the restroom and is looking weary as she walks down the hall toward her office when Barry steps around the corner. She's hoping he doesn't look at her too closely, but then he stops right in front of her and gives her a quizzical look.

"Kate, are you OK?"

"Yes, I'm fine. Just need a few minutes to put myself together. How do I look?"

"Uh, well, a little pale maybe, but otherwise you look just fine."

"I look like shit, don't I? White as a sheet. God, I can't believe this."

⚔

At the Las Vegas Division office of the FBI Special Agent in Charge Mathew McCain gets off the phone with the LAPD. He's fuming about what he was just told. It seems that Captain Tucker has been holding back info about locating Bobby Westbrook so he could get a head start on going after him. He got the info from an informant named Fast Eddie who claims to have cut a deal with Tucker and the FBI, something McCain knows nothing about. He slams down the phone as his face grows even more red. "Damn local yocals. Always wanting to play smart guys and one up us."

"Get choppers up in L.A., tell them to ready the jet, we're going down there, and get me Tucker on the phone, now!" A couple of the other agents in the room start gathering their gear knowing what's coming next. McCain didn't get his rank by letting others run the show.

⚐

"They're ready for you in the conference room, Kate."

"Tell them I'll be right there."

Kate breathes deeply, takes another sip of her Coke and heads down the hall to the conference room. Thoughts begin to bounce around in her mind spanning everything from childhood memories of Christmas, to sex at a frat house with some guy named Arlo. She's never been on camera before and her nerves are starting to feel it.

"I've got to be professional, get my story told in order to bring attention to what's going on in the LGBT community. I can do this. I can do this," she tells herself.

"Miss Simon, we are ready for you. Please have a seat and make-up will be right over. My name is Mark. If you need anything let me know."

"Thanks, Mark. I'm good for now." Yeah right. If he only knew.

"Great, the camera and monitor will be right in front of you. Anderson will ask you questions and you will see him on the monitor. We have about three minutes until airtime, any questions?"

"Can I get a Xanax? Just kidding, just kidding."

Kate sits back in her chair as the make-up person pats her cheeks and forehead with whatever it is they put on people to make them look more photogenic. Right now she's very grateful for a little bit of color on her face.

"All right, everybody, we are on in one minute. Cue the lights, camera and monitor, go live.

Kate is surprised by the intensity of the lights and squints a little, then Anderson Cooper appears on the monitor.

"Good afternoon, Miss Simon, I'm Anderson Cooper. How are you today?"

"Just fine thank you."

"I'll be asking you a few questions about some of the articles you have written. Is there anything in particular you would like to emphasize?"

"Yes, I definitely want to bring attention to the lack of equality in the LGBT community when it comes to how law enforcement treats them."

"Got it."

Mark steps in clipboard in hand. "We're on in ten seconds. . . and 5,4,3,2,1. . ."

"Good evening, I'm Anderson Cooper and we're back talking with reporter Kate Simon of the *Las Vegas Sun*. Miss Simon is the reporter who broke the story about a serial killer at large who is terrorizing people in the transgender community. She also has taken issue with how various local law enforcement agencies have responded or lack thereof."

"Hello, Miss Simon. Can you give us a little background on your story and tell us where things stand at the present?"

"Yes, Anderson, thank you. As you know there have been five transgender citizens murdered in the past six months, four in Reno and one in Las Vegas. All the victims received letters telling them they would be killed and when. And each note was signed by someone calling himself Leviticus."

"I take it that refers to the passage in the bible that speaks about men lying with men?"

"Yes, that's right. He quotes the passage in his letters."

"When did law enforcement become aware of the murders and how did they react?"

"They haven't given an answer to the first part of that question yet. As for their reaction, it has been very slow until recently, after I broke the story. They would not admit to a serial killer being on the loose until the death of the last victim, Mavis Rodgers."

"Has the FBI been involved?"

"The FBI was notified after the murder of the last victim and is now investigating."

"Do you think that law enforcement was trying to cover this up?"

"I don't know, Anderson. Obviously having a serial killer on the loose in cities where tourism and entertainment are their bread and butter isn't good PR."

"What would you like to see happen with the case at this point?"

"There certainly needs to be more transparency by law enforcement. The public has a right to know when something like this is happening. I also believe one of the reasons for this response is the lack of respect and equality for the LGBT community, especially transgenders. They simply are not given the same priority most of the rest of us enjoy."

"Are you aware of the two black transgenders killed in Baltimore and the report that claims such murders are becoming more frequent and occurring in various geographic locations across the country?"

"I am, Anderson, and three of the people murdered here were black."

"Thank you, Kate Simon, for talking with us and shining a light on this alarming problem. Please come back and update us as you continue your work on this matter."

"Thank you, Anderson."

"We'll be right back after this break."

"And we're off the air, kill the lights please. Great job, Kate, you looked like a pro."

Terry the intern rushes up to Kate all excited after seeing the interview. "Kate, you were wonderful. Good job, girl!"

Kate looks up at Terry. "Thank, thank. . .*blaarghhhhh*. . ." The words don't come out but the Coke and PowerBars do just as Terry bends down to listen to her.

⅄

We've been on the road for several hours now and everyone seems to be settling in. Julio's song was so moving there seems to be a new emotional bond that's brought us all together. Julio and Roxy are dozing off as the bright blue sky melts into an amazing display of orange, red and yellow on the western horizon.

Wayne is on his phone flipping through messages and updating his latest Friend requests on Facebook. Saleem never seems to waiver, he's always alert and aware of everything around him. Whether in the car or outside on the road, nothing escapes him. I can hear him humming along with the music he has softly playing up front.

Me, I'm sitting here thinking about Kate and the baby and a hundred other things, all rushing in and out of my mind simultaneously. There's one thought that's starting to come through loud and clear though: I have to piss.

"Saleem, how long to Barstow?"

"Oh, about twenty minutes, Mr. Nick."

"Good, let's make a pit stop there. I think everyone needs to stretch and use the facilities."

"Oh yes, Mr. Nick, I know just the place for us to rest."

I decide to strike up a conversation with Wayne to kill some time and take my mind off my bladder. "So, Wayne, are you working in Vegas now?"

"No, I've been touring lately. Just finished a show at the Edgewater in Laughlin."

"When's your next date?"

"Well, we only have one scheduled right now and it's a few months down the road. I've been cutting back and spending more time with the family. I have a teenage daughter, you know."

"Bet she keeps you busy."

"Yes, she does. So what do you do for a living, Nick?"

"I'm a private investigator."

"Really, how interesting. Bet you've got some good stories."

"Yeah, in fact here's one you might appreciate. I was tracking this celebrity for six months for a major casino in Vegas. They wanted some inside background on him. I found out he was all mobbed up and was part of a deal to buy the casino who hired me."

"That's not true and you know it. I wasn't in with the Mob. It was a drug cartel putting up the money. The Mob was just a front."

"What? What did you say?"

Wayne leans in toward me, looks me straight in the eye and starts to smile. "Gotcha, didn't I, Nick?"

"Damn, Wayne. That was a good one."

Just then Roxy wakes up. She brushes her hair back from her face and stretches out one arm. "Are we there yet?"

"Nope, but we're almost to Barstow. Saleem knows a good place to stop."

"I have to pee," Roxy grimaces and squeezes her legs together to stress her point.

"Well, that makes two of us. Can you wait about five or ten minutes?"

"I guess so. What have you guys been talking about? Politics? Religion?"

"Neither, Roxy. Wayne was just telling me about all the famous women he's slept with. Right, Wayne?"

Wayne snorts. "Yeah right, I'd go back over the list but we don't have time now."

"Oh, you guys are messin' with me, aren't you?" Roxy elbows me twice in the side.

"Here we are everyone, Barstow Station." The smile on Saleem's face widens as we pull into what looks like a giant truck stop. "Please to note the new Dunkin' Donuts. Mmmm, my favorite."

Roxy and I both make a beeline to the restrooms while Wayne makes a call to let his manager know what's going on. Saleem and Julio head for the Dunkin' Donuts located just a half dozen tour buses away. Throngs of sightseers destined for Vegas exit the buses like cargo on an assembly line while Saleem navigates through the camera-laden masses.

I'm feeling a little odd as I take my place in line at the urinal, wondering if Roxy is about to step up next to me or if she uses the ladies' room. Ladies' room, I'm sure.

Eerily, the emotions and feelings I was having earlier in the day, the ones Walter Pickles referred to as a spiritual awakening, start flooding back, even more intense than before. Much more intense. As I wash my hands I look in the mirror and don't even recognize the person staring back at me. It's like I'm in another world, another existence. Or maybe somebody slipped me some acid.

I take a few deep breathes, exit the restroom and walk into the gift shop area where dozens of senior citizens are shuffling through the aisles. An old man picks up a T-shirt with a dirty slogan on it and shows it to his wife. "Will ya look at this T-shirt,

Shirley? What the heck's this mean?" The silver-haired, pants-suited Shirley spins around and, loud enough for the people in the parking lot to hear, says, "It's a fucking T-shirt from Grandma, Henry. . .can't you read?"

I finally find a little cafe where I can sit down and pull myself together, but when the waitress comes to take my order and I look up, I'm speechless. I know she's talking to me but when I hear the words their meaning is completely different. It's as if I know what she's really thinking as she speaks, and it's certainly not related to the words I'm hearing. I seem to have some laser insight as to who this woman really is, what she knows, believes and loves. Yet I've never met her. She's rattling off the day's specials, trying her damnedest to push the $9.95 top sirloin, but I'm not buying. I'm too intent on this privileged glimpse into another person's true nature and this new understanding of the human condition I find impossible to describe.

Her warm smile and friendly greeting can't hide the frightened little girl standing in front of me. I want to say something but I don't have a clue of what the hell to say. She probably wouldn't understand anyhow and I'm not sure I would either. This is all very strange and bizarre. So I look down at the menu and order a coffee to go.

As I make my way back to the car I keep my head down trying to avoid anymore contact with people. I'm more than a little troubled about what the hell is going on with me. Is this shit real? Do other people in the world have this ability? Am I going nuts?

I'm trying to keep it together but all I can think of is looking into someone's eyes and watching their life flash before me as I invade their inner sanctity. I suddenly have a thought about waking up in a monastery in Tibet. Maybe this is all a dream.

As I walk up to the car, I see Roxy standing outside having a cigarette. Wayne looks like he is still on the phone. Saleem and Julio are coming from the other direction with a bag of goodies bearing the name Dunkin' Donuts.

I look at my watch, "OK guys, we better get on the road if we're going to get Wayne to L.A. on time."

"Yez, Mr. Nick, ready to go. Would you like a donut, please?"

I look at Saleem and *BAM!* Everything in him hits me. Then Julio looks at me and it happens again, straight to the core of a confused young soul.

Wayne gets out of the car and stretches. "Do I have time to go to the john?"

I nod but don't look at him and take the opportunity to pull Roxy aside. "Roxy, it's time you call your contact and get the info for the meeting, we're only two hours out, here's my cell."

Before Roxy says anything I connect with her eyes and am stunned and confused by what I suddenly seem to know about this person. The sensation is so unsettling I don't know how long I can keep this up, and yet to instantly understand a person in this way. . .well, I don't know how many how many people could handle such insight into the human psyche. It's so intense I can hardly breath when it happens.

"Good idea, Nick. Should I tell him you are with me? Nick? *Nick?* Did you hear what I said?"

I look away. "Sorry, Roxy. Yes, I heard you. Tell him you needed me to get the boy."

I walk out to the parking lot on the edge of the road to be alone for a minute or two and try to get a grip on the here and now. I keep an eye on the car, watching for Wayne to return so we can get going.

More than a few minutes go by and I'm beginning to wonder where Wayne is. I scan the parking lot and notice a throng of silver-haired ladies wearing name badges moving toward our car. There, in the middle of the pack, is Wayne, signing autographs and kissing cheeks. He finally works his way past the adoring 70-somethings and gets to the car. He turns, puts both hands in the air as if he's giving an encore, and says, "Thank you all so very much. Catch my next show in Vegas. Love you!" Ever the consummate showman.

Wayne climbs into the car all smiles and hyped-up over the attention. He claps his hands and points forward. "OK, are we ready to go? Let's hit it, Saleem, on to L.A."

Once we're back on the road I sit quietly thinking about my newfound gift, power, or brain tumor, whatever it is. Maybe I'm cursed. Who knows? I suppose time will tell. I listen to the conversations in the car but no matter what each person says I seem to be hearing more than the actual words. It's as if I have some new insight that goes beyond the words I'm hearing. I can't even begin to describe it. Maybe I need my blood pressure checked, or more likely a shrink. All of a sudden a question comes to me and I just blurt it out: "Do you believe in God?"

Roxy turns and raises an eyebrow. "Are you talking to me?" she says in her best De Niro which is terrible.

"I'm just throwing it out there. I don't know why, the thought just came to me, so I'm asking."

Roxy nods, looks at me rather strangely, gives me an, "uh-huh" look, then rests her chin on her fist doing a stellar imitation of "The Thinker." Entertainers, always ready to perform.

"Well, Nick, depends on which God we're talking about. There have been a whole lot of them throughout history. For the sake of conversation, let's talk about the one God, you know the one in the Bible."

"You can talk about whatever you like, Roxy. Have at it."

"OK, well, when I was a little boy my mother would take me to church every Sunday. I don't really remember the denomination. I don't think it was Catholic, I would've remembered that. All the rest of them are pretty much the same. I really enjoyed it, especially the singing. But then she married my stepdad and started drinking with him so Sundays were spent in bed with a hangover.

"Like most people I've had times in my life when I've prayed to God asking for this or that, sometimes begging for help or understanding. Guess that's what a lot of people call 'foxhole prayers'. Maybe it's just human nature to want to believe in some all- powerful being that can fix things for us, you know, give us some hope. Honestly, I just don't know. I mean I'd like to believe and have faith, but something in me won't or can't do it. Turning my life over to a spirit in the sky seems a little far fetched to me. I do believe there is a higher power in this world but just what it is I don't think we have the capacity to understand, at least not yet. So did any of that make sense, Nick?"

"Yeah, it did. Thanks, Roxy."

Looking around the car everyone seems like they're thinking about what they might want to say, if they want to say anything at all. Saleem slightly raises his hand as if in a classroom.

"How about you, Saleem, do you believe in God?"

"Ah, such a question you ask, Mr. Nick. Let me say I am an empirical thinker and as such I must require provable or verifiable evidence by experience or much experiment.

"In Western religion your God is characterized a metaphysical ultimate being, who is timeless, simple and supreme and has no human qualities. Ah, but Eastern religion, there God is thought of as force contained in everything, the essential substance, and oh yez, the most high principal of nature."

"So, Saleem, it sounds as if you make an argument for the existence of God."

"Oh yez, Mr. Nick, there are many arguments for existence of God, empirical, rational and deductive, but can all be denied by demonstrating they are meaningless, contradictory and at odds with known scientific or historical fact. Also many a conclusion about existence of God Saleem find divided by beliefs and religions. May I give example?" Saleem pauses for a moment glancing over his shoulder at me as I nod 'yes'.

"I consider myself agnostic though I believe in karma which in itself may be thought of as belief in God."

"Damn, Saleem. Wow, I don't quite know what to say. You've really given this God thing some thought."

"Oh yez, I study with the elders in my country before coming to the U.S."

"How about you, Julio? Any thoughts?"

"I don't know, Mr. Nick. Right now, it very confusing for me. As I told you all, I was brought up in a very strict religious family. We were Catholic and practiced our faith every day. My father very strict, if we break rules he beat us. He quote Bible that say spare rod and spoil child. But I like being part of Church, it was like big family. It made me feel safe.

"Then, when I confess who I am, everything change for me. They say I sinner and God hates me. They say I sick and need to repent or I go to hell. I don't understand. I same person I was before and they don't hate me then, why now? Because I not like them? Are they afraid of Julio? I thought God loved all people not just those who straight.

"Now I have no family, no church and no faith, but I still love them. Is that wrong? Maybe someday it all changes. I don't know but I have hope."

Roxy leans forward in her seat and places her hand on Julio's shoulder, patting it gently. "Hallelujah, sweetie. I love you. Don't you ever change. You're a good boy. Trust me, someday it will all work out."

"Thank you, Miss Roxy. You good person." Julio chokes out the words as a tear rolls down his cheek.

I smile at Julio and give a wink and a nod as he smiles back at me. Then I turn to Wayne. "So, Wayne, you've been awfully quiet. Want to jump in?"

"Yes, yes I would." Wayne looks up toward the ceiling of the limo and crosses himself. " I believe in God, the Father Almighty, Maker of heaven and earth, and in Jesus Christ his only son our Lord, who was conceived by the Holy Spirit, born of the Virgin Mary, suffered under Pontius Pilate, was crucified, died and was buried. He descended into hell. On the third day he rose again from the dead, he ascended into Heaven and sits at the right hand of God the Father almighty. From thence he shall come to judge the living and the dead. I believe in the Holy Spirit, the Holy Christian Church, the communion of saints, the resurrection of the body and the life everlasting. Amen.

"Are there any donuts left?"

"Well, Amen, Wayne. Amen. Saleem, can you get Wayne a donut, please?"

Wayne sits up, straightens himself, turns his head and raises his chin as he takes a donut from Saleem. "So how about you, Nick. What do you believe in?"

"I guess that's what I'm trying to figure out. Today has been a very strange day and things have been happening to me that I don't completely understand. For the first time in my life I'm beginning to have an understanding of some higher power or God, whatever you want to call it, but I'm not sure what to do about it. It's comforting and scary at the same time. I mean I feel like I'm two different people and one has never been aware of the other until now."

Saleem strokes his beard as if in deep thought, turns his turban-covered head and gently says, "Ah, you have unmasked the facade that we all wear."

"What do you mean, Saleem? Are you saying we all wear masks, we're all fakes?"

"Yez, to some degree, that exactly what I say. We all wear a mask that we show each other to function in society. It necessary for survival because it help us control our feelings, thoughts, and behavior. It compromise between our true selves and what society expect of us."

"So do you think there are people who can see through these facades to the true self of another?"

"I do, yez, I think to some degree many people can, but the true seer is very rare and only sees the true nature of the other. I have known a few in my life but they have very difficult time."

"Why's that?"

"It too much responsibility to know true nature of another, too much like being God. You can't play game that humans play with one another. Many true seers slowly go crazy, some kill themselves. The lucky ones lose the ability after a while and go back to being like everyone else. Duality is invention of modern man. He can't survive without it."

CHAPTER 16

SAVING GRACE

Back at the offices of the FBI, no sooner does Special Agent Mathew McCain hang up his phone when it rings again.

"Hello, McCain?"

"Yes, this is Mathew McCain."

"McCain, this is Captain Tucker."

"Tucker! What the hell is going on? Why haven't you kept me up to speed on the Mavis Rodgers' case?"

"That's what I'm calling about. We just got info less than an hour ago about Bobby Westbrook being in the L.A. area. I wanted to confirm it before I called you. Wanted to make sure it was true. I know what a stickler you are for accuracy."

"Is that right. I heard a slightly different version of that story but tell me what you've got."

Tucker clears his throat and snorts. McCain wants to gag when he hears him cough up a hocker. Then Tucker tops it off when he blows his nose.

"Yeah, well, we got a tip from an informant named Eddie Cologne that Westbrook had contacted a friend of Mavis' named Roxy Lynn. She and a P.I. named Nick Ross are driving down to L.A. to meet up with Bobby."

"This Cologne guy, does he go by Fast Eddie?"

"Yeah, that's him. We may need to drop some charges he has pending if we nail Bobby. That was the deal."

McCain sighs, his irritation with Tucker rising. "Do we have a tail on them yet?"

"We had them triangulated by a phone signal in the car but that went dead. We know the car and the plate number so the highway patrol should be able to spot them pretty easily. We can't spook them though. If they know they're being followed they might break off the meeting with Bobby and then we can't pick them up for questioning 'cause they'll just deny all of it."

"I'll get LAPD and our boys on it right away. Are you on the way down there?"

"Yeah, I'm getting on a plane now with a couple of my detectives should be there in an hour."

"I'm leaving too. I'll meet you at the airport when we land then we can coordinate with the locals. Oh, and Tucker?"

"Yeah?"

"You keep me informed, got it?" McCain hears Tucker mutter a profanity or two just before the phone slams down.

A

The God talk eventually winds down and everyone seems to be fine with the silence. I shut up, but my brain's gone into overdrive.

Saleem has opened up a whole new line of thought for me with his comments about duality, a concept I've never considered. If duality is a creation of modern man then wouldn't God and religion be the ultimate weapon in that creation? Did God create man or did man create God? Saleem breaks my mood when I see him staring in the rearview mirror, raising his right hand and pointing toward me.

"Mr. Nick, may I have a word, if you please?" Saleem motions for me to lean forward toward the front seat so he can speak in private.

"I have observed what seems to be unmarked police cars following us for last several miles. They keep switching off so not to be noticeable but I am certain we are being followed."

"Are you sure, Saleem? Maybe they're just looking for speeders."

"Well, let us find out. I will take next exit and then get right back on highway."

Sure enough, when we take the exit the first car keeps going but the second stays right behind us. As we get back onto the highway the car following us pulls over knowing he has been made. Within a few miles the first car picks us up again.

At this point Wayne and Roxy are beginning to wonder what's going on. Wayne looks at his wristwatch, then at me.

"Is there a problem? Are we going to get there on time?"

"No, no problem. I was just discussing which routes to take with Saleem once we get to L.A."

"Well, don't take the 5 that's always a mess." Wayne looks at his watch again. Same result.

"OK, Wayne, got it."

I lean forward toward Saleem. "We can't meet our contact if we're being followed, Saleem. Any ideas?"

"Yez, sir, I do. Saleem used to work in L.A. for limo service. My good friend and old boss own it. It where I purchased this car when I left to go to Vegas. I think he can help us. If you would be so good as to let me use your phone I will call him and tell him our dilemma."

I sit back and listen as Saleem speaks to his friend in Farsi. When he's done he hands me back the phone and gives me a thumbs up. I don't know what the plan is only that we have one.

▲

After spending another millennium in the ladies room, Kate has emerged and returned to her office. Well-wishers poke their heads in offering symbolic pats on the back for a job well done in the interview.

She tries Nick's phone again but it's still turned off. Wondering just what kind of out of town business he has that he's not able to share is getting the best of her. She leaves yet another message for Nick to call her when he can. Feeling a bit better, she gets up and goes to the lunch room for a snack and a Coke. More accolades from fellow reporters come her way as she stands in front of the refrigerator looking at offerings she knows will make her sick. Enjoying the attention, she starts to wonder if pursuing a job with CNN might be her next career move.

As she walks back to her office and starts to swing around her desk to sit down, there on the chair is a brownish-red spot.

She bends down to look at it more closely and suddenly jumps back, grasping her desk. It's blood.

At LAX Captain Tucker, Mitch Sutton and Lyle Carson are met by the LAPD. They will be joining up with the FBI as soon as they land. Waiting is not something Tucker is good at. He paces back and forth, fidgeting with his cell phone, accomplishing nothing.

"Why can't we go and get started? The FBI can catch up with us later. We're just wasting precious time." Tucker barks impatiently at the patrolman who calmly turns and faces him.

"Following orders, sir. I'm just a patrolman here to pick you up."

Finally Mathew McCain and two of his agents come walking through the gate. As soon as he sees Tucker, McCain straightens his lapels and cocks his head up. "All right, men, let's go," he snaps, walking past the detectives, motioning circles in the air like he's rounding up the troops.

The ride downtown is dominated by McCain's constant conversation on his phone. The other two agents are in a different squad car but they all seem to be on a conference call with someone who is feeding them info. Finally McCain gets off the phone and turns to Tucker.

"The CHP has spotted them on the 15 and has been tailing them for the last thirty minutes. One of the officers thinks he may have been made, so we're sending up a chopper to take over in hopes they don't break off the meeting."

"Damn it, I told you we had to be careful." Tucker looks out the window and huffs angrily. "If they have the slightest hint we're on to them they'll break it off and we're too close to let that happen."

McCain's confidence clicks up a notch, a striking balance to Tucker's anxiety. "Well, we'll know soon. They're coming into L.A. now on the 10."

▲

As we approach downtown Los Angeles, Saleem begins to have a much harder time determining if we're being followed, too much damn traffic. Since we can't take that chance, I'm ready to break off the meeting until Saleem turns and winks at me.

"I will be heading to my friend's place of business now, Mr. Nick. It's about 10 minutes from here, just off Wilshire."

I still don't know what Saleem has up his sleeve, but I nod in agreement. For some reason I feel comfortable with whatever it is.

Ten minutes go by before Saleem turns into a parking lot where a sign reads *Diamond Jim's Limo Service*. At the back of the lot is a small office situated next to a multi-story parking garage. Saleem pulls up to the office, gets out and goes in. An agonizingly long five minutes later he returns to our car.

"We are ready, sir."

As if on cue, out of the parking garage come six limos, all black Town Cars exactly like the one we are driving. We merge in line with them as one after another leaves the lot, each heading in a different direction.

"Where would you have me go, sir?" Saleem smiles, a wry grin on his face.

I take a minute to think, knowing this smokescreen won't last very long if we are being followed. I decide we better split up and take a taxi to our destination. "Take us to the Beverly Wilshire, Saleem."

Traffic's a bitch but once at the hotel I let Roxy and Julio know it's time for us to go and then turn to Wayne.

"Wayne, glad we could help you out. Hope your event goes well tonight. Saleem will take you wherever you need to go."

"Thank you so much for helping me, I won't forget it. I must say it's been quite an experience meeting all of you, but a very enjoyable one. Look forward to seeing you at my show in Vegas sometime. Roxy darlin', I'll definitely drop by and see your show," says Wayne. "And, Julio, now don't you forget to call me so I can get you that audition with my record company, OK?"

"I will, Mr. Wayne, thank you so much." Julio extends his hand as Wayne reaches forward with a double-hander.

Roxy walks up to Wayne to give him a big hug. Wayne hesitates in a moment of gender-preference etiquette confusion, then throws his arms around Roxy in a huge bear hug. Amazingly, I'm able to hail a cab quickly for us and pull Saleem aside.

"Saleem, we will be flying back to Vegas when we are done here so you can head out anytime after you have dropped Wayne off. I'll settle up with you when we get back. Thanks for all your help. Here's your cell phone, you can turn it on now."

"Oh yez, Mr. Nick, that is fine but I will be taking this opportunity to visit my daughter at UCLA. So if you need my services, just call. Saleem is very happy to have made your acquaintance and looks forward to our meeting again."

CHAPTER 17

L.A. Woman

Once in the cab, Roxy gives the address to the driver. I'm told it's somewhere in Beverly Hills, the part with the $6000 mailboxes, not in "the flats". We pull on to Wilshire, but are evidently headed in the wrong direction so we have to go a couple blocks before we can make a U-turn. As we pass back by the hotel again, I see a half dozen black-and-whites along with several motorcycle cops swarming the entrance of the hotel and surrounding the black town car we just exited minutes before. Not a good sign.

Wayne's the first to step out of the car. He has his hands in the air and from our cab I can see a look of alarm on his face. The cops seem to ready to forcibly assist Wayne in placing his hands behind his back. Wayne seems ready to maintain his gentlemanly stance at all costs.

Saleem follows, climbing out of the car as a dozen officers with guns drawn close in. Roxy and I look out our window, astonished by the spectacle. Julio, who is in the front seat, doesn't see what is happening. Just as well. Roxy leans over and whispers in my ear. "Do you think they'll be all right, Nick?"

"They'll be fine," I reply, more or less confident of my answer. "Saleem doesn't really know anything and all he has to say is that he was just a driver taking us to L.A. They don't have anything on him. As far as Wayne goes, I'm sure they'll be in for a big surprise once they find out they just busted Wayne Newton for nothing. Wait till the media gets a hold of that. Hell, Wayne might even like it. You know what they say about publicity."

We wind our way back through several residential streets that are lined with some of the city's most classic old Hollywood estates. It's obvious that Julio is mesmerized by the affluence on display. Each house more lavish than the next, each driveway sporting a six-figure vehicle or three. This isn't a part of town he's very familiar with I'm sure. After a few minutes, our cab pulls into the driveway of a beautiful, two-story 1930's style mansion where we're immediately stopped by a huge, ornate iron gate. Roxy leans out the window and taps the buzzer, but before she can even say anything the gate swings open. As we near the entrance of the house on the circle drive, I see a well-dressed woman standing out front on the sidewalk. Roxy, Julio and I all pile out of the car while the cabby starts hauling our luggage out of the trunk.

As the woman walks toward us I can see she is probably in her late forties or early fifties, quite attractive and dressed to the nines. As she extends her hand, the carat-count is difficult to calculate but huge would probably cover it. I adjust my sunglasses a bit as the sunlight plays off her diamond-dressed fingers.

"Hello, welcome, you must be Roxy Lynn. I'm Stella Jo Vance."

"Hello, yes, I'm Roxy, nice to meet you, Miss Vance."

"Please just call me Jo. And who are your friends, dear?"

"Hi, I'm Nick Ross, a friend of Roxy's and this is Julio, the young man Bobby asked us to liberate from Wesley Kootz."

"Ah yes, nice to meet you, Mr. Ross. And, Julio, I am so happy you're safe. Bobby will be very pleased." Julio nods and offers a shy smile, knowing he's clearly out of his league. I feel the same way.

Jo leads us inside through a simple but classic entranceway and into what I assume is a living room, although I'm not up on mansion lingo. The room is warm and inviting with a spectacular visual display of walnut, oak and ebony woodworking. The scent of recently polished wood and fresh-cut flowers certainly do trump the dirty socks and leftover pizza smell at my place. I glance up at the ceiling beams that look to be three feet thick. Thirty feet up in the air, they give the room an old time elegance one might have seen centuries ago. The walls are Eastern Black walnut panels that provide a perfect backdrop for the bright, splashy contemporary art that hangs on them. The floors are wide planks of dark, polished ebony. I'm guessing Jo does OK.

Roxy looks around in amazement, taking it all in. "Wow, Jo, you have a beautiful home."

"Thank you, Roxy. I've been very lucky. Say, why don't we all go out on the veranda and I'll have Rosa get us some refreshments."

We all follow Jo through one of several sets of French doors that lead outside to a patio large enough for a full-size tennis court. I'm fairly certain Jo has one of those some-where on this property, just haven't seen it yet. Each of us settles into a deep, weathered teak chair piled with pillows and situated to take advantage of another visual masterpiece. We look out over extravagantly landscaped gardens, thick with all colors of roses, dotted with patches of wild lavender and bordered with carefully manicured boxwood. Fragrant, blooming jasmine vines hang from wooden trellises. Kate's love of flowers creeps into my psyche. I shake it off and gaze out at the classic mid-century, kidney-shaped pool with tiles of dolphins and whales sparkling in the bright, sunlit water. Nice place.

Rosa emerges from the house and sets down a tray heavy with a ridiculous variety of drinks. Everything from craft beers to organic lemonades and sodas.

"Julio, are you hungry?" Jo kicks her mothering instincts into high gear and everyone is grateful, albeit for different reasons.

"Oh yes, ma'am, I am."

"Why don't you follow Rosa into the kitchen and she will get you something to eat."

"Yes, thank you, Miss Jo. That would be great."

After Julio leaves, Jo turns to us, eager to get to the point of this visit. "So, I guess you're wondering where Bobby is?"

Roxy looks troubled bordering on very annoyed. "Well, yes, we were told we were meeting him here in L.A. Is that not the case?"

"Yes, Roxy, I know what you were told but Bobby couldn't take the chance of you being followed so we had you come here to me first. Do you know if you were followed?"

"It looks like we were but we lost them and I don't see any way they could find us now. Right, Nick?" I nod, ready to supply details if asked but no one's asking, at least not yet.

"What does the boy know about all of this?"

"He doesn't know anything about Bobby being a suspect. He just thinks his friend Bobby sent us to find him and bring him down here where he will be safe."

"Good, let's keep it that way. If there are no signs of the law we will be leaving in a few minutes. I'm monitoring the police channels and checking my Waze app for locations. So far the only thing I've come up with is they mistakenly busted Wayne Newton and are very embarrassed." Jo giggles. Wayne's gonna' love the publicity. And his attorneys won't mind either, what with the cost of living in L.A. and all.

▲

"McBride, you stupid son of a bitch, didn't I make it clear not to apprehend them?"

"Hey, I don't give a shit if you're a Division boss, McCain. The FBI doesn't run the LAPD. It was my call and I'm the Assistant Chief of Police."

"Yeah, well now they've gotten away and we're sitting here holding our dicks in our hands looking like idiots for busting Wayne Newton." McCain glances up at the TV on the wall of the Precinct and grimaces. Hotel security cameras captured the bust and the networks are airing it continuously. The next 24 hours will be all Wayne Newton, all the time. It won't be long before the SNL crew will be working on the skit.

"I'm telling you we'll find them, McCain. I've got an APB out. Did we get any info from Newton or the driver on where they were headed?"

"My guys questioned them, they don't know a damn thing. We've apologized to Mr. Newton and sent them both on their way. Now we need to get the tech people involved in this. Have pictures sent out of all of them, including Bobby, to the departments in L.A. and Orange County. Start running those facial recognitions through the computers on all cameras available."

"You do like to give orders don't you, McCain."

"Somebody's got to."

The pissing match is officially on.

⋏

"OK guys, I've talked to Bobby and he's good with us heading down to meet him. Why don't you get ready to go. There's a bathroom down the hallway if you would like to freshen up. I'll have Vic bring the car around and put your bags in it."

A few minutes later we all walk out of the house together toward a silver exotic sitting in the circle drive. I recognize the classic symbol on the hood immediately, but Roxy's not the car buff I am.

"Nice car, Jo. What's a Ghibli? asks Roxy.

"It's a Maserati, honey. Good car for a road trip. If we were staying in town I'd have Vic drive us in the Bentley but this is more fun on the freeway."

After we all settle in, Jo makes her way through town and on to the 405 heading south. Traffic is the usual stop-and-go crap. One minute we're doing eighty and the next we're at a standstill.

"Mind if I ask where we're headed, Jo?"

"No, of course not, Nick, I should have said something before. We're headed to Laguna Beach, it's a little over an hour from here depending on traffic."

"Oh wow, I've always wanted to see to Laguna, I hear it's a beautiful place. A couple of the girls in my show use to live there and they always raved about it." Roxy says.

"It is a beautiful place, I have a house there and that's where Bobby is staying. Did you know it's the home of the original 'Boom Boom Room' not like the one in Vegas."

"So, Jo, do you know Fast Eddie? He owns the 'Boom Boom Room' in Vegas."

"Knew him from when he was here in L.A., Roxy. This is where he got his start by supplying drugs to some of the gangs. How he managed to stay alive and out of jail is a mystery to me. Though I did hear he had become an informer. All I know is, I didn't trust him."

"Well, that makes two of us."

As I listen to Roxy and Jo, I'm becoming more and more curious about Jo and how she has made her money. Julio's in the front seat listening to music with some high-tech earbuds Jo gave him. I figure it's a good time to ask questions I may not want him to hear the answers to.

"So, Jo, mind if I ask you what you do for a living?"

"No, of course not. I own a half dozen escort services in L.A. and Orange County. We cater to the LGBT community a lot, but I serve straights too."

"Really? I don't mean to offend you but most of those operations in Vegas offer quite a variety of choices, if you know what I mean?"

"Sure, I know what you mean, but prostitution isn't legal here nor is it in the city of Vegas, just in some counties. My people are strictly legit. They play by the rules when they're working for me or they don't play. Now what they do on their own time is up to them."

"You get hassled by the cops much?"

"I did when I was first starting out but in the last few years I've built a good relationship with them."

"How's that?" Now she's got me really curious.

"The modern day slave trade. I get a lot of info from my people about human trafficking in Southern California and I pass it on to the authorities. We've helped put away some real bad guys and I'm proud of it. I can't stand those lowlife sons of a bitches preying on young girls and boys."

"Good for you, Jo, I'm impressed. I hate 'em too. Did you know that Julio was taken in L.A. and sold in Nevada?"

"Yes I did, Nick, and it's one of the reasons why I'm helping Bobby, that and the fact that I believe he's innocent."

"Well, we're all up shit creek if he isn't. So how did you get to know Bobby?"

"After Bobby left the NFL he decided to go back to school and get his degree in sound engineering. He never got the big contract and only played a couple of years so he needed a part-time job."

"He worked as an escort for you?"

"He did, and was one of my best. You can't imagine how many gay men loved being seen with a former pro football player who was now openly gay."

"Nope, I'd never thought of that."

Roxy leans in and elbows me. "That's because you're straight, Nick."

"He was bringing in upwards of two grand a night working for me. I hated to lose him."

▲

Kate puts her head in her hands, takes a deep breath and tries to pull herself together. After all that has happened, she can't be losing this baby. She reaches for her phone and calls her doctor. She gets a recording that nonchalantly informs her the offices are closed and if there's an urgent medical need call 911 or go to an emergency room.

She calls Nick to leave another message. "Nick, I'm on my way to the emergency room there may be a problem with the baby. Call me when you can. I love you."

CHAPTER 18

WELCOME TO LAGUNA

Except for this being my first ride in a Maserati, the trip to Laguna Beach is pretty boring until we get to Newport Coast. As we crest the hill and start to descend toward PCH, the view suddenly opens up and all I can see is a stunning Pacific Ocean. The sun has just set over Catalina Island and the few scattered clouds across the horizon are lit up in deep red and orange hues. Julio pulls out his ear buds and is visibly awed by the sight.

"Oh my God, so beautiful!"

"It is, isn't it Julio? I love the sunsets this time of year and this is a good one."

"How much farther to Laguna Beach, Miss Jo?"

"Just a few miles down Pacific Coast Highway. My house is in the north end of town right next to Emerald Bay."

Roxy perks up, energized by the sunset. "Wow, incredible sunset. . .Emerald Bay. . .I feel like I'm off to see the Wizard."

As we approach Laguna, the ocean pulls our attention to the right, while the high ridges of open wilderness rise up then roll off into deep canyons on our left, the view only spoiled by a brief stretch of McMansions on the hillside. As we enter the city limits I spot a sign that reads, "Welcome to Laguna Beach." I can't read fast enough but it says something about an Art Festival and some kind of Pageant.

We pass by gated communities on our left and right. I'm wondering if they require you to show your tax returns to enter. Jo points out Irvine Cove on our right with its multi-million dollar homes perched on cliffs that overlook the ocean. On the left, the homes of Emerald Bay sit in a canyon that winds back to a high ridge adjacent to seven thousand acres of wilderness area. Hard to believe there's a wilderness area this close to such pricy real estate. Jo turns left soon after we pass the Emerald Bay gate and heads up the hill to a secluded street that dead-ends on a ridge.

"This is it, guys." She seems relieved as she pulls into the driveway and opens the main door of a three-car garage attached to a sleek contemporary home. Situated on a hill overlooking Crescent Bay and the ocean beyond, the stainless steel and glass structure is nestled in between three Royal Palms and two huge California Oak trees. Julio sits up and cranes his neck trying to see more.

"Is Bobby here, Miss Jo?"

"Yes, Julio, Bobby is here. He's waiting for us."

Julio opens the car door and jumps out looking around for a sign from us to turn him loose. Just as I'm about to say something the front gate opens and out steps Bobby.

"Bobby, Bobby!" Julio runs around the car and launches himself straight at Bobby. Bobby's outstretched arms catch Julio, almost in mid-flight.

"Julio, you're safe. I'm so glad you're here, buddy."

"Oh, Bobby, thank you. Thank you so much for sending Miss Roxy and Mr. Nick for me. I didn't think I'd ever see you again."

Bobby hugs Julio again and gently pats his head with his large hand. "So, Jo, any problems getting here?"

"No, none at all. I'm sure we weren't followed if that's what you mean."

"Guess I'm a little paranoid. I owe you big time, Jo, for all you've done for me."

"I take care of my own, Bobby. Last thing I want to see is another innocent black man railroaded for something he didn't do. There's a lot of that going around these days."

"Thanks, Jo. And Roxy, you don't know how much I appreciate you coming and especially for managing to get Julio away from old Kootz. I see you're wearing the necklace."

"Yes I am, just hope it sheds some light on things. As far as Julio goes, I'd do it again in a heartbeat," says Roxy. "And by the way, this is Nick Ross. He's a P.I. who's working for me and who helped me get Julio. I couldn't have done it without him."

Bobby extends his hand and gives me a warm but serious smile. "Hi, Nick, glad we're on the same team."

"Well, I hope I can help."

"C'mon let's all go inside. I've fixed some pasta, hope you're hungry."

"I'm going to put the car away, Bobby, but you go ahead and show them around, I'm sure we're all starving."

⟁

After sitting in the emergency room for more than an hour, Kate is beside herself. She doesn't know what is happening to her as she sits watching the dead and the dying being wheeled in and out of the corridors down the hall.

"Nurse, please, can you tell me how much longer? I think I may be losing my baby. I need to see a doctor."

"I'm sorry, ma'am. We've had two gun shot wounds, three heart attacks and an attempted suicide hit us all at the same time. Please be patient."

"You don't understand. I've had blood spotting for hours." Kate's voice quivers as she pleads with the nurse.

"I understand, ma'am, and I don't want to sound callous, but if you're having a miscarriage there's nothing that can be done about it. Once they start they can't be stopped. We have to take care of the life-threatening cases first."

"And you don't think losing my baby is a life-threatening case?" Kate says indignantly.

"Sorry, ma'am, we'll get to you as fast as we can."

Kate sits back down in the waiting room and looks around. There are homeless people passed out in chairs and mothers with young children coughing uncontrollably. An elderly man sits alone next to an oxygen tank on wheels and the young man directly across from her is ghastly pale except for his red-rimmed eyes and looks scared to death.

Then a doctor walks in. She thinks finally someone is coming to see her, but he passes her by and sits down next to the young man in the chair. She can't hear the entire conversation but the first words are, "I'm sorry. Your wife didn't make it."

Kate sits in her chair watching with discomfort as the young man doubles over sobbing until someone comes in, gently takes him by the arm and leads him away. She sits back, puts both hands on her belly and takes a deep breath. Then she stands up and walks out.

⌄

As we sit around the dinner table I watch Bobby very carefully. My "gift", as I'm beginning to think of it, seems to allow me to listen to what someone is saying and sort the truth from the bullshit. Call it some newly developed intuition but I think it's more than that. And what it's telling me is that Bobby has a lot of issues and conflicts—not unlike many of us—but that he is not a killer. Of that I am sure.

"Wow, Bobby, this pasta is fabulous, did you make it?"

"Thanks, Roxy, yes I did. I like to cook."

"Hey, Nick, how about passing the bread around if you can pull yourself away from your plate for a sec."

"Sorry, I'm starving. Here ya' go. Anything else?"

"I see you've grown your beard out, Bobby."

"Yeah, Roxy, thought it might be a good idea to have a different look for awhile. If you know what I mean."

"Yep, got it. So when are you going to test the necklace?"

"I'm sure the batteries in it are dead by now and it's too late to get any tonight. Maybe you and Jo can get some for me in the morning?"

"Sounds like a plan, sure hope there's something useful on it."

"Yeah, me too. My life may depend on it."

"So, Julio, what do you think of Laguna Beach?"

"I love it, Miss Jo, it's beautiful. I've never been out of L.A., not until I was taken to Nevada. I don't think that counts though."

"No, it doesn't, Julio, and that's something I'd like to talk to you about. Are you OK with that?"

"Sure, Miss Jo."

"Do you remember what the person looked like who got you off the streets in L.A. and took you to Reno?"

"Yes, ma'am, he was an Asian man, kind of short and stocky."

"Did he have any distinguishing marks? You know, like a tattoo, a birthmark, facial hair?"

"Yes, Miss Jo, he did. He had a tattoo of a dragon underneath his left ear. I never forget that."

"Ah, I thought so. I'm guessing that's Kim Van Hune. They call him, 'The Blade'. Do you think you would you remember him if you saw him again, Julio?"

Julio looks at Jo as his hand makes a fist. "I will never ever forget him, Miss Jo."

"Well, it's about time to turn in, Julio," Jo says folding her napkin and standing up. "Why don't you take the office and den area. There's a sofa bed in there that's very comfortable. I'll get you some pillows and sheets."

After Jo returns from getting Julio settled in for the night, we all sit in front of the open pit fireplace. Jo pours some cognac for Bobby and Roxy, but I decline.

With the lights down, the fire sparkles and cracks. The flames reflect in our eyes and as I look around the group I can tell that each of us is wondering about the days ahead. Jo takes a sip of her cognac and an irritated look comes over her face.

"I've been hearing about Kim Van Hune for years," she says, "but he's almost like a ghost. He brings in children from the Far East and Mexico in addition to those he picks up in southern California, then sells them to anyone looking for slave labor. The garment district, pimps, the porn industry, you name it. The guy's scum."

"How the hell does he get them into the country, Jo?"

"He brings a lot of them in through Mexico, up from Central America. Quite a few of Asians get smuggled in the hulls of freighters to just outside U.S. territory where they're picked up by fishing boats and brought ashore. A lot of the kids are half dead by the time they get here."

"What an evil son of a bitch. Why can't they catch him?"

"I don't know, Roxy. He's either really smart, really lucky or both. I've got two girls who work for me that escaped from him but they're still terrified he will come looking for them."

Bobby leans in. "Yeah, that's what Julio told me when we were in Nevada working for Wesley Kootz. He said he was too scared to run away because if he got caught he would be killed."

"He scares the hell out of all of them, Bobby, and rumor has it he puts "kill dates" on many of the children he brings in."

"What the hell does that mean, Jo?"

"Well, Nick, you know how they put expiration dates on food? He puts expiration dates on many of the people he brings into this country."

"*What?*" You got to be fucking kidding me."

"No, I'm not. After a few years he found out it was better to kill off some of his imports before they started to assimilate into society. Too many were causing trouble or running off, sometimes even going to the authorities and that was causing real problems for their owners. So he put kill dates on them which scared the hell out of the rest of the kids. Kept them guessing as to who might be next unless they did as told. That way he keeps his clients happy and makes more money by continually replacing the ones he eliminates."

"Oh my God! I've never heard of anything so evil. I hope he rots in hell."

"I'm sure he will, Roxy, but I'd like to see him swimming with the fishes first. Know what I mean?"

Sitting in front of the fire, we all stare at the flames in silence, thinking about what Jo has said. It might just be me, but there seems to be a feeling of gratitude in the air despite each of our current circumstances.

CHAPTER 19

DEAR DIARY

*H*ear my prayer, oh Lord, thy will be done. *The shemale can run but she can not hide. God is everywhere and sees all. I will find her and carry out his law, the law of the gospel in Leviticus: "For you must not profane the name of your God. I am Lord. Do not lie with a man as one lies with a woman. That is detestable."*

I pray to you, God the Father, maker of Heaven and Earth. Hear my words as I do your bidding. Guide me and give me strength to cleanse evil from this world and bring the word of God to all those who sin. In your name justice will be done. Amen.

CHAPTER 20

Hungry for the Truth

"**Well, good morning,** everybody. How did you sleep last night?"

"I slept great, Jo, thanks," says Roxy. "It's so nice to be able to have the windows open and no bugs flying around."

"Yes, Miss Jo, I agree with Miss Roxy, but even better was hearing the sound of those waves crashing on the beach."

"I love that too, Julio. It never gets old. So how about we all go into town for some breakfast? I'm starving. You up for getting out of the house for a little bit, Bobby?"

"Hmm, that's a little risky, but. . .sure, why not? I'll put on some sunglasses and wear a hoodie. Just kidding, better make it a ball cap."

Jo puts down her coffee mug and turns towards the open French doors that lead from the kitchen to an expansive redwood deck and a 180-degree ocean view. "Nick, what about you? Hungry, sweetie?"

Mesmerized by the glistening white caps and the deep blue variations of the Pacific, I've been oblivious to the morning chatter of Jo and the other houseguests. It's been more than 24 hours now since I've talked to Kate, heard her voice, asked about the baby – my baby – but it feels like it's been much longer. Too much drama screws up the pace of daily life and can make minutes seem like hours, or hours shoot by like seconds. And I've been dealing with a lot of drama lately.

"Nick? Eggs, bacon, French toast? You awake out there?"

"Oh, yeah. . .hey sorry, Jo," I reply and take one more deep breathe of the cool, salty air before I step back into the kitchen, the thought of Kate still lingering. "Yes, I'm starving. Let's go."

"Great. Bobby, would you please back the Explorer out of the garage? It'll give us more room."

We descend Jo's winding street and turn on to PCH towards Laguna's downtown. We've got the windows open and are enjoying the sea breeze heavy in the air until traffic suddenly comes to a standstill.

"You know several years ago you could pretty much count on Laguna streets being almost empty mid-week between Labor Day and Memorial weekend," Jo grumbles as she slowly inches the Explorer down Forest Avenue past art galleries and trendy restaurants. "Not any more. Now it's tourist season 24/7, 365. Town's turned into a damn Disneyland."

Jo hits the brakes hard when the BMW in front of her nearly rear-ends a Lexus trying to claim a parking spot. "And the City Council's *got* to do something about this traffic, it's ridiculous and dangerous. Maybe they should put up gates and sell admission tickets."

Jo cautiously turns the corner, waiting while three cyclists blow right past the stop sign. "This is why it seems like everyone in town needs a yoga class. It's either that or blood pressure medication." Jo shakes her head as she maneuvers the Explorer into a tree-shaded spot across from the Presbyterian Church.

As we walk toward the beach we pass five art galleries, four over-priced T-shirt stores and three ice cream shops.

"Anyone in this town sell anything useful, like nails or light bulbs?" I ask.

"Sure, we've got a great hardware store one street over. More expensive than Home Depot but you don't have to fight the traffic in the canyon."

As we wait at the light to cross PCH, I can't help but notice the cars going by. So far I've seen two Ferraris, three Maseratis, a Bentley and a Rolls Royce. Every other car is a Beemer, a Lexus or a Mercedes. Not a Ford and Chevy anywhere in sight.

Jo leads the way down the sidewalk ushering us past a bigger than life-size wooden statue of a bearded old man. I need to know more. "Hey, Jo, who is this guy? Why the statue?"

"That's 'The Greeter', a true Laguna icon. His name was Eiler Larsen and for 40 years, day in and day out, he stood on various street corners here in town, greeting everyone and wishing them a pleasant day. He never asked for anything and was never paid for his kindness, he just did it. Yes, he's somewhat of a legend here. So this statue stands here in front of the restaurant that bears his name. Other 'Greeters' have tried to pick up where

Larsen left off, but none have been as genuine or as beloved by the locals. You can't turn back time."

We get a table outside on the patio just a stone's throw from the water's edge—and with a great view of young women playing beach volleyball. The morning sun shimmers on the ocean like a thousand shooting stars sparkling in a deep blue sky. After we've settled in and ordered coffee, Bobby turns to Julio with a serious but kind demeanor.

"Julio, I have something to tell you."

"What's that, Bobby?" Julio says, innocently staring back at Bobby.

"When I was in L.A. I tracked down your family and talked to your mother."

Julio's expression changes instantly from curiosity to apprehension.

"She wants to see you, Julio. Your whole family wants you to come home."

"Really, Bobby? But what about. . .you know?"

"You being gay? She told me they had a hard time dealing with it at first. She explained to me how your family has always taken God's word literally but that after talking with several different priests they came to have a different understanding. She says they found acceptance through prayer. She just hopes you can forgive them."

"Oh. . .I do miss them." Julio looks away as if he might start to cry.

"I think the new Pope should get some credit for persuading people like your family to open their minds and hearts to the gay community even when it's uncomfortable for them. I think his comments have had a positive impact on a lot of people, not just Catholics. And I think your family now realizes how much they love you and miss you."

"What about father, does he want me home? He threw me out."

"Your mother said he's had a hard time but you're his son and that's all that matters."

"But, Bobby, can't I stay with you?"

"You're a good boy, Julio, but you belong with your family and you need to finish school. Besides, I have some legal issues to deal with right now so it wouldn't be possible."

The sound of the waves fills the uncomfortable silence at the table.

Julio stares out at the ocean for several minutes until the waitress returns with our coffee.

"Are you OK, Bobby?" he asks.

"I'm fine, Julio, don't worry about me. I'll check in on you from time to time. I'm not going away. Jo will take you back to your family when she heads up to L.A."

"I will miss you, Bobby."

"I'll miss you too, Julio. Come on, buddy, give me a hug."

We all offer simple but sincere words of encouragement, grateful when our waitress returns to take our order. We all know it won't be easy for Julio, or his family, and that his journey is taking him right back to where he started.

After breakfast Roxy, Julio and I stroll the boardwalk past Main Beach and climb the stairs to Heisler Park. Jo and Bobby head to the hardware store to get the batteries Bobby needs to work on the necklace back at the house. Despite the laid-back atmosphere of the beach, I'm feeling nervous. I have a murder threat looming for my client and I have a huge ache in my heart about Kate. I just want to get back to Vegas or at least be able to turn my phone on and call her. I miss her terribly.

CHAPTER 21

The Calm Before the Storm

"**H**ey, I've got three hits on facial recognition in a group of five people. Call the Chief. We've found them." Despite the urgency of news, it gets only momentary attention from most Department staff all of whom are immersed in their own overwhelming workloads.

Within fifteen minutes however, Assistant Chief of Police Scott McBride has assembled everyone in the conference room, no excuses accepted. Captain Tucker, Lyle and Mitch sit waiting, eager to find out what's up when McCain marches into the room.

"What the hell is going on, and where's the Assistant Chief?"

Everyone turns toward McCain, most with cautiously amused expressions, a visible testament to a strong locals versus Feds resentment. Tucker shrugs his shoulders, then scoots his chair back, intentionally making enough noise to be heard down the hall. He stands, clears his throat and places both hands firmly on the table as if ready to pounce.

"Hey, you're the FBI." Tucker smirks as he leans forward. "Don't *you* know what's going on, McCain?"

Just then McBride walks into the room. "Gentlemen, I've been informed that we've located the whereabouts of Bobby Westbrook and the persons of interest you have been pursuing. Our plan is. . ."

"Great, McBride, where the hell are they?" McCain interrupts as he stands and walks to the head of the table.

"As I started to say, Agent McCain, we know they're in Laguna Beach. I've contacted the Chief there and made him aware of the situation. I've told him not to do anything but locate the subjects and observe until we arrive."

McCain tries to direct another question at McBride but Tucker ignores him and cuts him off. "Any vehicle I.D. or plate number?" he asks. McCain is now clearly pissed.

"No, not yet, Captain," says McBride. "But now we can focus all our resources on Laguna so it shouldn't take long if they show themselves again. I'm putting the Sheriff's Department on standby in case we need the SWAT team."

"Sounds like a good plan, McBride," says Tucker, intentionally lobbing another comment right past McCain.

"Sit down, Tucker, I'll take care of this," McCain seethes. "And McBride, isn't this a little out of your jurisdiction? I mean, I'd hate to see your boys end up arresting Wayne Newton again."

"Real funny, McCain, I'm sure that plays well in Vegas but this is L.A. It's Laguna's jurisdiction along with the Orange County Sheriff's. I'm merely advising till they take over."

"I don't want this getting screwed up again, McBride. Understand? Now how long will it take us to get down there?"

McBride pauses for a three second stare-down with McCain, then takes a deep breath. "About an hour and a half, less if you use lights and sirens."

"Tell them we're on our way and keep me updated on any more sightings, especially if you get a plate number."

"You ever get tired of barking orders, McCain?"

▲

"Nick, is that you, Nick Ross?"

We're standing on a path in Heisler Park overlooking "Rock Pile" a favorite surfer's cove when I hear my name called out.

"Nick, it is you."

When I turn around I see Rick, Jasper's boyfriend and business partner from Vegas standing there. He's dressed in his usual Bermuda shorts, a Tommy Bahama flowered shirt and flip flops, with a leather man-purse hanging from his shoulder.

"Hey Rick, good to see you. Jasper mentioned you were spending a lot of time here but I certainly didn't expect to run into you."

"Well, it's a small world isn't it, Nick?" Jasper says in his trademark bitchy pseudo-polite tone. "So, who are your friends?"

"This is Roxy Lynn and this is Julio. We're just here for the day."

"So nice to meet you both," Jasper gushes as he throws one arm around his companion's shoulders. "And this is my friend from Laguna, Baldemar Firetto, but everybody just calls him

Baldy." The fit and 50-ish gentleman wearing a weathered "Save the Canyon" t-shirt and Quiksilver boardshorts tips his hat revealing his shiny dome.

"We're on our way to Las Brisas for breakfast, have you eaten?"

"We just finished eating down at the Greeter's but I hear Las Brisas is nice, a little pricy but nice. "

"Will you be letting Jasper know that you saw me?"

"That depends, Rick, do you want me to?" I ask, not wanting to get caught up in Rick's bullshit but trying to be civil in front of Roxy and Julio.

"Well played, Nick," Rick chuckles. "Now that's a good question. I know he's a little upset with me right now, so I'm thinking yes. . .why not?" Rick smirks and tosses his hands skyward with a casual who-cares gesture.

"Good to see you, Rick, but we really have to go. We're meeting someone. Nice to meet you, Baldy." With polite nods from Roxy and Julio, we continue down the path that hugs the cliff above Rockpile toward the local lawn bowling club. I can't help but wonder what the hell Jasper sees in Rick and why he puts up with his petty game-playing, especially since Jasper does the majority of the work at their restaurant. But the thought quickly passes. I've got bigger issues to deal with.

▲

Kate's been up half the night worrying and checking for more blood. Finally with the morning light streaming in through her bedroom window, she crawls out of bed and goes into the bathroom. In a couple of hours she will see her doctor and her questions will be answered. As she reaches for her phone her hand starts to shake. The only messages are all work related, nothing from Nick.

"God, I wish I had someone to talk to, but nobody knows I'm pregnant except Nick. My mother would flip out if I sprung it on her. She'd be on the first flight out of Georgia and that's not what I need right now. Can't talk to anybody at work about it, too many questions—and the gossip. Oh, the gossip. Maybe I should see a shrink? No, I just have to keep telling myself everything is going to be all right. Everything is going to be all right."

Kate goes to the living room and curls up on the sofa. Just a few more hours.

⏷

Danny Alvarez had always wanted to be a cop. He grew up on the streets of Santa Ana and learned at an early age what kind of power police officers have at their command. As soon as he was old enough, he applied to the police academy eager to become part of the Sheriff's Department.

Despite some borderline psychological test results he became a Sheriff's Deputy and joined the force in Orange County. Soon afterwards he married his high school sweetheart Maria and started a family.

And now, after only being on the force a couple of years, he has already made a name for himself as a no-nonsense tough cop who takes crap from nobody. His reputation has even brought him respect in the gang-infested areas he patrols.

Within the last nine months though, Danny has been in two officer-involved shootings and has killed both suspects. The incidents took place soon after he came off rookie status. His commanders love him and are very happy with what they've seen, especially since both the shootings were seen as open-and-shut cases by the Police Review Board with slim chance of litigation. Their only concern was the fact that both people killed were black.

But Danny just saw it as life on the streets. He sees himself, as his family and peers see him, a good man and a fine cop. So when his Captain suggested to him that he apply to the SWAT team, Danny enrolled immediately.

After completing training the veterans on the team always likes to have a little celebration for the new recruit. The special night out, however, took Danny by surprise when he found out that half of the team was female. The tradition is somewhat akin to the hazing in a fraternity. So the night before Danny is to start his new assignment, he is taken from one bar to another where the shots of tequila flow like water. By the time he gets home at 3 a.m. he's shit-face drunk and can barely walk. Unfortunately his wife has been up all night with a sick baby and now demands his help. By the time 7 a.m. rolls around, Danny is sick with a hangover, has had no sleep and is irritable as hell as he gets ready for work. It's his first day on the SWAT team.

⋏

"Call McBride and tell him we have another positive ID on facial recognition of the suspect in Laguna Beach. He just got into

an SUV with a Caucasian woman and is headed east on Forest Avenue. I think we can enhance a frame and get a plate number."

Within twenty minutes, McBride is on the phone with McCain. "We've got a hit in Laguna on our boy, got the vehicle and the plate number. It's registered to a Stella Jo Vance on Dartmoor in Laguna."

"That's damn good news, McBride, tell your boys job well done. We'll take it from here." McCain pumps a fist in the air as he turns toward Tucker.

"Tucker, you and your men contact Laguna P.D. I want that house under surveillance but no black and whites, only unmarked. I don't want to tip our hand. Then contact the Sheriff and schedule a meet-up nearby with the SWAT team. You got all that?"

"Yeah, McCain. I got it, anything else?"

"If you believe in God, pray that he's our man."

⅄

"So this is lawn bowling, huh? Kinda' looks like a grown-up version of bocce ball," I comment as Roxy and Julio stand on the sidewalk overlooking the exquisitely manicured greens of the Laguna Beach Lawn Bowling Club. The club, which was started in 1931, sits on the cliffs overlooking the pounding surf of the Pacific that stretches to Catalina and beyond. The Club's greens are about the size of half a football field and sit smack in the middle of some of the most expensive real estate in the world.

"Looks like Jo's here already, over by the clubhouse. C'mon let's go in."

Jo sees us and waves for us to come over to her. She's standing on the edge of one of the greens talking to a trim, tanned woman all dressed in white, who looks to be in her 60's.

"Well, I see you found the place. What do you think? Beautiful, isn't it? How would you like to play a game, Julio?"

"I don't know how to play, Miss Jo."

"Oh, don't worry about that, I'll show you what to do. We'll just play for fun. Come with me, I'll get you some bowls and give you guys a quick lesson."

CHAPTER 22

The Storm

Just outside Laguna's city limits at Crystal Cove State Park, mountain bikers, trail runners and hikers traipse through the parking lot on their way either into or out of one of south Orange County's favorite playgrounds, the beach notwithstanding. Most barely glance at the Sheriff Department's SWAT team as they gather in a parking lot getting ready for their deployment. They are met by the FBI's McCain, Captain Tucker, his detectives from Vegas, the Chief from Laguna and some of his officers. Looks more like a staging for a military invasion of the entire town rather than a law enforcement effort to capture one man.

After a briefing by McCain to get everybody on the same page, the battalion moves into action. The plan is to have a small number of SWAT officers surround the house but remain unseen. This should be reasonably simple due to the location of the house at the end of the street. Only one house sits next to it with the other three sides bordering the wilderness area. They intend to wait to move in until they get confirmation from one of these spotters that the subject is in the house. When confirmed, the rest of the team will move to secure entry to the premises and take Bobby Westbrook into custody.

With the first team in place, it isn't long before Bobby is spotted walking on to the deck at the back of the house. He leans over the rail, stretches and takes in a deep breath of coastal air then walks back into the house through the floor-to-roof sliding glass doors.

With confirmation made, the second group of helmeted robo-looking forces move into position to enter the house. McCain and the SWAT team leader take their command post overlooking the operation. "Tell your men nobody makes a move until I give the go ahead, got it?"

"Yes, sir, it's your call." The team leader relays the message to his men through the microphone in his helmet. "All troops stand by and hold your positions, orders are eminent."

▲

Jo is about to roll a bowl on the green at the club when her phone rings.

"Jo, it's Bobby. I've been working on the necklace and I think I have something. I've got a voice. Where are you guys? I'll come meet you."

"Bobby, that's great news. We're down at the lawn bowling club, come down and join us. We'll meet you in the clubhouse and celebrate."

"I'll be there in a few minutes."

Jo turns to me, Roxy and Julio with a big grin on her face. "That was Bobby. He sounds very excited. He found something on the necklace and is coming down to join us."

"Thank God," Roxy cheers throwing an arm in the air. "That's really good news. Maybe we can get the cops onto the real killer now."

⋏

The office where Bobby is working looks out over the cliffs and ocean below. He's eager to get outside and enjoy what he hopes is his new found freedom. As he walks from the office through the kitchen and heads to the garage he has no view of the street in front of the house. He gets into the Explorer, starts it up and hits the remote to open the garage door. As soon as he backs on to the driveway he is cut off by an armored humvee blocking his exit. A dozen officers drop into position, rifles aimed and ready.

⋏

Back at the club an alert goes off on Jo's phone flashing WAZE. She hurriedly opens the app and sees it showing a dozen police vehicles at the location of her house. Immediately she calls Bobby back to warn him.

⋏

"Exit the vehicle slowly and put your hands in the air" the speaker on the bullhorn calls out.

Bobby slowly gets out of the car, puts his hands in the air and takes a step forward. "Do not move," the voice announces again in a threatening tone.

Then, out of habit or instinct, Bobby reaches for the phone vibrating in his pocket. "Gun!" yells rookie Danny Alvarez. Within a second a dozen high-powered assault rifles let go a barrage of death. Bobby's body gyrates as the exploding projectiles rip through him in all directions. Literally dead on his feet, he begins to sink and falls forward uncontrollably, collapsing onto the driveway. A pool of deep red blood begins to form under him and slowly starts to run down the drive into the street and finally the rain gutter.

McCain screams at the top of his lungs, "Hold your fire. Hold your fire!" but it's too late. "God damn it, who yelled gun! Who's the fucking idiot that yelled gun!"

Nobody says a word. The code of silence already in place.

Jo hustles us into the car and we're at the house in no time. I jump out as soon as we stop but tell Roxy to stay in the car with Julio. The police are already putting up crime scene tape but I make it far enough to see Bobby lying in a pool of blood on the driveway.

I turn and head back to the car. My hands are shaking and I can barely catch a breath. I want to scream obscenities but know better than to bring any attention toward me. I hear the warning shriek of a siren, just before I see an ambulance turn onto the street and make its way past us to the body that has no need for its services.

The SWAT team closes its perimeter sealing off the house, the car and Bobby. Within minutes one of the team bounds out the front door yelling, "All clear."

As I near our car I try to settle myself with little success. Roxy and Jo are straining to see what's going on when they spot me coming towards them. I motion for Jo to get out of the car. As she walks toward me I can see the anguish on her face which I'm sure is a direct reflection of my own.

"They shot him, Jo. He's dead"

"Oh my God. . . no, no!" Her head falls against my chest and I can feel the pain of her muffled sobs. "He was innocent. Why the hell would they shoot him?"

"I don't know but Julio can't see this. He needs to stay in the car."

Jo hugs me, still sobbing she hesitates for a moment, takes a deep breath and says, "I'll get Roxy."

Roxy breaks down as she walks towards me, arms outstretched. She senses the worst. Tears are rolling down her cheeks as she sobs uncontrollably falling into me.

"He's dead, isn't he?" she says with a gasp, embracing me.

"I'm sorry, Roxy. Yes, he is."

"Who's going to tell Julio? I can't do it, Nick."

"I think we should all do it together, Roxy. So we can all be there for him."

Together we walk back to the car to face Julio, who is about ready to jump out and run to see what is going on.

"What's happening, Mr. Nick, is Bobby OK? Why are all the police here? Is Bobby OK? Is he OK?" panic swells in his voice.

"Julio, I'm sorry. This is very hard."

"No, Mr. Nick, no! Tell me Bobby's OK!" Julio grabs me by the arm shaking it.

"Bobby has been shot Julio. I'm sorry but he's gone."

Julio screams and beats his fist on the back of the seat, sobbing and then tearing at his hair. "No, no, not Bobby, he good man. Why? Why would they kill him?"

"We don't know what exactly happened Julio, but we'll find out."

"I want to see him. Let me out I want to go see him." The police are cordoning off the crime scene and moving closer to us as Julio looks out the window sobbing.

"Julio, I can't let you do that. Please, you need to trust me. You do not want to remember Bobby like this."

Roxy moves in and puts an arm around Julio, trying to calm him down. That's when I see Lyle walking toward a cruiser about half a block away. I motion for Roxy to take over as she hugs Julio and puts his head on her shoulder. "Jo, I'm going to go talk to someone I know and find out what happened."

Lyle spots me about fifty feet away coming at him and motions for me to walk behind one of the squad cars on the side of the street.

"What the hell are you doing here, Nicky?"

"A better question is what the hell happened, Lyle? Why did they kill him?"

"He made a move for his pocket and somebody yelled gun. It was over in five seconds."

"Shit! Did he have a gun? Do you know if he had a gun."

"No, it was just a cell phone."

"Are you fucking kidding me? How many times is this shit going to happen, Lyle? Bobby was innocent and he could prove it."

"So why didn't he, Nick?"

"Because he had just gotten the proof a few minutes ago and was on his way down to meet us. Now he's dead, fucking dead."

"What proof? What are you talking about?"

"The necklace, Lyle, did you find the necklace?"

"I don't know, they're searching the house now. What's a necklace got to do with the murders anyway?"

"The necklace was a recording device that Bobby had made for Mavis to wear. She was wearing it when she was killed. It could have the killer's voice on it."

"I'll check it out, Nick, but you need to stick around. I'm sure McCain and Tucker are going to want to talk to you."

As I walk back to the car I see that Julio is sobbing on Jo's shoulder. Roxy's in the front seat staring at me in disbelief. Before I can reach for the handle she throws open the door.

"What's going on, Nick?" she says sharply. "What did he say?"

"He doesn't know if they found the necklace or not but they want to talk to us." I wince in anticipation of her reaction.

"No, you know I can't do that. We need to get the hell out of here," she says, her panic rising with each word.

"We can't, they've closed off the road."

"I *have* to get out of here, Nick. I'm not taking the chance of going to prison for something I didn't do." Her glare at me intensifies while her eyes fill with tears.

Jo sees that Roxy is visibly upset and tells Julio to lie down and rest for a few minutes until she comes back. "What's going on, you two? Roxy, you OK, sweetheart?"

Roxy squints hard, adding another level of intensity to her anguished reply. "They want to question us about Bobby. I can't do that, Jo. They might arrest me."

"What? Why on earth would they arrest you, dear? You haven't done anything wrong. There wasn't even a warrant out for Bobby's arrest yet."

"It's not that, Jo. I got caught up in something really awful a long time ago. I'm innocent but the cops won't think so. I have to get out of here. I can't take the chance." Roxy's visibly nervous, her eyes darting around looking for an escape.

Jo sighs and shifts into control mode. "I have an idea. See that sign at the end of the road that says trailhead?"

Roxy nods. "Yes."

"I've got a daypack in my trunk I always carry for emergencies, there's a ball-cap in it. Put on the pack and tuck your hair up under the cap. Walk to that trailhead like you know what you're doing and just keep on going. There are always hikers coming and going so stay calm and no one should notice you."

"But where am I supposed to go, Jo?"

"Follow the trail for about two miles till you get to Bomber Ridge, watch for the trail sign. Stay right on the trail and it'll take you all the way down into the canyon. There's a rental car place just a couple blocks from the trailhead. Do you drive, dear?"

"I still have my license. I just don't like to drive."

"Well, we all have to do things we don't like sometimes, sweetie. I'll call my contact there and tell him I have a friend who'll be coming off the trail and needs a car. But if you're going to do it you'd better go quickly. I'll get the daypack. Why don't you tell Julio goodbye."

"Thank you, Jo. I really appreciate your help. Nick, I'll call you when I get back to Vegas."

"Yeah, do that as soon as you get back. Here's your phone but don't turn it on till you're home. Now, give me a hug and be careful. I'll see you in Vegas."

Roxy quickly says goodbye to Julio, then throws on the pack, tucks up her hair and heads towards the trailhead. Jo and I watch as she hikes out to the path framed by wild sage and disappears slowly into the horizon.

"Nick, can you keep Julio company for a few minutes? I'm going to call my lawyer here in town just in case we need him."

We wait in the car in silence. Julio sobs from time to time but mostly just stares out the window toward the house where Bobby was shot. Words seem worthless, just improvised band-aids trying to stop a torrential flow of pain. I can't imagine what the poor kid is feeling. Especially after all he's been through.

I want to scream as my anger builds about the injustice that has taken place. In contrast, Jo is calm, almost too calm, like she's already plotting to get even in some way.

I look up to I see Lyle, Captain Tucker and McCain walking toward our car. Jo and I both get out after attempting to reassure Julio that everything is fine. McCain steps forward, introduces himself and turns to Jo.

"Is this your house, Miss Vance?"

"Yes, it is."

"Why was Bobby Westbrook hiding here?"

"Hiding? I beg your pardon. He's a friend of mine and welcome here anytime."

"Did you know he was wanted for questioning for a murder in Las Vegas?"

"No, of course not. How would I know that?"

McCain turns to me. "What brought you here from Vegas and where's the other woman who was with you?"

"She had business in Vegas and flew back this morning. We came down to take the young man in the car back to his parents. Bobby was a good friend of his so we stopped by to see him."

McCain ramps up the intimidation factor. "You two aren't telling me everything," he says wagging an accusatory finger in my face. "How would you like to be taken in for questioning?" He doesn't scare me. I had a third grade teacher who was much better at this shit.

"Excuse me!" says a booming voice walking towards us. We all turn at once. "Excuse me, sir, I'm Miss Vance's attorney."

As he gets closer I recognize the guy as being the friend of Rick's we met earlier today at the park.

"Hello. My name is Baldemar Firetto and I represent Miss Vance and her protégé. Your questioning is over here. You can direct further inquiries through me."

"The questioning is over when I say it's over Mr. whatever your name is, or I'll arrest both of them."

"The name is Baldemar Firetto, sir. What's the issue here?"

"Harboring a fugitive, Mr. Firetto. Your client and her friend here knew he was a suspect."

"Is that right? Was a warrant out for Bobby's arrest?" The stare-down is officially on.

"No, we had intended to charge him after taking him in for questioning. Standard procedure, we have evidence."

"And that's never going to happen now, is it? My clients will be getting in their car and leaving now, sir, unless you plan to arrest them under false pretenses." Firetto wins.

McCain is seething. He looks at Tucker and then back at Baldy. "Fine, get the hell out of here but you haven't heard the last of it."

CHAPTER 23

There's No Place Like Home

Roxy nervously but steadily makes her way up the steep rocky path to the top of the ridge. Up ahead she can see the Santa Ana mountains in the distance with a dusty haze surrounding them. As she glances back, she sees the village of Laguna as it sprawls down from the hilltops and spills into the ocean. Beyond the city lies the Pacific, its deep aqua waves pushing past Catalina Island, out to the horizon where it joins billowing clouds and deep blue sky. Roxy stops for a minute to take in the beauty but fear soon regains its grip so she presses on.

There are only a few people on the trail. It's the hottest part of the day and up on the ridge it's ten degrees warmer than down below on the canyon floor. As she starts to climb a particularly rocky part of the trail, Roxy is startled when she hears something up ahead. At the top of the rise she freezes. Face to face with a rattlesnake coiled and ready to strike, a new kind of terror overcomes her.

The heavy bodied diamondback is nearly six feet long. The black and white bands above its tail quiver making its distinctive threatening sound. The snake's triangular head stretches and shifts from side to side, fangs showing, ready to strike.

Roxy is paralyzed with fear. Heart racing, she freezes not knowing quite what to do. She's known stage fright in Vegas but that was just anxiety that would pass. This is real danger and she's scared to death. Just then from the other direction a mountain biker comes barreling around the corner. He sees the snake but it's too late. He runs right over it, panic-cranks to the right and catapults himself off the bike and into the scrub sage below. The snake makes a failed attempt to strike, lunging at the rider-less bike and getting caught up in the spokes of the rear wheel. The bike stays upright for a few yards as the snake gets tossed round and round in the wheel. Finally its head gets wedged between the chain and the gears. It tries desperately to free itself but its whip-like motions only serve to tear its own head off.

"Amen!" says Roxy as she runs over to the man lying in the bushes. "Are you all right?"

"Damn, he was a big one. Yeah, I'm OK. . .I think."

Though reluctant to step too far off the trail, Roxy extends her hand. "Here, let me help you up."

"Is the snake still out there?"

"No, I think your bike killed it."

"Really? Damn, good bike."

"I also think maybe you saved my life, thank you."

"You might want to thank the man upstairs for that. All I did was fall off my bike, he did the rest." The young man picks himself up, brushes the dust off his jersey and bike shorts, straightens his helmet and pulls his sunglasses down over his eyes.

"You sure you're OK?"

"Oh, I've taken worse falls than that. Just gotta get back on it. You take care now."

"But, I don't even know your name."

"My name's Casey. You?"

"Roxy. My pleasure for sure. One more favor, could you tell me how much farther it is to Bomber Ridge?"

"No more than a half-mile, you can see it from here. It's that next big rise."

"Thank you again. Can I shake your hand? I want to make sure you're real." As Casey extends his hand, Roxy sees a tattoo of a cross on his arm just above his wrist.

▲

Kate sits in the waiting room of her Ob-Gyn with a half dozen pregnant women and three husbands who look like they're experiencing another dimension. Hardly anyone says a word except for two of the husbands who are speculating on the odds of the Denver Broncos making the playoffs this year. Everyone else is intently focused on their cell phones no doubt attending to urgent Facebook and Twitter business. Kate wonders if the art of conversation is truly dead and buried. She's glad her type of work helps her keep that skill alive, but she's too exhausted to put it to practice right now.

The door connecting the waiting room to the hallway filled with examining rooms opens and a young woman steps out on her way toward the exit. She is visibly shaken. Her eyes are puffy and red. She hangs her head trying to hide whatever it is that has upset her. There's a sadness about her that lingers throughout the room.

Everyone is silent for a moment, heads down, no one wanting to make eye contact with her or each other. As soon as she's out the door, one of the men shouts out a score in the football game and everyone goes back to checking their phones and texting. The nurse steps through the door, clip board in hand. "Kate Simon."

⚚

Roxy's now on snake alert. Her eyes sweep the trail left to right before each step, while she strains to pay attention to every sound, every movement in the wind.

Heading up the last rise she stops twice to listen, caution and fear ruling each move. Out of breath but relieved to reach Bomber Ridge, she begins her descent into the canyon. Her anxiety eases when she sees the highway cutting its way through the limestone rock walls and willow trees below. Almost there.

She quickens her pace down the path as it gets closer to the canyon floor, surprised at her own ability to maneuver the rocky trail. "Not bad for a showgirl," she mutters to herself. As she approaches the road, the traffic is bumper to bumper on the narrow highway heading out of town. She walks along the narrow shoulder, relieved cars are moving so slowly since they're not much more than an arm's length away. On the other side of the road two men with backpacks trudge along pushing shopping carts filled with empty cans and various belongings. Roxy spots what looks like an encampment about a hundred yards up the road. Nearby day laborers sit waiting for work. Directly above them on top of the hill, multi-million dollar houses line the ridge and overlook the city below.

Finally Roxy sees an Enterprise Leasing sign. She waits for what seems forever to cross the road and go rent a car. She hopes for something small and simple to drive but when she gets to the lot all she sees are SUV's.

⅄

Lyle's surprised by how relieved Captain Tucker seems to be about Westbrook being dead. Maybe it's just an easy way to close the book on the case.

"Captain, Nick told me there's some sort of necklace," Lyle says pulling the Captain aside. "Something Bobby made for Mavis that has a recording device in it. He said Bobby had found evidence on it and was on his way down to tell them about it. Said it could prove his innocence."

"You think this thing has the killer's voice on it?"

"There's a good possibility. If it exists we sure as hell need to find it."

"It would certainly change things. I'll talk to McCain about it. You take Mitch and do a thorough search on the car."

Tucker heads back into the house to find McCain but first he goes to the office where Bobby was spotted by the SWAT team. If Bobby was working on the necklace there he hopes to get a look around before anyone else can, especially McCain. "Smart-ass, know it all," Tucker mutters under his breath just as he enters Jo's office through the double French doors. He's surprised when he sees McCain sitting at the desk.

McCain slams a drawer shut and without even looking up says, "What took you so long?"

Roxy pulls on to Laguna Canyon Road, or the 133 as non-locals call it, as traffic comes to a halt. She's only driven a car twice in almost five years so some of the technology is a little overwhelming. Hands-free systems for your phone, GPS software that talks to you and satellite radio all make her wish she was in Nick's old Thunderbird, the kind of car where all you have to do is drive.

Once out of the canyon the traffic speed picks up quickly. As the speedometer hits seventy-five, her nerves kick into high gear as well. With everything she has to worry about, she didn't need SoCal traffic to be one of them.

She heads north on the 405 towards L.A. and starts to think about the last time she saw her mother. She wonders if it's been long enough. It was less than a week after the bank robbery and her stepbrother had already been caught by the police. She was getting ready to leave L.A. for good and make a new life somewhere else, but couldn't bring herself to leave without seeing her mother one last time even though the risk was high.

In the middle of the night she had snuck back into her mother's house and gently awakened her. Her stepfather was in the next room passed out drunk. A train could have run through the house and he wouldn't have known. She remembers thinking, "Poor mom, she deserves better."

She and her mother sat in the kitchen talking all night until the sun's shimmering rays glistened through the window on to the table where they sat. They talked about the past, the present and each of their uncertain futures. When she'd heard her step-father begin to stir she knew it was time to go. She had no desire to ever see him again. She hugged her mother tightly and kissed her on her forehead. They both knew it might be the last time they would ever see each other. When Raymond Tisdale walked out the door that night, Roxy Lynn was born.

She misses her mother terribly at times and on occasions had come close to breaking down and contacting her, but fear always won out. Now just a few miles outside of Inglewood the desire to see her again is overwhelming. She carefully maneuvers the rental car through the heavy stop-then-go traffic, blinking away intermittent tears.

"Damn, why did I run? Why did I run back then and why am I running now? I get so tired of hiding, of always being afraid that I'll get caught. I just want to see my mom. Just for a few minutes. They can't possibly be watching her after all these years and, damn it, I could be dead in a couple of days. I'm going."

Roxy makes her way to the old neighborhood where everything looks pretty much the way it did when she left. Trash still lines the alleys and the occasional junk car sits by the curb waiting to be towed off by the city truck that never comes. She drives by the house a couple of times in hope of seeing who may or may not be at home. There's no car on the street in front of the house so she suspects that her stepfather may not be there. Besides, this is the time of day he usually hangs out at the bar with his drinking buddies before stumbling back home for dinner.

Roxy parks a few doors down and walks past the house slowly. Her feet are filthy from her get-away trail hike in flip-flops. She's tired, thirsty and apprehensive as hell. Then she sees her mother through the window in the front room. Her heart begins to race as she catches her breath and heads up the walk to the front door. She tries the doorbell but hears nothing so she knocks. A minute that feels like ten passes before the weathered wooden door partially opens. Her mother unlocks the rusty metal security screen door and sticks her head out.

"Yes, may I help you?" she asks in that good neighbor tone of voice that Roxy knows so well.

"It's me, Mom."

"I'm sorry you must be mistaken. Who are you? I don't know you. Why are you calling me mom?" The door begins to close.

"Mom, wait. . .it's me. . .Raymond." Roxy can see the expression change on her mother's face from questioning to shock.

"No. . .you're a woman. I have a son." The door closes another inch.

"I know, Mom. It's really me. I'm your child. I need to explain. Can I please come in?"

"You're not going to hurt me, are you?"

"No Mom, never. Please, it's all right. I'm Raymond, your son."

She steps back and looks carefully at Roxy. Her eyes light up and a smile grows wide across her face. "Oh my God," she says placing her hands on her face, "now I see it in you. I see Raymond, come in. Come in, son."

For awhile they sit quietly, neither knowing quite what to say. Ray's mom stares at Roxy only to quickly look away when their eyes meet. Roxy looks at her mother's face and sees the toll the last ten years have taken. Her hair greyer, the lines deeper and an unmistakable sadness in her eyes that Roxy had never seen before. High on her right cheek there's what looks to be a bruise dabbed over with makeup.

"It's OK, Mom, I know this is a shock to you but is it really that surprising? I mean you know what I was like when I was a kid. I never fit in."

"Oh I know, your face used to light up whenever you saw a beautifully dressed woman, the same way little boys get excited about a new pair of basketball shoes. And you were always very sensitive. So how long have you been. . .I mean. . .when did you decide. . .?"

Roxy sees that her mother is struggling to understand that she no longer has a son but that she now has a daughter who loves her very much. She reaches over and takes her hand.

"Just about ten years ago. It was almost right after I left here. I wanted a new life. I needed a new life, but I'm still the same person I've always been."

"I can see that now, but are you happy?"

"I am, Mom. Yes, I am."

"Do you have a partner, are you married? I mean you can do that sort of thing these days, right?"

Roxy smiles warmly. "Yes, you can but no I'm not with anyone right now."

"What do you do? Where do you live?"

"I'd like to tell you everything, Mom, but I don't know if I should. I still have a problem with the bank robbery so it might be better if you don't know."

"That damned bank robbery and your crazy stepbrother. He ruined everything."

"I know, Mom. In a way it set me free but in another it more or less sentenced me to a life of constant worry about being arrested." Her hand tightens around mine as she leans in closer to me.

"Why after all these years have you come back? I thought maybe you were dead."

"I needed to be in the area to help out a friend, but things have gotten a little crazy. As I was driving here I couldn't stop thinking about you and the day I left. It was so long ago, too long. That's when I made the decision to come by."

"Your stepfather will be home soon. Do you want to stay?"

"No, I can't see him, he wouldn't understand. He never did. How's he treating you, Mom? Has he ever hit you again?"

"We get along most of the time," she says shifting her gaze away from Roxy and out the front window.

"Mom, look at me. Why do you stay with him? I know he's hurt you before."

"Habit I guess. I don't really have anywhere else to go."

"Well, it's a bad habit and one day soon I'll help you. I promise. In the meantime, don't put up with it, call the cops if you have to."

"You'd better go, Ray. Oh. . .I'm sorry. What is your name now?"

"My name is Roxy, Mom, and yes, I'd better go."

"Will I see you again, Roxy?"

"I don't know, Mom, I hope so. I love you."

"I love you too, son. Give me a hug." Roxy stands and embraces her mother, choking back tears then walks out the front door.

A police cruiser is parked directly in front of the house.

CHAPTER 24

ANTICIPATION

The first thing I do when I get in the car is turn on my cell phone which I haven't been able to do since I left Vegas. Dozens of messages and texts take up space but I'm only looking for Kate's. Then I find it, an email and several voice mail messages. Something's wrong, Kate sounds worried. Something is wrong with the baby. I frantically call her, but there's no answer.

⋏

The doctor is running late. Kate waits anxiously in the examining room wearing only a one-size-fits-nobody medical exam gown. She runs through a litany of things the doctor may tell her most of which she knows she won't want to hear. Will she be the next woman to walk through the waiting room head down, tears in her eyes, the pain of loss on her face?

Finally the doctor knocks on the door and enters the room with a nurse by his side. After the initial compulsory questions and a vain attempt at humor, he has Kate lie down to examine her. He says little but tells her they want to run an ultrasound.

$$\blacktriangle$$

I fumble with my phone as we leave Jo's house and drive back down the hill.

"I really need to get back to Vegas as soon as possible."

"What's the matter, Nick?" Jo asks. "Something wrong?"

"It's an emergency. My girlfriend is sick and she really needs me."

"No problem. I'll take you up to John Wayne. We can be there in fifteen minutes. I'm sure they have flights to Vegas every hour."

"Thanks, Jo, I'd really appreciate it."

On the way to the airport I try to talk to Julio. He's huddled in the backseat, eyes red from crying, head resting against the window. It's obvious he's hurting. In addition to what happened to Bobby, I'm sure he's confused and worried about going back home to his mother and father, mostly his father.

I turn around and try to get his attention. "Julio, I want you to know what a fine young man I think you are. I know you're going through a lot and losing Bobby is very difficult for you, but you'll get through it. There are a lot of unanswered questions right now, but I promise I'll let you know about the investigation just as soon as I hear something"

"Thank you, Mr. Nick. I needed to hear that," he says softly.

"Here's my phone number. Promise me you'll stay in touch. I know you might not want to think about it right now but I really do think you should contact Wayne Newton and get that audition he mentioned."

"Yes sir, Mr. Nick. I promise to do both."

"Good, because Jo and I will be checking on you."

Jo glances at the sad young man in her rearview mirror. "That's right, Julio, Nick and I are sort of adopting you."

"For that I am happy, Miss Jo, thank you."

Jo pulls into the lane for arrivals and stops at the curb for my airline. "Here we are, Nick."

"This is where I get out, Julio. I have to go." I reach over and give Jo a hug and then turn back to Julio. "You take care. . .love you."

"Good-bye, Mr. Nick. I love you too."

"Take care, Nick. Let me know how things turn out."

"I will, Jo, and oh, I almost forgot. I put my ankle holster and my gun in your trunk. Would you mind sending them to me? I can mail you a check."

"No need. I'd be happy to. Have a good flight."

I enter the airport and immediately search for the departing flights screen. There's a Delta flight scheduled to take off in fifteen minutes. I head towards the counter but see that the line is backed up. No one's checking in for first class so I walk over there. The woman at the ticket counter is busy at her computer. She doesn't look up but says she will be right with me. She's probably in her fifties with a bit of grey hair and slightly plump but in a very appealing way. She's definitely one of those seasoned airline employees who has seen it all, both the good times and the bad.

"Yes, sir, may I help you?" Her name tag says *Delores W.* but her demeanor tells me she's an airlines war-weary veteran for whom customer service still means something.

"The flight to Vegas leaving in fifteen minutes, can you get me on it? It's an emergency."

"I don't know, sir, let me check." Delores' fingers fly across the keyboard. "That's a pretty full flight." Her eyes search the screen while her fingers click-click on the keys. More searching, more clicking. "I'm very sorry, sir, first class is full."

"Is there anything else?" I ask, my voice cracking unintentionally.

"There is a seat in coach, but you probably won't be able to clear security in time to make the flight."

"Please. If there is anything you can do, I would really appreciate it. We may be about to lose our baby."

She looks at me and studies the anguish in my face for a second then starts typing, She swiftly checks my credit card and ID.

"Here's your ticket, sir," she says, glancing at me only briefly but long enough for me to see her eyes welling up. "This first class ticket will let you get through security quickly but I'll contact the gate and let them know we overbooked so they'll seat you in coach."

"Thank you, thank you. You're an angel."

"Well, I don't know about that, but you'd better hurry. They won't hold the plane," she says with an apologetic shrug. "And good luck."

She was right. There is virtually no line in first class and I breeze through security. I make it to the gate just in time and board as they are about to close the aircraft's door. As soon as I get to my seat I pull out my phone and try Kate again, no answer. I text her that I'm on my way back.

⅄

Although nervous, Roxy tries to walk nonchalantly toward the curb as she leaves her mother's house, keeping an eye on the officer getting out of his squad car and coming toward her.

"Excuse me, Miss. Do you know a Mrs. Tisdale?"

"Well, yes, she's a friend. Why do you ask?"

"I'm here following up on a domestic abuse call one of the neighbors made. They heard a woman screaming last night from that house, Mrs. Tisdale's house."

"I'm sorry, officer. I don't know anything about it, she didn't say anything to me but you'll look into that, won't you?"

"Yes, of course. Thanks for your time, Miss."

"You're welcome."

Roxy turns to walk away feeling somewhat relieved and hoping her nerves didn't give her up. Then the officer approaches her again.

"Just one more thing, Miss. You wouldn't happen to know where Mrs. Tisdale's son Raymond is, would you?"

Roxy shrugs and brushes her hair away from her sweaty brow. "Uh, no. . .no I don't, sorry. I mean, why would I?"

"Just a long shot. Thought I'd ask. There's an old case file I saw in the report. I'm sure he's long gone by now." The officer barely glances at Roxy as he focuses on his note pad. "Thanks again for your time, ma'am."

Once in the car Roxy can hardly stop shaking. She fumbles in the daypack for the keys before remembering that all she has to do is push a button. She checks the rearview mirror repeatedly until the squad car is out of sight.

"Oh my God, I can't believe that just happened," she says to herself. "I've got to get out of here. Out of this town and back to Vegas. That was too close."

Roxy turns the corner and heads to LAX.

CHAPTER 25

Would You Like to See a Video?

Within minutes of the shooting the media begin to show up at the scene. Everyone from the local newspaper reporters to NBC's satellite van, all ready to broadcast live.

As police scramble to control the crowd, reporters push forward with cameras rolling and live mics. Nobody wants to look like the bad guy and force them back.

"Who's in charge here? Who can we talk to?" shouts the reporter from NBC.

"Please stay behind the yellow tape, sir. This is a crime scene investigation. I'll try to get someone to talk to you," says a young deputy looking a little overwhelmed.

McCain is talking to Captain Tucker about the necklace when the deputy taps him on the shoulder. "Excuse me, sir, but there's a crowd of reporters out front wanting to talk to someone in charge."

"Go get the Sheriff or the Chief. They can talk to them," McCain snaps, barely glancing at the young deputy, clearly a rookie with regards to murder scenes.

"I'm sorry, sir, but I already talked to the Sheriff and the Chief. They told me to go find you. They said you're in charge."

"Fine, go tell the bloodhounds I'll be out in a few minutes. Shit, here we go again."

McCain grabs his suit jacket, pulls it on and heads for the bathroom. He flips on the light and walks over to the sink. He stares at the mirror and practices smiling like he's trying to nail an on-camera audition. He straightens his tie, musses his thick, black but graying hair and adjusts his jacket. Looking in the mirror one last time, he crosses himself, flicks the light off, walks out and heads straight for the reporters.

"Good afternoon. I'm Special Agent in Charge Mathew McCain with the FBI. I'll be glad to take your questions but please remember this is an ongoing crime scene investigation. There is very little I can tell you at the moment," he says, chest out, shoulders back, feet firmly planted.

A barrage of questions come flying from the crowd of reporters, each jockeying for position to be heard. Boom mics hover in front of McCain's face.

"Please, one at a time," says McCain volleying with the crowd. "You, with NBC, you first."

"John Michaels, Channel Four News. What can you tell us what happened here?"

"Right now all I can tell you is that a suspect in the investigation was apprehended."

"We have reports of multiple shots being fired. Has anyone been injured? Any Laguna locals involved?"

McCain calmly looks out at the small crowd of media, knowing he has their full attention and weighing each word carefully. "Upon taking the suspect into custody he made an aggressive move for what we believed to be a weapon and said suspect was shot."

"Did the suspect have a weapon?"

"Did he fire the weapon?"

"What kind of gun?"

"What did he look like? Is he a local?"

McCain can only catch bits and pieces of the questions flying at him but relishes each more than the next.

He raises his hands to the mic to signal he's finished. "That's all the questions for now. We will be holding a news conference when more information becomes available. Thank you."

The media doesn't give up easily. "But, Agent McCain, *did* the suspect have a weapon? What was he wanted for? Can you answer the questions, sir?" The reporter from NBC's frustration is evident as he makes one last attempt for specific information.

McCain turns and walks away ignoring the reporter's comebacks while two officers hold back attempts to get his attention. Finally the reporters and their crews give up and start to back off, loading up their cameras and mics.

"Excuse me, sir," says a twenty-something kid in dusty boots and carrying a hiking pole as he approaches John Michaels.

"Yes, what is it? Can I help you with something?" says Michaels, barely looking up as he continues to help his assistant load up their gear.

"Hi, my name is Colt. Maybe *I* can help you with something."

Michaels straightens up and faces the young man. "What exactly do you mean?"

"Well, I was hiking back in the wilderness area and just when I was coming in off the trail I saw all these cop cars everywhere."

"Really? Show me where you came in from."

"Up there, at the end of the road. See that trailhead sign and the gate?"

"Yeah, go on."

"I stopped up there on that ridge to see what was going on and that's when all hell broke loose."

Michaels takes the kid's arm and gently moves him out of earshot of the other reporters. "What happened, Colt?"

"I saw a man standing in the driveway with his hands in the air. One of the cops was on a bullhorn yelling at him not to move. But then he did." Colt brushes his hair out of his eyes and squints at Michaels. "I mean I couldn't see it all that good, but it looked like he went to put his hand in his pocket for something."

"Did you see him pull anything out?"

"No, but somebody yelled 'Gun' and that's when the shooting started. Scared the hell out of me so bad I almost dropped my iPhone."

"What? You have a video of it?

"Yeah, just thought it was a good idea."

"Maybe. C'mon let's go sit in the van and have a look. What did the guy who got shot look like? Have you told anybody else about this?"

"No, no sir, I haven't told anyone else. He was a young, black guy about 6 ft. 3, maybe 200 lbs. or more, very muscular. I don't know, something just didn't sit right with me after seeing the whole thing."

CHAPTER 26

DREAMS VS. REALITY

Thank God, I got a window seat. I don't think my tendencies toward claustrophobia could tolerate sitting in the middle right now. Those strange, but somehow comforting, feelings are back again and rushing through me. What did Walter Pickles call it, a spiritual awakening? Not sure about that but at least I'm not seeing straight into the souls of everyone I come in contact with now. That seems to have subsided somewhat though I'm still getting this rather unsettling sense of deeper understanding, a shift in consciousness, a crazy, new perception of the world around me. And that's sure not something I've ever known to be part of my DNA, at least not like this. Maybe I've just become more aware of other people's thoughts because of the stress Kate is going through. Maybe it's alcohol withdrawal, or maybe I'm just getting used to "my gift". All I know is I think I'm a better man because of whatever this is that's happening. Very strange.

For me plane rides have always been a great opportunity to do a little self- reflecting, think through issues, do some mental housekeeping. But not today. The only thing I can think about is that tomorrow is Halloween. The day the killer told Roxy she would die. But I'm still not sure I know just who that killer is, or was.

I can't get Bobby off my mind. Was he really the killer just luring Roxy in to fulfill some crazy, transgender-hating prophecy? I don't think so but the cops claim they have evidence linking him to the other murders. I almost hope it's true he was the killer. It would make things much simpler. But the voice in my head keeps telling me he's not the one.

Once we are in the air I feel the cabin pressure beginning to wear on me. The cool air blowing on my face from the vent above makes me sleepy. I lean back in my seat enough to rest my head, but not so far as to be in the lap of the person behind me.

Before I know it I'm asleep and dreaming. Now there are two things that seem to happen over and over in almost all my dreams. The first is, I'm always at a party. The second, there's always sex involved. I'm not always the participant, but there's always sex. But this dream, this dream is different.

I'm at the Follies where Roxy headlines. All the "girls" are wearing masks and they seem to be acting out parts on the stage, but nobody speaks. Roxy sits in the middle of the stage on a throne. She's wearing a white silk robe with gold trim and the necklace that Bobby made for Mavis.

The girls all dance around her in some sort of celebration, bowing and twirling. Just as the dancing reaches a frenzy, Roxy stands up and they all drop to their knees. Roxy slowly steps forward, removes the necklace and holds it out in front of her. A deep voice commanding, "Listen to the Truth" echoes through the theater once, twice, three times.

From the side of the stage out walks a man in a long, black hooded robe, a sword hanging from his waist. I can't see his face, darkness is still upon him. The girls on their knees stand and run as if they know the shadow's intent. As he walks into the light his face becomes visible. It is the Shakespearean face of comedy, the eerie mask casting a chilling stare out from under his hood. He turns to Roxy and holds out his arm. Roxy places the necklace in his hand and hangs her head.

He turns and raises his hand holding the necklace high into the air. The shadow that had obscured his mask clears. The mask is no longer the mask of comedy, but is now the mask of tragedy. The theater goes dark.

I scream for Roxy but there is no sound. The next thing I know, I'm running outside in an open field. I scream again for Roxy and this time I hear a faint voice, far away, crying out my name. As I keep running the voice keeps getting louder until I begin to approach the top of a hill. I stop, terrified. Twelve men in dark, hooded robes are kneeling and chanting in front of a cross. Roxy is on the cross. Her robe is torn open and blood is trickling down her chest and between her legs. She has been castrated and her breasts have been removed. The hooded men pay no attention to me as I walk by them and stand next to Roxy.

"Roxy, I've got to get you down."

"It's too late, Nick," she whispers.

She can barely speak and has no strength to support herself on the ledge of the cross. Her arms have pulled out of their sockets from the weight of her body. She looks at me calmly and says:

"I know the truth, Nick. I have seen the future. I know the truth."

Just as I start toward her the hooded man in the tragedy mask pulls his sword and thrusts it into her side. She falls limp, her head hanging down on her chest. The man then turns to me but his mask has changed back to comedy. He stares at me and laughs an evil laugh.

I jump up in my seat and scare the hell out of the guy sitting next to me.

"Hey, you OK, buddy?" he says.

"Oh, yeah. Sorry, guess I was dreaming," I say as I run both my hands through my hair trying to shake off the thoughts.

"Must a been one of those weird ones, huh?"

"Yeah, you could say that. More like a nightmare I'd say."

The pilot comes on and tells us we are approaching our landing as the seat belt sign lights up. I slept through the entire flight. As soon as we touch down I pull out my phone. There's a text from Kate:

Nick, got your message about your flight will pick you up at the airport. I have news. Love Kate.

Within hours after the shooting of Bobby Westbrook the news has gone viral. Social media sites are posting comments and videos of the scene where the shooting took place. All lead off with, "Another unarmed black man executed by the police."

Channel 4 News in L.A. has the exclusive video of the incident and are set to release it nationwide at 6:30. Due to the graphic and violent nature of the footage the report will no doubt be preceded by a warning to viewers about the content since the SWAT team virtually blows Bobby to bits.

Things are heating up fast. People are already starting to march in L.A. carrying signs that read, "Black Lives Matter" and " Hands up, don't shoot." But the actual death of Bobby Westbrook may be just the tip of the iceberg. Rumors begin to circulate about a conspiracy to cover up the serial killings of the five transgender women in Nevada. Law enforcement anticipates a firestorm of protests if the black community joins forces with the LGBT's.

McCain is deflecting all interviews with the media by telling them a news conference is being scheduled. Behind the scenes he is catching hell from his superiors who are catching hell from the White House not to mention several congressmen and senators. Captain Tucker is getting the third degree from his Chief but is told to stay in L.A. and show support at the press conference. His detectives, however, have been ordered home.

"Lyle, you and Mitch need to go back to Vegas. There's no point in you staying here and the Chief wants you back."

"We'd rather stay, Tuck, even if it's just for moral support."

"Can't do it, Lyle. You have to go back."

Lyle scratches his head and pulls at his ear lobe with his thumb and index finger.

"You know, Captain, I just don't get it. I mean about the necklace not being found. Nothing in the house, on Bobby or in the car?"

"No, Lyle, not a trace of it."

"But I don't get it why would Nick tell me that if it wasn't true? It doesn't make any sense. He's got nothing to gain by lying."

"I don't know, Lyle. Maybe Bobby was lying to Nick, trying to buy time."

"Maybe. I guess that's possible but something doesn't feel right about it."

Tucker shrugs his shoulders and looks away. "Well, it doesn't make much difference now, Bobby's dead."

"Makes a hell of a difference if Bobby wasn't the killer, Tuck."

"He was the killer in my book. Anyway you boys gotta' head back. Next flight out, got it?"

"Tucker, I need to talk to you," yells McCain from the front porch of the house.

"Gotta' go boys, see ya back in Vegas."

Tucker walks up to the house where McCain is frantically typing away on his Blackberry. "Just a second," he says and tells Tucker to go on in.

After a few minutes McCain enters the room where Tucker is waiting, walks over and pulls up a chair in front of him.

"We got a shit load of trouble, Tucker. This shooting is bad but it may be the least of our problems. I just got off the phone with headquarters and they told me there's evidence of a cover-up in Reno in the four transgender murders. They think the same may be true for the one in Vegas."

"What the hell you talking about, McCain? What kind of cover up?"

"Looks like three of the four killed in Reno all went to the police asking for protection but were turned away. They were told to just get out of town if they were worried about their safety. Sounds like the same thing happened in Vegas with Mavis Rodgers. You know anything about that?"

"Fuck no. Never got to me, first I've heard of it."

"What about in Reno? Weren't you there on that task force when the murders took place?"

"I did hear some scuttle going around after the third murder but nobody gave it much thought. Really a shame, but it's a little hard to take those people seriously some times, if you know what I mean."

"I hear where you're coming from but I wouldn't say that out loud if I were you."

"It's just me and you, McCain. I'm not stupid."

"There isn't anything left for me to do here, I'm heading back to my hotel to get ready for the press conference tomorrow. You staying over, Tuck or going back to L.A.?"

"My detectives are heading back to Vegas but I'll stay here tonight. Have one of the Sheriff's deputies drive me up to L.A. in the morning."

"Going to check out Laguna, Captain?" McCain says slapping Tucker on the back. "Well, don't have too much fun. Press conference is at nine and I need your ass there to answer questions about the Mavis Rodgers' case."

"I'll be there."

McCain takes a taxi to his hotel, a small place south of Laguna's downtown village. The young man at the front desk checks him in and asks if he's familiar with Main Street Cabaret.

"Tonight is the big LGBT fashion show. You might want to check it out." McCain sneers at him, says nothing and walks to the elevator.

Tucker now in his room, grabs a beer from the mini-fridge and flips on the TV. Every channel is reporting on the shooting.

McCain gets an update on the video that's gone viral and background on the young man who shot it. He slams down his phone, pushes his laptop shut, changes into board shorts and heads down to the beach.

Tucker heads down to Main Street Cabaret.

CHAPTER 27

RELIEF, LOVE AND MURDER

We taxi up to the gate and wait to disembark. All I can think of is Kate. What's the news she has to tell me? Is she all right? Is the baby all right? Why didn't she just tell me in her text what is going on? Do women and men communicate differently? Never mind, I know the answer to that, along with every other guy on this planet. She must have good news, that's why she wants to tell me face to face. Yes, that's it, good news. . .I hope.

I'm toward the back of the plane so my frustration builds as the slow motion exit procession takes place. The airlines really ought to give people lessons on how to get off a plane. I mean I've never seen such a large collection of people who don't seem able to move together in a forward direction. Some people have to wait for others who aren't getting out of their seat. No help for the little old lady whose bag was put in the overhead by the flight attendant. And then there's the guy who had to put his carry-on five rows back from where his seat is.

Finally I'm in the terminal and headed for the baggage area where Kate is meeting me. As I come down the escalator I see her standing by the wall. She looks up, sees me and a big smile comes across her face.

I stretch out my arms to embrace her and we melt into each other feeling a warm familiar passion. I kiss her gently, then pull her to me and hug her tenderly with all the restraint I've got, the warm scent of her hair driving me crazy. I don't want to let go—ever—but reluctantly I step back and look at her, my hands cupping her shoulders.

"How are you? I've been going crazy thinking about you."

"I'm OK" she says, resting her hands on my chest. "Let's go to the car, we can talk there."

I pull her close to me as we walk out of the terminal and head for the parking garage. I can't stop looking at her. Her eyes are sparkling and her face is beaming.

"I sorta missed you," she says as she flashes her big blue eyes at me and winks.

"I sorta missed you, too." I give her a sharp squeeze. "Guess you've heard the news about Bobby Westbrook."

"Can't avoid it, it's all over the media. We've got a lot to talk about, Nick, but first I have to tell you about the baby."

Once in the car Kate turns to me and takes both of my hands in hers.

"After my CNN interview when I went back to my office I noticed some bleeding. Not a good sign. I was pretty scared and there was no one I could talk to since I've kept my pregnancy a secret. I wound up going to the emergency room because my Ob-Gyn had already gone for the day. That was a disaster. I never even got in to be examined. They told me if I was having a miscarriage there was nothing they could do about it, so I left.

"This morning I called my doctor and he had me come in right away. God, sitting in that waiting room, alone. . .it was awful. I know you tried to call me but I had to keep my phone turned off in the doctor's office."

"And?"

"The doctor did an exam but didn't tell me anything. He wanted to do an ultrasound first." Kate's eyes fill with tears just as her mouth widens into a beautiful smile. "Our baby's alive, Nick. I was so scared, but the baby is fine."

I drop my head on to her shoulder. "Thank God," I whisper, then look back up at her. "I'm so sorry you had to go through this alone, Kate."

"Well, you're here now and that's what counts, " she says, softly touching my cheek. Then she laughs. "But, no messin' around for a few weeks until I go back to see the Doc, sorry."

"As long as you and the baby are OK, that's all that matters." I pull Kate toward me, cup her head in my hands and kiss her. A kiss straight from my heart that suddenly overwhelms me with more emotion than I can ever remember. I feel as if time's been suspended for a brief moment and my life has suddenly changed. The awakening, my awakening, has kicked into high gear.

⋏

Roxy is sitting at her gate at LAX watching the news on an over-head monitor. NBC is getting ready to run the video of Bobby being shot. The newsman gives a stern warning that the video contains graphic scenes of violence and may not be appropriate for children.

A young mother sitting next to Roxy looks like she just left her yoga class. Her two kids who look to be around six and eight are piled up next to her, pawing her arms as they all watch the monitor. Roxy watches with quiet disgust as the mother, who has just heard the reporter's warning, shrugs it off with a so-what while the clip runs not once but twice.

After the video they cut back to the news anchor who imme-diately cuts to a reporter on the street who's interviewing several black people who have just watched it.

"They shoot us down like dogs," says a young black man wearing a hoodie and pounding his fist into his palm.

"When will this stop? Dear Lord, don't we matter?" asks an elderly black woman carrying a bag of groceries.

"Here we go again," says the mother of the two children sitting next to Roxy. "Like I'm sure this guy was completely innocent," she says loud enough for anyone three seats away to hear. "Right. If he was so innocent why was a SWAT team after him? I heard he was a serial killer. I say he got what he deserved."

Roxy takes in what the woman just said then leans over and whispers in her ear. "Is that what you want your children to see? Is that how you want them raised? And by the way, I knew Bobby Westbrook. He was innocent, you racist bitch."

Roxy gets up, walks over to the Corona Bar and orders a double vodka rocks.

⋏

On the way into town Kate fills me in on what's going on with the Bobby Westbrook shooting. She tells me about the video that a twenty-something hiker shot of the actual sequence of events. Then she lets me know there's a rumor about a cover-up, victims who contacted the police for help but ignored because of their sexual orientation. Supposedly the Attorney General is looking at ordering a full investigation.

"Sounds like they're trying to get on top of this before any major protests start. What do you think?"

"I think you're right. I've heard talk that the LGBT and black communities are joining together for a march on the Strip this weekend. Could be thousands there."

"You know, there's someone I think you should interview."

"Who's that?"

"Remember that client of mine I told you about? The showgirl in Vegas? Her name's Roxy Lynn. We were just in California to see Bobby Westbrook." I brace for her reaction. She knows I haven't been able to share any details with her but good reporters always want to be the first to know and Kate's a very good reporter.

"*What!* Oh my God, Nick! You saw him just before he got shot?"

"Yep, we spent the night in the same house with him. Even had breakfast together the next morning in Laguna."

"Who's house? How did you find him? Who else was with you?"

Kate starts in with some rapid-fire questioning and I try to keep up with answers. I explain about the relationship between Jo and Bobby, Reverend Kootz and Julio, but Kate can't get the questions out fast enough.

"What did Bobby say about the killings? Did he. . .? Did he do it? Did he know who did?"

"He said he didn't do it. He told us that Mavis had gone to the police but they told her to leave town if she was worried about her safety. Nice guys. And he said he had proof he was innocent."

"Proof?"

"Yeah, he asked Roxy to pick up a necklace for him in Vegas that Mavis was wearing when she was murdered. He claimed he'd wired the necklace to record any conversations Mavis had since he worried about her safety."

"So the killer's voice was recorded?"

"Maybe. At least that's what Bobby told Jo. He was just leaving her house to meet us downtown when he was shot by the cops."

"Why haven't I heard about this on the news yet?"

"I don't know. I told Lyle about the necklace at the house after the shooting. He said they would look for it."

"This is a game-changer, Nick. I need to get to my office. Can you set up that interview for me with Roxy?"

"I'll try, Kate, but she may be hesitant."

"Why's that?"

"She's the next victim."

▲

"Mind if I join you?" inquires a voice from behind Roxy's right shoulder. A bit startled, she turns to see a man standing next to her at an open bar stool smiling. He's smiling in a way that catches Roxy off guard and, despite all the crap in her life that's going on, it piques her interest.

"No, be my guest," she says removing her purse from the stool.

He's a good-looking, executive type, 50-ish with graying hair that's just long enough to curl slightly over the back of his shirt collar. He's dressed in casual clothes with logos that come with high price tags, but wearing a sports watch that says he's no idiot. As he moves onto the stool next to her she can tell he's in good shape. A tricep flexes through his polo shirt as he sets his Maui Jim's on the bar.

"Hi, my name's Pence, Pence Moorhouse. Where you headed?"

"Hello, Pence. My name's Roxy. I'm headed back to Vegas, how about you?"

"On my way to China out of New York. I have a long layover here."

"Ah, business trip in China?"

"Yes, I represent a group of investors over there that have some real estate holdings here and in Canada."

"Are you an attorney?"

"Used to be. Now I'm just a glorified real estate agent." Pence smiles broadly and signals the bartender. "What do you do, Roxy?"

"I work in Vegas. Ever hear of the Follies?"

"Can't say that I have but I've only been to Vegas once. I'm not much of a gambler."

The bartender approaches. "Can I help you, sir?"

"Yes, I'll have a vodka martini on the rocks, olives with a little dirt, easy on the vermouth."

"Any particular vodka, sir?"

"Stoli. And get the lady whatever she's having."

"Yes, sir. Would you like another vodka rocks, Miss?"

"No, no thanks. I wouldn't be able to walk. Make it a white wine. A pinot grigio would be fine."

"So, Roxy, when does your flight leave?"

"We board in about 30 minutes."

"Hmm, I was going to ask you to have dinner with me. I'd like to get to know you better. There's always a later flight to Vegas."

"Well, thanks, you do work fast, don't you? I'd better pass though. Besides, I might not be quite the woman you think I am."

"OK, you're going to have to explain that one. What do you mean?"

Roxy's been down this road before and has learned that the best explanation is a straightforward one. "I'm transgender."

Pence is unfazed. "Yes, I know that. While you were ordering your drink I Googled the Follies. That's why I asked you to dinner."

Roxy grins, leans back on her barstool and gives Pence a long, ruminating look. "You know what, give me a few minutes to check on another flight. I'll be right back."

Roxy walks back to her gate to talk to the agent about changing her flight. As she approaches the counter she can feel an icy stare coming from the woman with the two kids. Roxy doesn't bother to look back, doesn't want to give her the satisfaction. Within a few minutes she has changed her flight to one scheduled four hours later.

On the way back to join Pence, she stops in the ladies room. One look in the mirror sends her into a frenzy. "Oh my God, I need makeup. And my hair, good Lord. I can't go to dinner in these clothes. I hiked out of a canyon like this just a few hours ago."

She does her best to freshen up, then heads back to the bar where Pence is sipping his martini.

"Well, that was quick," Pence remarks as he turns to Roxy and smiles.

"Yes, they make it pretty easy, but I need to tell you something."

"Now what?" he laughs.

"I can't go to dinner with you looking like this. I hiked in these clothes this morning and have hardly any makeup with me, just a few necessities. I had to leave in a hurry. It's a long story."

"Don't worry about it. This place practically has its own mall. Let's go get you some clothes and whatever else you need to feel comfortable. Then we can go to dinner, OK?"

▲

"I need to pick up my car at police headquarters, Kate. Lyle had it driven down from the desert for me." I buckle up and pull out my phone as Kate pulls out of the airport parking garage.

"No problem. I'll drop you there then head to my office. I need to make some phone calls and work on this story. I'm on deadline so it has to come out before the FBI's press conference tomorrow morning."

"When's that?"

"My editor told me it's at nine in L.A. You want to meet later at Ronnie's for dinner? Maybe eight o'clock?"

"Sounds good, I need to check in with Alice and catch up on some paperwork myself."

⚔

The brilliant fall sunlight Laguna is known for is starting to fade as Colt walks on the sand near Thousands Steps beach. The normal deep green and blue colors of the ocean have faded. A milky gray overcast blurs the horizon into a cold lifeless merger of sea and sky. The marine layer has returned stealing the sun's last light.

"What a crazy day," he says looking out at the silhouette of Catalina as it fades from view. He shoves his hand into his pocket and touches his phone, wondering if maybe he could have made a few bucks from that video he shot earlier today. Too late now he guesses. Still shaken from the shooting he witnessed, Colt tries to relax as he strolls deserted beach, walking close to the water's edge. The sound of the waves crashing on the shore have a completely different feel when the crowds are gone. He loves the solitude and the beauty he finds in the fading light on a day like this.

Out of sight, a pair of eyes are trained on Colt. They watch his every move and track him as he casually moves on down the beach.

Colt shuffles along to a place where the sand ends and rock formations break the incoming waves like fortresses defending the cliffs. He scrambles up and around the rocks then climbs down into a secluded cove. The eyes follow him and begin their approach.

CHAPTER 28

DEAR DIARY

The time has come to do your bidding, dear Lord. I kneel before you in prayer asking for guidance so that I may carry out your will.

The day of justice for the shemale is at hand. God's law shall be served and those who break it will know His wrath. They must repent their sins and ask the Lord to cleanse their souls. They must read the words of Leviticus and heed the warning.

I myself was once a poor miserable sinner who denied God's word. I lived in a world of lies and deceit until I was shown the light. Now I am a proud disciple who carries out God's will and brings the heathens to justice.

May the heavens reign down from above and bring us all the true word of God. May those who deny the almighty be caught up in the rapture and burn in hell through out eternity.

In your name, dear Lord, thy will be done.

CHAPTER 29

'Twas the Night Before

After Kate drops me off to pick up my car I head over to my office. Traffic is heavy and the going is slow but for some reason it doesn't bother me. Getting cut off by the young woman in the Lexus talking on her cell doesn't even raise my blood pressure or cause me to spew expletives in her direction. That's a first. I feel at peace but I don't know why. Colors seem brighter, the music on the radio seems clearer and makes me smile. Next thing I know I'm turning into the parking garage at my office, the entire drive feeling to me as if it only took a few seconds.

Every time I think I might be getting back to my "normal" self, something like this happens again. Maybe this *is* my new normal and I've graduated to another mindset, or maybe this is what it's like to be sober. Nah.

I walk into the office and see Alice on the phone. What a surprise. Her legs are crossed and she's leaning sideways in her chair with one elbow resting on the desk. When she sees me a big smile comes across her face.

"Hello, Alice, I'm back."

"Oh, just a sec. Let me call you back in five, sweetie." She hangs up the phone and straightens herself in the chair. The aroma of Alice's favorite coffee fills the air.

"Hey, you look good. How was L.A.?"

"It was a blur. Have you seen the news about Bobby Westbrook?"

"Yeah, sorry. I guess it didn't go very well."

"No, it didn't. What do I need to catch up on here?" I glance at the neatly organized piles of assorted mail. Thank God for Alice.

"Not much. I did manage to get the research started you wanted on the detectives who were involved in the Reno murders."

"Turn up anything?"

"I'm working on it. I think you may be surprised."

"Really? That would be great, but why?"

"Well, before you give me a raise, maybe I should finish it."

"Look, Alice, there's some urgency here. What have you got?"

"I understand, but I really do need to check out a few more things first. How about first thing in the morning?"

"OK, but if you finish sooner let me know. By the way I'm staying late so I'll lock up. Kate's meeting me for dinner later. You have any plans?

"I have a date," Alice says with a coy little smile. "That's who I was on the phone with."

"Oh really, who is he?"

"I can't say yet but it might surprise you."

I can't be sure but I think Alice is blushing. "Somebody I know? You can tell me."

"Oh no, you're not getting it out of me that easy."

She *is* blushing. Very un-Alice like and it makes me wonder why. "Fine, be that way. You have a good time with your mystery man. I'll see you in the morning."

"I always have a good time, Nick. That's what life is all about."

▲

"How about that store, Roxy?" says Pence pointing at the high-end designer clothing store on the concourse.

"Oh no, they're much too expensive."

"Don't worry about it, Roxy, it's just an outfit. It's not like I'm buying you a Porsche or something. Come on, let's go in."

Roxy and Pence enter the store and are greeted by the manager. He's a well-dressed man in his 40's, lean with just slightly too much hair product to be cool.

"Welcome. How may we help you today?"

"The lady needs an outfit for dinner. Anything she wants with all the accessories."

"Yes, sir, right away. Dina, would you please help this couple find what they're looking for? Something perfect for the lady. Sir, Dina will take care of your every need but please do not hesitate to call for me if you have a question. Here's my card. My name is Winston Barklage, please enjoy."

Roxy stifles a giggle at the gushing demeanor of the store manager, but loves the attention and Pence's generosity. She can't remember the last time anyone treated her this way.

She tries on dress after dress and starts to get a little silly parading around like she's in a fashion show. Pence takes the cue and offers applause, even letting out a low, admiring whistle. Dina the sales person is starting to show some impatience but plays along to get the sale. Finally Roxy decides on every woman's go-to, a little black dress. When she steps out of the dressing room to look in the mirror, Pence voices his approval.

"It's perfect, Roxy. We'll take it. OK with you?"

"Yes, I love it," she says, giving Pence a big hug.

"I'm pretty certain you're going to need shoes, but anything else?" Pence asks smiling at Roxy but talking to Dina.

"Ah, yes, if you don't mind? I saw the perfect shoes and a great bag," Roxy says pointing Dina in the direction toward the door.

"Whatever you want," Pence says. "But no Porsche."

Roxy laughs and Dina looks confused. "I know just what you're talking about. Good choice. I'll get everything all together so you can try it on and see how you like it."

Ten minutes later Roxy comes out of the dressing room and a big smile broadens across Pence's face.

"You look amazing, Roxy. Are you ready for dinner?"

"Yes, I'm famished. Picking out new clothes is hard work."

"Do you like seafood?"

"Yes, I love it."

"Great, I know the perfect little place in Santa Monica. We should have plenty of time."

⏶

When I get to Ronnie's I realize by the crowd it's Thursday night specials. Everything is fifty percent off until eight o'clock and the place is packed. I make my way to the bar to find Jasper. As I look around my eyes catch the big screen TV over the bar. NBC is running the video of Bobby being shot, again.

I think to myself how every day it seems all we hear about is murder and terrorism. I wonder what it's doing to us, to our world. With all our great strides in technology and communications, respect for human life and empathy for each other seems to be backsliding. Maybe I'm just feeling pessimistic, I don't know.

"Nick, you're back," shouts a voice from the crowd. As I turn, I see Jasper walking towards me.

"Hey, Jasper, I just got in. Looks like you're really busy tonight."

"Thursdays are always crazy, Nick. Can I get you something?"

"Think I'll just have a Coke, Jasper. Thanks."

Jasper walks around the bar and grabs a Coke and a glass of ice. "Here ya' go. How was L.A.? Wacky as ever?"

"Well, I sure as hell don't know how people stand the traffic, it's crazy. We went down there to see Bobby Westbrook and you know the rest. It's right up there." I point to the TV and shake my head.

"Oh shit, sorry, man. I didn't know. I can't believe they show that kind of thing on television. Looks like they blew him apart."

"Yeah, I know. It's hard to take when you actually know the person. And I happen to believe he was innocent."

"Really? Well, if you're right I certainly hope they catch the real killer."

"Me too. Oh, by the way, we ran into Rick while we were in Laguna."

"You did? And just what did my dear friend Rick have to say? Was he by himself?"

"He said to tell you hello and that he was doing fine. Had a friend with him name of Baldemar Firetto, called him Baldy."

"Baldy!" Jasper's face reddens as he slaps his hands on the bar.

"Yeah, turns out he was a lawyer for the lady who took us down there."

"That son of a bitch. Baldy is Rick's old boyfriend."

"Shit, sorry, Jasper, I didn't know. Maybe I shouldn't have said anything."

"No, no, you did the right thing. Besides if Rick didn't want me to know he would have told you not to say anything. I think he wanted me to know, the son of a bitch."

"Jasper, here comes Kate. Any chance we can get a table as soon as one comes open?"

"You got it."

Kate is making her way through the crowd when she spots me. That beautiful smile of hers I love gets bigger as she approaches. She kisses her index finger then presses it against my lips in a frisky sort of way.

"Guess who's going to be front page tomorrow? They decided to run with my story. I'm hoping the headline will be: 'Feds

Roll the Dice in Vegas with Transgender Lives'. My editor seemed to like it. What do you think?"

"I think I love you. You've got guts, Kate. But you know they're going to come back at you."

"Yeah, I know, but I'm sick of it. I'm sick of what's happening here and all over the world. I just read a report that says they're killing transgenders for sport in Brazil. It's so damn pathetic. And very, very sad."

"Well, I hope your article can make a difference, but I think it's going to be a big challenge for long time. Lot of bigoted people out there."

"God, I hope so, the making a difference part I mean. But right now, I'm starving. Can Jasper get us a table?"

"He's working on it."

"Did you get that interview with Roxy lined up for me? It'd make a great follow- up to tomorrow's story."

"You're not just using me, are you?" I ask teasingly. Kate gives a look that's says not funny so I move on. "I left her a message but haven't heard back yet. I'm starting to get a little concerned."

⚔

Pence hails a cab as he and Roxy head for Santa Monica. He speculates the restaurant they are headed to may not be what Roxy is expecting. It's a quaint little neighborhood restaurant in an older section of town where the tourists rarely go.

Run by the same family for over fifty years, one of the founders still heads up the kitchen every night. Rafael Caselli was born in the lake region of Lombardy and migrated to the U.S. with his parents when he was a teenager. Soon after, he and his father Fino started the restaurant and their reputation for seafood and pasta is second to none in L.A.

Pence met the Caselli family twenty-five years ago when he was travelling with his mother and he always makes a point of eating there whenever he's in town.

The taxi turns down the narrow little street and pulls over in front of a small building with a red awning.

"This is it," Pence says as he opens the door for Roxy. "You do look fabulous in that dress. Have I said that too often?"

"Not often enough." She grins, reaches for his hand and notices the sign above the door: FINO'S RISTORANTE, FINE SEAFOOD AND PASTA. It reminds her more of a neighborhood tavern than the restaurants she used to seeing in Vegas.

"Not what you were expecting?"

"No, it's fine. I'm sure it's very good."

"It's a tradition of mine and a very special place. I always come here when I'm in L.A. I think you'll like it."

"I'm sure I will. And I'm starving."

They walk through the front door and are immediately greeted warmly by Rafael's granddaughter Isabella who is the hostess. "Oh, Mr. Moorhouse, it's so good to see you! I'll go get my grandpa."

Isabella doesn't get far before her grandfather Rafael, wiping his hands on his apron, bursts through the kitchen in full chef apparel and walks over to greet Pence. He throws his arms in the air, his eyes crinkling as his smile broadens. "*Buona sera,*

Pence! Pence Moorhouse. Ciao, cosi bello vederti." Rafael shakes Pence's hand then embraces him like family.

"Ah, Rafael, bello vederti anche."

"And who is this lovely lady with you?"

"This is Roxy. Roxy, this is Rafael."

"So nice to meet you, Rafael."

"Ciao, bella, Miss Roxy," Rafael says opening his arms. "The pleasure is mine."

As Rafael's granddaughter Isabella shows Pence and Roxy to their table they can hear Rafael shouting out orders for antipasto and wine selections. Within minutes, Mario the head waiter is at their table.

"Your antipasto, sir, and might I suggest a vino to accompany dinner?"

"Yes, please do."

"Yes, sir. The 2010 Paolo Scavino Barolo is near perfect. Would you like to taste it?"

"Yes, please." Pence glances at Roxy and she returns a sly grin along with raised eyebrows. Mario pours a small amount into Pence's glass. Pence subtlety swirls it and brings it to his nose, then smiles as he slowly sips the wine, savoring it before he swallows.

"This is exquisite, Mario. Please, pour a glass for the lady." As soon as the waiter obliges and leaves the table Roxy reaches for Pence's hand and playfully gives it a slap.

"You didn't tell me you were a wine snob, Pence."

"Hey, I'm not really. Well, maybe a little. Is that a turn-off, Roxy?"

"No, well, maybe a little. All things considered, I'm a pretty down-to-earth sort of gal." Roxy smiles and raises her glass for a toast. "Here's to new beginnings."

Pence raises his glass and touches it to Roxy's. "Yes, to new beginnings."

They enjoy the antipasto and wine while quietly looking over the menu. After a minute or two, Roxy closes her menu and lays it on the table.

"Pence, I'm exhausted and overwhelmed. Why don't you order for both of us. You know this place so well."

When Mario returns Pence begins to order. "We'd like to start with the butternut squash risotto. And follow that up with cioppino, then we'll share a caprese salad. For dessert cannoli and espresso. How's that sound, Roxy?"

"Fantastic."

"Very good, sir. I'll get things started."

As each course is served, Roxy and Pence savor every new taste and smell, sharing guesses about herbs, sauces and cooking technique. Their conversation is enthusiastic and light-hearted.

"Oh, Pence, this is amazing. I'm so glad you brought me here. I can't remember the last time I had such a wonderful evening."

"That makes me very happy, Roxy. It's so nice to share this experience with someone. I'm glad it's you and I'm glad you enjoyed the food."

Roxy places her utensils side by side on her plate as a signal to the waiter, then looks thoughtfully at Pence.

"Can I ask you a personal question?"

"Sure," Pence replies. "What is it?"

"Well, can you tell me a little about yourself and maybe something about your orientation?"

"Getting down to brass tacks, eh?. . .Sure, that's fair. My father's British, he's a professor at M.I.T. My mother's Canadian and she's a pediatric surgeon at Children's Hospital. I was born while they were living in New York, so I have dual citizenship. I went to Georgetown law and was a corporate attorney with Chase before I went to work with my current clients.

"Let's see, I got married when I was thirty. She was also an attorney, a public defender. We were married for five years when we both decided it just wasn't working. We never had kids, though that's probably evident. As far as my orientation goes, I've experimented over the years. Gay, bi, straight, I've tried all of them."

"Is that what I am, Pence, an experiment?"

"Maybe, is that what you want to be, Roxy?"

Roxy leans forward, picks up her drink and swirls the glass a few times staring at the table. Then she looks up at Pence. "Maybe, I'll have to think about it."

Pence reaches across the table and squeezes Roxy's hand. "We'd better be heading back. My plane leaves in two hours. I wish I could stay over but I have meetings scheduled in the morning."

"I have to get back too, Pence." Roxy pauses, then gently removes her hand from his. "Maybe another time?"

"When I'm finished with this trip I have some free time. How about I stop by Vegas on my way back?"

"I'd like that. I'd like that very much. I hope I'm still. . ."

"Still what, Roxy?"

"It's a long story, Pence. Let's talk in the cab on the way to the airport."

CHAPTER 30

D-Day

On the steps in front of LAPD Headquarters reporters are assembling for the nine o'clock press conference. On the sidewalk, a line of protesters, coffee cups in one hand and banners in the other, extend the length of the block. Signs that read, "Black Lives Matter" and "Time for Justice" seem to float above the crowd as the chanting grows louder. Policemen in riot gear have taken positions between the protesters and the media.

John Michaels of Channel Four News gets a call from his editor while he's running sound checks. "Michaels, have you seen the breaking news in Laguna Beach?"

"Have not. What's going on?"

"The kid who took the video of Bobby Westbrook being shot turned up dead on a beach down there this morning."

"Shit. What the hell happened?"

"They're calling it an accidental drowning. A spokesperson for the Laguna police said it looks like the boy got caught in a cove at high tide and couldn't get out. The waves pounded him into the rocks."

"You believe it?"

"Not sure. That's why I called you. You just talked to him when you were there yesterday, right? What do you think?"

"He looked like he was in pretty good shape to me. I find it hard to believe a kid who has lived there all his life and knows the beaches would get trapped like that."

"That's what I was thinking. How about you head back down there after the press conference and ask some questions."

"Will do. I'll give you a call later and let you know what I come up with."

As the news conference is about to start McCain, Tucker, the Orange County Sheriff and Assistant Chief McBride all gather together just inside headquarter's front doors to review each of their talking points. McCain makes a last comment before they head outside to meet the press.

"Remember, if you don't know the answer to a question just say, 'I don't know' and leave it at that. Don't try to bullshit them or deflect the question with some answer that will get us in more trouble. Let's go." McCain straightens his tie and opens the door.

The Assistant Chief takes the podium and adjusts his mic as the cameras roll. "Good morning, everyone. I'm Assistant Chief Scott McBride. We are here this morning to brief you on the Bobby Westbrook case and answer any questions you may have regarding it. I will remind you that this is still an ongoing investigation headed by the FBI. Now, let me introduce you to the head of the investigation, Special Agent Mathew McCain."

"Good morning. Thank you for coming. First, I would like to make a statement about what led up to the current situation and the outcome. Then I will take your questions."

"Bobby Westbrook, also known as Robert S. Westbrook, was wanted for questioning in the murders of five transgender individuals in Nevada. A recent break in the case led us to L.A. and then to Laguna Beach, in Orange County. Although no warrant had been issued for his arrest we had substantial evidence pointing us in his direction. It was our intent to find Westbrook, take him into custody and, after questioning, charge him with those murders. This is not unusual; prosecutors often use this tactic. Unfortunately, upon confronting Westbrook at a private home in Laguna, he ignored orders to remain still with his hands in the air. He made an aggressive move for what we perceived to be a weapon at which point the Orange County SWAT team did what they are trained to do. Now, I'll be happy to answer your questions. Please state your name and news organization."

"John Michaels, Channel Four News in L.A. Was Mr. Westbrook carrying any sort of weapon when he was shot?"

"No, he was not."

"Then what was the aggressive move he made? Can you be more specific?"

"He reached into his pocket."

"Was there anything in his pocket?"

"Yes, there was some change, keys and a cell phone."

"So, is it possible he could he have been trying to answer his phone?"

"I don't know, but our officers perceived an imminent threat to their lives. Next question."

"Aaron Constance, Channel Two News in L.A. What is the substantial evidence you have on Bobby Westbrook?"

"I can't go in to all of that right now, but I will tell you that his DNA was found on four of the five victims. Yes. You, next question."

"Roger McNamara with CNN. There's a story in the *Las Vegas Sun* this morning that states there was a necklace with a recording device in it. It said Bobby Westbrook rigged it for his girlfriend Mavis Rodgers and it possibly has the killer's voice on it. Was this necklace found, and if so, did it have any recordings on it?"

"We do have information about the possible existence of such a necklace. However the crime scene was thoroughly searched and no necklace, or any type of recording device, was found."

"Do you think the necklace exists?"

"I don't know." McCain again adjusts his tie and quickly points to the next reporter. "Yes, your question?"

"Dick Houston, Channel Seven News in L.A. This question is for the Sheriff. On the video it sounds like someone yells something right before the SWAT team opens fire on Westbrook. Rumor has it this person yelled 'gun'. Can you confirm or deny this?"

"I did not personally hear anyone yell anything however I was in a command position back from the team. Maybe someone else on the panel can respond to your question."

The Assistant Chief leans in and says, "Sorry, I wasn't there." Tucker and McCain simply shake their heads no and move back a step.

"I have a question for Agent McCain and Captain Tucker," the CNN reporter shouts.

"Go ahead," McCain says and motions for Tucker to step up to the microphone.

"The same reporter who raised the question about the necklace in her *Las Vegas Sun* article this morning also states that four of the five victims all went to the police for help and were essentially turned away and ignored. She also says that these facts have been covered up by the departments in both Reno and Las Vegas. Would either of you like to comment on this?"

Tucker steps up to the microphone. "Sure, I'll go first. I am not aware of any such report. Nothing was brought to my attention in Vegas, nor when I was on the task force in Reno."

"How about you agent, McCain?"

"I can assure you that this investigation will be thorough and completely transparent. We have nothing to hide and justice will be served. Thank you all."

McCain turns away from the mic quickly and signals the others to move inside. As Tucker moves toward the door he glances back at the CNN reporter Roger McNamara who he's had run-ins with in the past.

"Fuck you," Tucker mouths and enters the building.

CHAPTER 31

HAPPY HALLOWEEN II

"Hey, wake up, sleepyhead." I nudge Kate with my nose and push on her neck.

"What time is it?" she mumbles into her pillow.

"It's almost eight o'clock, how about some coffee?"

"I'd rather have sex," she says as she scoots up next to me.

"Well, that makes two of us but you know what the doctor said."

"Yeah, I know but we could still mess around. I just can't. . .you know."

"Oh, you mean something like this?" I put my head down on Kate's thigh just below her thong and start kissing her leg. Kate begins running her hand down my stomach and into my boxers.

Just when things are getting good my phone rings. "Shit. I'd better get that, sweetheart."

Kate laughs. "No, it's all right, go ahead. I'll go get the paper. I'm anxious to see my article."

"Hey, Nick, it's Roxy. I'm sorry to call this early."

"No problem, Roxy, are you OK?"

"I'm fine. In fact I'm great. How are you?"

"Wow, you sound. . .different. I thought you might be freaking out considering what was happening the last time I saw you."

"I know but sometimes life throws you a curve and I just caught a major one."

"Really, what happened? You sound, well, a little giddy. What's going on?"

"Let's just say L.A. was eventful, in more ways than one."

"Haven't had my coffee yet but I'm all ears." There's a lull in the conversation as Roxy takes a minute to think.

"Go get your coffee, Nick. We'll talk later. I got your message about an interview with Kate. Does she still want to do it?"

"Hold on, let me ask her. . .Kate, I've got Roxy on the phone. Do you still want to do the interview?" I yell into the kitchen.

"Yes, you bet. Ask her if we can do it later this afternoon or early this evening."

"Roxy, she definitely wants to do the interview. How about late afternoon or early evening."

"Early evening would be great. She can help with the trick-or-treaters, how about around six?"

"Six, Kate?"

"Great."

"It's a go, Roxy, but listen to me, you know what today is. Be careful and don't take any risks. Despite what the FBI says I still don't believe Bobby was the killer."

"Don't worry, Nick. I'll have my boys with me all day. I'll be just fine."

"OK, I'll bring Kate over tonight. See you then."

I walk into the kitchen and see Kate sitting at the table drinking coffee and reading her article in the newspaper. I wish I could see her sitting at that table every morning.

"Barry really is a good editor. He made this read even better than what I wrote."

"I think that's what editors are supposed to do," I reply, grabbing a mug from the shelf.

Kate looks up from the paper and shoots me the look. "Really?"

"OK, OK. I want to read it when you're done."

"Here, you go ahead. I need to check my messages. I just got a text from Barry. Must have heard us talking."

As I sit reading Kate's article I hear her giggle and look up to see her beaming.

"Now what?"

"Looks like Anderson Cooper read my article in this morning's paper and now CNN wants to do a follow-up interview with me. Seems it got picked up by the major networks."

"Congrats. That's really great. I'm proud of you. Sounds like you'll be heading to the office soon. What time's that press conference this morning? I'd like to watch it."

"It's at nine and, yes, I'd better get going so I can prep for the interview. Oh no. . . shit not again. I think I'm going to throw up."

Ten minutes later I gently knock on the bathroom door after pacing through the house. "Are you OK in there, Kate?"

"Yeah, I'm fine. Really. Just give me a minute. Do you have any Coke or Pepsi? It usually helps."

After I retrieve a Coke for Kate and she's had a few sips, she gets dressed and is ready to head out. "And what are you going to do today, sweetheart?"

"I've got some research to go over at my office and I think I'll try to get over and see my dad this afternoon. It's been awhile, better see what the old man is up to."

After Kate leaves I'm not far behind. I put the top down on the T-Bird and head for my office.

As I pull up to a stoplight I look over at the SUV next to me. A lovely young lady with long blonde hair is sitting in her Land Rover. Her visor is pulled down so she can look in the mirror while putting on some sort of eye make-up. In her other hand is her phone which she hasn't stopped talking into since I pulled up. Pathetic a scene as it is, I'm cracking up, but I have to see what happens when the light turns green and we start moving. Sure enough, she continues with the eye make-up only occasionally glancing at the road. The phone is still attached to the right side of her head and her mouth keeps moving. She's definitely knee-steering. How do women do this? And why? I resist the temptation to honk and wave fearing a multi-car pileup. Show's over. I turn on to a side street, head into my parking garage and go up to my office.

Alice is in her usual position talking on the phone. Everything looks normal except for her outfit. She is in full costume for Halloween. Now I haven't seen all the Batman flicks but I'm pretty sure she's Cat Woman. I'm definitely sure after she claws her hand in the air and hisses at me.

"Good morning, Nick."

"Good morning, Cat Woman."

"Oh, just call me, Kitty. What do you think of the outfit?"

"Suits you perfectly, Kitty. Ah, I'm going to go dig into that research you did for me while I was gone. It's ready I hope."

"Aw, come on. That's it? Suits me perfectly?"

"Yep, pretty much."

"Well, OK then, Mr. All-Work-and-No Play. I'll think you'll find most of the detectives' backgrounds are pretty boring, nothing really stands out. No red flags. But when you get to Captain Tucker, well, that's a different story."

Alice is right as usual. Each of the other detectives' files is fairly mundane. There are the usual divorces, substance abuse and child support issues but, so what, that stuff could happen to anybody.

Then I get to Tucker's file. It seems he was in charge of the investigations for all four murders in Reno. The task force he was on reviewed all the cases but never determined if they were committed by the same person. Their conclusion was that the murders were random or possibly copycats.

Even more interesting is Tucker's personal background. He grew up in rural Kentucky, an only child to his parents Fred and Mildred Tucker. His father Fred was killed when Tucker was sixteen, the apparent victim of a burglary in the middle of the night.

However, the investigating officer Ezra Dupree for the case had a different opinion and stated in his report that no forced entry was found and nothing seemed to be missing from the house.

I decide to give Mr. Dupree a call.

CHAPTER 32

EZRA DUPREE

"**G**ood morning, Shelbyville police department. How may I help you?"

"Good morning, I'm looking for officer Ezra Dupree."

"Oh, gosh, old Dewey retired, must be goin' on five years now."

"Do you have any idea where he can be reached?"

"I'm sorry, who are you?"

"Sorry, I should have introduced myself. My name is Nick Ross, I'm a private investigator from Las Vegas. I'm working on an old case that Mr. Dupree was in charge of."

"Well, I don't see any harm in putting you in touch with him. He still lives in town. I don't think Dewey's goin' anywhere. You want his number?"

"Yes, thank you. . . .Miss?"

"Sally Jo, and you're very welcome. Here it is."

I call Mr. Dupree and let the phone ring five, six, seven times. I'm just about to hang up when the ringing stops.

"Hello?"

"Hello, Mr. Dupree?"

"Yep, this is him. How long was it ringin'? The wife yelled at me to pick up but I was out in the garage workin' on my truck."

"It was just a few times, sir, no big deal. My name is Nick Ross. I'm a private investigator from Nevada."

"Well, hello there, Mr. Ross, and what can I do for you today?"

"Well, sir, I'm calling about an old case you investigated back in the early '80s, the Fred Tucker case."

"Oh yeah, old Fred Tucker. I remember that one."

"Would you be willing to tell me a little bit about it, Mr. Dupree? I've read the file but I'd like to hear more from you."

"Well, it is a matter of record so I guess it can't do no harm." Dupree hacks into the phone loudly and I get a sense that he's not well.

"Sorry. Damn cigarettes. So why not, be glad to and you can call me Dewey, that's what I go by."

"OK, Dewey, thanks." I can hear the shuffle of foot steps, more hacking and the pull of a chair across the floor.

"Sorry. Needed to sit down Mr.. . .what'd you say your name was?

"Ross. Nick Ross."

"Ah, OK, Nick. So ole Freddy turns up dead layin' on his own couch in the middle of the night. The wife and son were in the upstairs bedrooms sleepin' and never heard a thing. The wife said Freddy must a passed out cause he'd been drinkin' a bit."

"Were there any signs of forced entry or a struggle, Dewey?"

"Nope, backdoor was unlocked and standin' wide open. Freddy's throat was slit ear to ear. Most likely done while he was still sleepin', best we could tell."

"But nothing was taken, right?"

"Nothin' that was obvious. We looked around, things seemed in order. The Mrs. and the boy didn't think anything was gone, but the Mrs. said Freddy used to hide money a lot so maybe that's what they were after."

"So do you think that was the motive? Or could it have been something else?"

"Oh, I got some thoughts on it, I reckon. Never really talked about it much though, wouldn't be right to speculate without any evidence."

"What do you mean, Dewey?"

"Well, since your an 'out-a-towner' I'll tell ya', but it stays between me and you, got it?" More hacking, so I wait a second to give him a chance to recover.

"Of course, Dewey, I got it."

"Well, ole Freddy was what we called back then a little light in the loafers. It was pretty well known he'd switched sides. But Shelbyville was old school and if you had a hankerin' for that kinda thing you best hide it or be ready to get the shit kicked out a ya'.

"I know his boy got into fights all the time from bein' bullied and teased about it. The word gay back then still meant happy round these parts. They called him a fairy, a fag, or a queer. Well, I do go on now, don't I?"

"No, no please, I appreciate your time. I'd like to hear more."

"Well, what I was gettin' at is ole Freddy was talkin' bout headin' for New York City or Cali-forn-i-a. You know. Someplace he could be himself and not hide anymore."

"Was he going to leave his family behind?"

"Looked that way."

"So, how do you think they felt about that?"

"I'm sure it didn't set right. Freddy might a been a queer but he had a decent job workin' for the city in the water department. They would've been left with almost nothin'"

"What do you think happened?"

"Well, rumor has it Freddy was friendly with some high school kid. The kid was about the same age as his son. This kid got really angry when he found out Freddy was leavin' town. Maybe angry enough to kill him. So that's one possibility. But me, I think the boy did it. Now whether or not the Mrs. knew I couldn't tell ya. But she'd a never given him up. He was her everything."

"Did you question him?"

"Sure we did. Couldn't get nothin' out a him except that he was sleepin', never heard a thing. No blood on him, no murder weapon found, so not much we could do."

"Nobody was ever charged? It's still an open case?"

"Yep, that's right. Freddy's wife got his pension and a healthy check from the insurance company. The boy didn't have to put up with the teasing and bullying anymore and maybe ole Freddy is in a better place. Sometimes things just are what they are. Life has a way of dealin' out its own justice, if you know what I mean."

"I guess so, Mr. Dupree, I mean, Dewey."

"So would you happen to know what happened to the boy, Nick? It is Nick, right?"

"Yes, it's Nick and I do know what happened to him. He's a cop in Vegas, a detective."

"Well, if that don't beat all. Would've never seen that comin'."

I pause for a brief, but final, hacking session.

"Thanks a lot, Dewey, for taking the time to talk to me. You've been a big help."

"No problem, maybe me and the Mrs. will get out to Vegas sometime for one a those shows they have and I'll look ya' up."

"You do that, Dewey, I'll look forward to it."

I hang up the phone. Something is odd here. I can't put my finger on it yet but something is very odd.

CHAPTER 33

REASON TO BELIEVE

"**A**lice, I'm heading out. I'm going to see my dad for awhile so I'll check in with you a little later."

Alice looks up at me and strokes the painted-on whiskers her cheeks are sporting. She smiles at me and gives a little purr. "Tell him hello for me, Nick, and have a Happy Halloween."

"Thanks, I sure hope it's a happy one. You have a good one too."

On the way to my dad's place I can't help thinking about Roxy. First of all, I'm very curious about whatever it is she's so excited about. I mean today *is* the day she was told she would die. Worried, I could understand, but giddy seems an odd reaction. Something must have happened while she was in L.A. Second, I'm still wondering if this threat is really real? Maybe somebody is just screwing with her, trying to mess with her mind for some reason. Still it has to be taken seriously. Third,

I mean, why am I worried? I don't know how anybody could just walk right in past two bodyguards and snatch her out of the clear blue. Who the hell could do that? Maybe that's a question for the old man.

As I ring the doorbell at my father's apartment I hear voices. One of them is definitely a woman. The door opens and there stands my father in a wife-beater t-shirt with a sheepish grin on his face.

"You're early."

"Ah. . .sorry, Pop. Should I come back in a little while?"

"No, no come on in."

Dad steps aside and I step into the hallway where I see a woman walking out of the front bedroom. She glances at me and blushes. "Hello," she says in a diminutive voice. "I'm Martha."

"Hello, Martha, I'm Nick. Walter's son. Nice to meet you."

"Well, well. . .I was just on my way out so I'll leave you two boys alone. Talk to you later, Wally. It was nice to meet you, Nick." I watch my father's eyes follow Martha as she walks to her car.

As Martha's car pulls away I fold my arms in front of my chest and look at my dad with a questioning posture. "So, Pop. Or should I call you, Wally? Is there something you would like to tell me?"

"She's a friend and you won't call me that if you know what's good for you," he says as the post-romp grin fades from his face.

"A friend who just walked out of your bedroom, right?"

"Well now, what the hell. I didn't take a vow of celibacy you know."

"It's OK, Pop, I'm just giving you a hard time. I'm happy for you."

"Let's change the subject," Dad says, grabbing a shirt off his favorite armchair. "You ain't here to talk about my sex life. C'mon let's go in the kitchen. You getting anywhere on your case?"

"I was, thought maybe we had a big break. Then our break got himself killed. Have you seen the Bobby Westbrook video?"

"Yeah, they blew the hell out of him."

"He was our big break."

"Shit happens, son."

"I've been wondering, Pop. How the hell does a killer just walk right in and grab these people when they know he's coming for them?"

"Good question. I've thought about that a lot. Struggled with it myself until I went back to the basics."

"What do you mean, Pop?"

Walt leans forward in his chair and picks up the pack of Marlboro Lights. He retrieves one and taps the end of it on the table, an old habit left over from smoking Camels for years. He flips open his lighter and draws in until the cigarette glows.

"Well, it's like this, Nick. I use K.I.S.S."

"K.I.S.S.? What in the world does that mean?"

"Keep. It. Simple. Stupid."

"Oh, right, haven't heard that in awhile."

"Yeah, and what I came up with is this. There are only a few people who most of us trust enough to let into our homes. Family and good friends would be the first two and I think we can rule them out in this case. The next two would be priests and cops."

"I get it. One of them you trust and the other you wouldn't have a choice."

"Exactly, they could walk right in and grab you before you ever knew what happened. Of course, it could also be somebody impersonating them. Might not actually be a real priest or cop."

"I think we might be on to something, Pop."

Wally stubs out his cigarette and reaches for the next one.

▲

Kate arrives at her office and heads straight for the ladies room. A CNN crew has started setting up in the conference area.

"Terry, when you see Kate come in, send her to my office I need to cover a few things with her before she goes on the air."

"Will do, boss. I'll keep my eye on the ladies' room, that seems to be her hang-out lately."

When Kate finally emerges Terry the intern is waiting for her. "Barry is looking for you, Miss Simon. He needs to go over some things with you before you go on. Are you feeling all right?"

"Yes, I'm fine. Thank you, Terry. Tell him I'll be right there."

Kate heads for the break room to grab a Coke before she walks down to her editor's office. She's taking a sip as she walks through the door.

"Good morning, Kate. How're you doing? Ready for the interview?"

"I'm good, and yes, I'm all ready for the interview," she says stifling a burp.

"Good, let's go over the topics you want to cover."

Just then a staff reporter comes running into the office. "Turn on Channel Four, there's breaking news on the Westbrook case."

The screen comes to life just as the local network cuts to their reporter at the Las Vegas Metropolitan Police Department. The reporter stands ready, microphone in hand.

"This is Tag Phillips with Channel Four News reporting to you from the Metro Police Headquarters. We have been given information that there is about to be a statement made in the Bobby Westbrook case. We now take you live to the news conference in L.A."

Mathew McCain and his entourage have reassembled the press conference inside headquarters and called the reporters back for breaking news. Assistant Chief McBride walks up and takes the mic.

"Please give us a few minutes, we have some breaking news for you."

The Sheriff is talking into McCain's ear and pointing at a piece of paper. McCain starts nodding yes, takes the paper and walks over to the microphone.

"Thank you for your patience, everyone. As was stated we have some breaking news for you regarding this case. CSI has identified several items found at the home in Laguna Beach where Bobby Westbrook was hiding to be the personal possessions of the victims in this case. These items were found hidden in Westbrook's belongings. The items included jewelry and women's undergarments. Our lab has tested them and they do match the DNA in four of the five victims. Given the weight of this newfound evidence, we are now inclined to conclude that Bobby Westbrook was the serial killer known as Leviticus."

Kate leans back in her chair and lets out a big sigh. "Shit, you've got to be kidding me. I feel like everything I've written is worthless."

"Come on, Kate, don't give up so easily. You still have the cover-up angle to work on, not to mention the discrimination violations by the departments."

"Do you really think anybody will care now that they've concluded that Bobby's the killer?"

A quick knock on the door and the producer of the CNN crew enters the room.

"Sorry for interrupting but I just talked to Anderson. I'm afraid the interview has been cancelled. He said he would get back to you."

Kate hangs her head and throws both arms up. "I think I'm going to be sick."

CHAPTER 34

DEAR DIARY

Today is the day, dear Lord. Today I will do your bidding. I will carry out your word as you have instructed me to do. The shemale must die. I will pray for guidance in meting out the justice that is deserved.

A new prophet will take responsibility as Leviticus has done his job. Now we will show the sinners our legions are many and our will is powerful. We can not be stopped. God's will be done.

One after another I will take names and books from the Bible that speak the truth and tell of the abomination of man lying with man. They will be brought to justice, it is written.

Now with God's help and guidance I must prepare to take the shemale. The time draws near.

CHAPTER 35

CLOSING IN

I turn the key and the T-Bird roars to life. The radio is blaring "I Won't Back Down." Why is it that every time I get in the car lately a Tom Petty song comes on? I dial down the volume and start thinking about what my father and I just talked about, the possibility of the killer being a cop or clergy. A variety of suspects run through my mind. Wesley Kootz is at the top of the list.

As far as the cop theory goes, that's a little more complicated. I didn't have any suspects at all until I read the research Alice did and talked to Ezra Dupree. Now Tucker seems to be a possibility, or maybe that other kid whose name I don't know.

The thing is, I've had these moments when something seems to resonate. Times when I know there's something important that can tie everything together if I could just get it to click. My game plan now is to go back to the office and review everything, look for something I may have missed that might hold a clue.

I need to get Lyle on the phone and see if I can get more info about the crime scene. I also need to ask him what the hell could have happened to that necklace.

But first I need to talk to Kate and see how her interview went. I would have liked to have seen it but didn't have a chance at my father's place. He doesn't own a television and steadfastly refuses to get one. He says they turn people into ignorant clones who can't think for themselves and become corporate puppets. He still gets his news the old fashioned way, newspapers and radio.

From time to time I do wonder about this new intuition, or spiritual awakening as my "parole officer" Walter Pickles likes to call it. I wonder if it will last? Will it ever be as intense as it was at the truck stop? All I know is that I'd better tap into this energy while I still have it, go track down Tucker and Kootz and find out if they know anything about the murders.

I pull into the parking garage at my office and put the top up on the T-Bird. My phone rings, it's Kate.

"Kate, what's up? I was just going to call you."

"Did you see the news conference?"

"No, I've been at my dad's. How did your interview go?"

"It didn't. They cancelled it after the press conference broke the news about the new evidence."

"What? What new evidence? Did they find the necklace?"

"No, they found articles belonging to the victims in Bobby's personal possessions."

"You've got to be kidding me."

"It shocked me too, Nick. I don't know what to believe anymore. I mean it looks like Bobby really was the killer."

"Where are you?"

"I'm still at my office trying to figure out what to write now."

"I need to talk to Lyle, maybe he can help make sense of all this. I'll call you later."

I race up the stairs to my office and step through the door only to find Alice lying on the floor in front of me. She's on a yoga mat in some downward position chanting something I can't decipher.

"Is this a Cat Woman thing, Alice?"

"No, I was just taking a break and decided to work on my yoga practice. You know you might want to consider yoga yourself, Nick. I hear that it's better than AA for lots of folks and it does wonders for your back."

"Thanks, I'll think about it. When you're finished I need everything we have on the Roxy Lynn case."

"Namaste, coming right up." Alice moves into a sitting position that makes me cringe just looking at her. No way I'm going there. "Oh, and your father called. And your parole officer, that Pickles guy called too."

"That's weird, I was just at my dad's. Did he say what he wanted?"

"No, he didn't," Alice says as she lowers her forehead to the floor.

I walk into my office pick up the phone and call Lyle, no luck. I leave a message on his voice mail. I try my dad and the same thing, no luck. So trying for a perfect shut-out, I call Walter Pickles.

"Hello, this is Walter Pickles."

"Walter, it's Nick. My secretary said you called."

"Hey, Nick, I was just checking in with you to see how things are going."

"Do you mean my, ah, spiritual awakening as you call it?"

"Well, that's one of the things I was wondering about."

"Well, I'm not sure about it, Walter, but it has been quite an experience. Never really felt anything like it before. It's a little scary to tell you the truth."

"I understand. It can be pretty frightening. That's why I wanted to check in with you. Is it still as intense as it was when it first started?"

"No, but it's tough to explain. I mean the understanding is still there but that feeling of looking right through people into their souls has lessened, thank God. I don't know how much more of that I could take."

"I understand, Nick. If you need to talk don't hesitate to call me anytime. I've had some experience with this kind of thing and I think I can help."

"Thanks, Walter, I may take you up on that."

"Oh, and Nick, make it a point to get to a meeting soon."

"I will, Walter. It won't be today but soon, I promise."

▲

Roxy's sitting in her apartment looking up info on her new heart-throb. She knows she should be fearing for her life but she can only think about one thing, Pence Moorhouse. She's never believed in love at first sight. She's not even sure she believes in love. That is until now.

Pence has texted her twice since landing in Beijing and each time her face has lit up like a little kid's on Christmas morning. She wonders if it could be the real thing.

Her phone rings. "Roxy, this is Kate. Did you happen to see the news conference this morning about Bobby Westbrook?"

"Hi Kate. No, I didn't. What happened?"

"The FBI released new evidence. They found several personal items from the victims in Bobby's possession. It looks like he did it, Roxy."

"No," Roxy says emphatically. "That's just not possible, Kate. I saw him and talked to him, he couldn't have done anything like that."

"I know. Nick said the same thing but the evidence is overwhelming."

"I can't believe this. Do you know if the protests are still taking place today? I think I'll go if they are."

"I haven't heard anything yet but I plan on covering them if they do."

"Are you still coming over to do the interview this evening?"

"Well, I'm not sure if there's much point in it after what's happened, but yes, I'll be there at six."

Roxy hangs up with Kate then fumbles to open her purse and nervously pulls out her lighter and a cigarette. She opens her door, steps outside and lights up, looking out over the brilliant Vegas skyline. Her bodyguards both approach.

"Good morning, Miss Roxy, how was your trip?"

"Oh, good morning, guys. It was very interesting to say the least. Listen, I need to talk to both of you."

"Sure, Miss Roxy, what's up?"

"It looks like the threat against me is over. They found the murderer and killed him so I'm going to let you guys go for now. You can go and enjoy Halloween with your families."

"Well, that's great news for you, Miss Roxy, and my daughter will be very happy when she finds out her daddy is taking her trick-or-treating tonight."

"Please stop by with her if you can. I'd love to see her in her costume."

"Thanks, Miss Roxy. We'll definitely try and do that."

A pair of eyes watch as Roxy finishes her cigarette, then turns and walks back into her apartment.

⚔

"Guess who just walked in, Nick?" Alice says as she pokes her head into my office.

"Batman?"

"Very funny. No, it's Lyle."

"Great, send him in."

Alice walks back out to the reception area where Lyle is waiting and pivots around her desk.

"That's quite an outfit you have on, Alice. Do you have plans later?"

"Maybe." Alice bats her eyes.

"Just thought you might like to share a little catnip."

"You can go back now, Lyle." Alice blushes as she grins and turns away.

"Hey, Nick. Got your message and was in the area so thought I'd stop by."

"Thanks, even though you probably just wanted to see Alice, but I'd like to talk to you about that crime scene in Laguna."

"What about it?" Lyle says dodging the Alice comment and taking a seat across the desk from Nick.

"I saw that necklace with my own eyes, Lyle. Bobby was working on it the morning he got shot. What could have happened to it?"

"I don't know what to tell you, Nick. We didn't find any trace of it and the place was thoroughly searched, more than once."

"Any chance somebody could have taken it, Lyle?"

"What do you mean, Nick? You think a cop took it and didn't turn it in? Evidence tampering is a serious crime, you know that."

"Yeah, I know, Lyle, but it's possible. Maybe somebody decided to pin this thing on Bobby because the case was heating up and he was getting too close."

Lyle shifts in his chair, scratches his head and glances out the window, then turns back to Nick. "You got somebody in mind, buddy?"

"Yeah, I do." Nick leans back in his chair and studies Lyle's face hard. "Tucker."

"Oh, for God's sake, Nick. I know you don't like the guy but do you really think he'd do something like that? Why?"

"Think about it. He was under the gun to solve this thing and get it over with so the casino owners would get off the Mayor's back. And it's no secret Tucker isn't the most liberal-minded when it comes to social issues."

"You got a point and that may be true, but murder? That's a big step to take just because you're pissed off about this LBGT rights thing. And anyway, what about the other evidence?"

"I haven't figured that out yet but I'm working on it."

"Well, you let me know when you've figured it out cause in the mean time I think we got our man," Lyle says as he stands to leave.

"Would you do me a favor and at least question Tucker about the necklace to see what kind of a reaction you get?"

"I'll see what I can do but Tucker didn't come in this morning. Mitch said he flew back to Kentucky to see his mother, said she's pretty sick."

"OK, and there's one more thing."

"And that is. . .?"

"We rescued a kid from Wesley Kootz's compound who had been taken off the streets in L.A. and sold to Kootz as a sex slave. Kootz is a pedophile and a human trafficker, he needs to go to jail."

Lyle turns, pulls at his earlobe and walks toward the door.

"We'll look in to it, Nick."

CHAPTER 36

You Got to Have a Heart

In the desert outside of Laughlin, Wesley Kootz relaxes in his air-conditioned RV watching an Angels game on his wide-screen TV via satellite dish. He summons Max to his quarters.

"Max, I want you to get everybody together in fifteen minutes. I've got something to tell them. We'll all meet in the tent."

"Yes, sir, Reverend, I'll get right on it."

Kootz spends the next few minutes looking at emails then changes out of his velvet robe into blue jeans, cowboy boots and a t-shirt that reads, "Fear God".

The hot, dry Nevada air hits his face as he steps out of his RV and inhales hard. He strolls into the tent smiling and greets his small band of workers with a hearty, "God bless, you all." After a few handshakes and backslaps he steps onto the stage, surveys his band of followers and opens his arms to speak.

"Thank you, brothers and sisters, for the fine work you do helping to get God's word out every week. We've been on the road for months now and I know some of you are missing your families, so I've decided to give everyone the next week off with pay. I myself could use a little R&R so I'm heading up to Idaho for some trout fishing. Max has graciously agreed to stay on while we are gone and keep an eye on things. Thank you, Max. So have a real good time, everybody, and I'll see you all in a week."

Kootz walks quickly back to his RV grabs his suitcase and throws it into the F-150. Before he starts the engine he takes out his phone and texts: *Are you ready?*

⚓

As I pick up my phone to answer it I glance at the caller ID, *St. Rose Hospital.* Horrible thoughts flash through my mind as I quickly slide my finger over the phone.

"Hello?"

"Could I speak to Mr. Nick Ross, please?"

"This is Nick Ross."

"Mr. Ross, your father Walter Ross has been admitted to St. Rose Hospital."

"What? What's happened, why was he admitted?"

"He apparently had a heart attack and is currently in the ICU. The doctors can give you more details, sir."

"I'm on my way. I'll be there as soon as possible."

I jump in the T-Bird and take off for the hospital full of worry and fear. My old man has smoked cigarettes going on 50 years now. I can't imagine the damage they may have done to his heart among other things. Now I understand why he didn't answer when I called him back. I dial up Kate.

"Kate, I'm on my way to the hospital, my father's had a heart attack."

"Oh no, I'm so sorry, Nick. Is he going to be all right?"

"Not sure yet. On my way there now. I'll find out when I get there."

"Call me as soon as you find something out. I'm so sorry, sweetheart."

"Thanks. I'll call as soon as I know something. Why don't you go on over to Roxy's and I'll meet you there when I can."

"Are you sure you don't want me to come to the hospital?"

"No, he's in ICU. I don't even know if I'll be able to see him. You go ahead and do your interview with Roxy and I'll be by later."

▲

Roxy decides to get a cab and head down to Fremont Street where the protest march is supposed to take place. She wishes Saleem was available to drive her but it seems he's not yet returned from visiting his daughter in California.

As they near Fremont she sees that several side streets have been blocked off. She tells the driver to pull over so she can get out and walk and see what's really going on. As she approaches the main intersection from a side street she begins to see protesters. They probably only number about a hundred or so, not near what the media had projected.

Yesterday protests in other parts of the country drew thousands. The press conference this morning, and the news that evidence had been found in Bobby's possession, must have done its job in deflating the anger and injustice that people have been feeling, particularly in the LGBT community.

Even for Roxy who knows many in that community, it's hard for her to identify the composition of the crowd. Just as it should be, she thinks. "Black Lives Matter" signs wave against a strangely festive backdrop of PFLAG, PUSH and GLAAD rainbow banners. In contrast, a half a block away Roxy can see a solid line of police officers on both sides of the street in full riot gear. What she sees looks like something more out of a Star War's movie than a street in Vegas. She doesn't understand why this small crowd of impassioned activists would warrant such a massive show of force. As the march begins, Roxy is unaware of the pair of eyes that are tracking her like she's game being hunted, watching intently for the right opportunity to move in.

The march progresses past the rows of troopers who stand motionless behind their shields watching for signs of aggression. The demonstrators' destination is the Fremont Casino up ahead where news crews are waiting.

Roxy decides to peel off from the crowd and head down a side street that has been blocked off. The eyes close in ready to strike.

"Hey, Roxy, is that you?" a voice shouts from further down the street.

Roxy turns to see a woman approaching her. She hesitates for a moment looking carefully at the woman.

"Roxy, I'm Kate. I recognized you from your pictures with the Follies."

"Oh hi, Kate, it's nice to meet you. I'm looking forward to the interview tonight."

"Nice to meet you, too," Kate says shaking Roxy's hand. Nick was right, she can't believe how beautiful Roxy is in person. "Have you been taking part in the march?"

"Yes, but my heart just isn't in it right now. Did you come down to cover it?"

"I did. Got a couple of interviews and my photographer got some good shots. It's not exactly what I was hoping for but at least it's something."

"I was just going for a coffee, Kate. Would you like to join me?"

"I'll walk down there with you, but I don't have time for coffee. I need to get back to my office for a deadline. I'm glad I ran into you though. Nick's probably going to be late tonight. His father had a heart attack and he's at the hospital with him."

"Oh, that's terrible, I'm sorry to hear that. I hope he's going to be OK."

"Yeah, me too. I'm on pins and needles waiting for Nick to call and tell me what's going on. I'll come over to your place tonight by myself and hopefully Nick will be able to join us later."

"Why don't you come over and join me for dinner then. I'm just going to order a pizza and fix some salad."

"Thanks, that would be great."

"Perfect, come at six and park around back in the lot. That way you won't be on the street with all the trick-or-treaters. Just come to the back entrance, it's number 69."

Roxy heads into Starbucks while Kate walks back toward the crowd assembled in front of the Plaza Hotel and Casino.

A pair of eyes watch Roxy intently, waiting patiently for the right moment. Then a cab pulls up in front of Starbucks and Roxy gets in. The eyes look away.

⚔

I pull up to the hospital searching for a parking spot. Business must be good by the looks of the parking lot but I'm in a hurry. Finally a BMW pulls out and I slip into the spot.

I enter the hospital lobby and am immediately lost. Over to my right I see several grey-haired ladies with volunteer badges standing behind a counter that reads, "Patient Information".

"Hello, may we be of assistance, sir?"

"Yes, I'm trying to find out where my father is. He was admitted a few hours ago and they told me he was in ICU."

"What's his name, sir?"

"Oh, sorry, his name is Walter Ross."

"Well, let's see," the woman whose badge reads Ellen runs her finger down a list on a clipboard. "Yes, here he is. The ICU is in the west wing on the third floor. Just go down the hall and take the elevator on the right."

Not so simple. As I approach the elevator I'm stopped by a security guard. " Sir, you need to get a security badge from the front desk."

"Oh, sorry officer I'm in a big hurry."

"No problem. I understand. Happens all the time." The officer walks me over to the desk and I pick up the badge.

When I get to the third floor I head straight to the nurse's station. The staff seems to be in a continual state of flux, coming and going as they swap out charts and check medications. Finally I belt out a rather loud but appropriate, "Excuse me, could someone help me please, my father is in ICU here."

Finally the head nurse steps up to the counter across from me. "Sorry, sir, we're really busy here, how can I help you?"

"My father is Walter Ross. He's in ICU and I'd like to see him."

"Of course. He's in room 323. I can let you see him for a few minutes but please keep it short, he's being prepped for surgery."

"Surgery? What kind of surgery?"

"I'll get the doctor, sir. He can explain your father's condition."

As I walk down the hallway with the nurse, I glance into each dimly lit room through the viewing windows. In each bed there's someone helplessly hooked up to a machine with blinking lights, tubes and wires running everywhere. It scares the hell out of me.

When we walk through the door to my father's room I see the same array of technology monitoring his every breath. I lean against the wall briefly and pull myself together as the nurse steps up to his bedside.

"Mr. Ross, your son is here to see you."

"Nick?"

"Yes, Dad, I'm here." I take his hand in mine and give it a quick squeeze. "Love you, Dad."

I realize when I look into his eyes something I've never seen before. My "experience" is kicking in and I'm caught up by the sensation of wanting to look deeper and deeper into his weary eyes. What I see amazes me: the character of a good man, the honesty of his intention, the beauty of his capacity to love. And love me. Things I've never known about my father. I blink and am consumed with an overwhelming sense of gratitude and the intensity of how proud I am to be his son.

Dad sputters out a gravelly whisper. "Damn cigarettes. Guess they finally caught up with me. Doc says I need a triple bypass."

My father's voice suddenly snaps me back to reality. "The nurse tells me they're getting you ready to be operated on. I'll be here for you, Pop."

"Now don't you worry about me," he says waving off my hand. "I'll be fine. Too ornery to die, at least that's what the doc says."

Just then the doctor walks into the room, picks up Walter's chart and jostles his leg.

"Hey, Buck, come to give me some more good news?"

"Hello, Walt. How are you feeling? Your vitals look good."

"Feelin' like a million can't you tell, Doc? Oh, this is my son Nick. Nick, this is Dr. Morgan Buchanan, but I just call him Buck."

"Hello, Nick, nice to meet you."

"How's my dad doing, Doctor?"

"Why don't we step outside for a minute. We'll be right back, Walt."

"No need to talk behind my back, but, oh sure, go ahead. I'm not going anywhere."

Dr. Buchanan and I step into the hallway and I brace myself for bad news.

"Nick, I've known your father for about ten years now. I've treated him for heart problems and tried unsuccessfully to get him to stop smoking so this situation doesn't surprise me. I thought it would happen a long time ago."

"Wow, he never told me he had heart trouble, but I do understand the smoking issue."

"He needs a triple bypass. Thankfully, he was with a friend who is a retired nurse when the symptoms started happening so she gave him aspirin and called 911 immediately. She probably saved his life. I think his prognosis is very positive but let's see how the procedure goes."

"How long will the operation take?"

"He should be in recovery about two hours from now. If all goes well he can go home in a day or two."

"Well, this is better news than I expected, thank you, Doctor."

We walk back in the room and the doctor walks over to my father's bed and jostles his leg again. "You ready for an overhaul, old man?"

"Ready as I'll ever be, you old quack," Dad says doing his best tough guy imitation.

"They'll be coming to prep you for the procedure in a couple of minutes, Walter, so spend some time with your son. I'll see you in the operating room and we'll fix that ticker of yours."

For the next few minutes I just sit back and enjoy my time with my father until they come and take him to pre-op.

I decide to head down to the cafeteria and realize I haven't been in a hospital since my mother died. Not a very comforting environment which is odd since everyone here is in such need of it. The stark coldness of the place hits me as the prospect of my dad possibly not making it seeps into my mind.

As I enter the cafeteria I see the woman who surprised me when she walked out of the bedroom at my dad's house yesterday. She's sitting alone at a table sipping coffee. "Hi, I'm Walter's son, Nick. I think we've met. You're Martha, right? "

"Oh, hi, Nick, yes we did meet under some rather unusual circumstances." She smiles and motions for me to sit down. "Please have a seat and join me."

"So, were you with my dad when it happened?"

"Yes, I was. I've seen these things before but he scared me to death."

"Dad's doctor mentioned that a nurse called 911."

"Yes, that's me. I was a nurse for 45 years. Still miss it sometimes," she says gazing into her half-filled coffee cup.

"The doctor said that you recognizing the symptoms and acting so quickly to get help may have saved my father's life. Thank you. My old man may be a little cantankerous but I love him."

"I understand, Nick, and yes, he is a good man. I care about him a lot."

CHAPTER 37

Trick-or-Treat

Kate finishes up at her office and heads over to Roxy's apartment. She makes a quick stop at a Trader Joe's along the way to pick up a bottle of wine.

It's twilight and a few of the trick-or-treaters are already on the street. She takes Roxy's advice and pulls around to the back of the apartment house to park. Grabbing her briefcase and the bottle of wine, she heads for Roxy's apartment. She hopes Roxy will understand her not drinking but she's not ready to share the news about her pregnancy quite yet. She rings the bell.

"Hi Kate, come on in, I'm just making a salad. The pizza is in the oven staying warm. I hope you like vegetarian."

"Sure, fine with me."

"Can I get you something to drink?"

"Just water for me, but you go ahead. I brought some wine."

"You know, I think I will have a drink. I feel so relieved with this death threat mystery solved." Roxy sighs, pulls a wine glass from the cabinet, then smiles. "Maybe I can get my life back now and be able to sleep at night. And not have to pay bodyguards around the clock."

"I can't imagine what it's been like for you, Roxy. I think I would have freaked."

"It's been tough. There were times when I was very close, believe me. I've never really been afraid of being alone, but this. . .fortunately something always happened to pull me through."

"Sounds like you had someone watching over you."

"Yes, I think so and his name was Nick." Kate nods in agreement, feeling proud that Nick had no reservations about helping Roxy. Some detectives she knows would have looked the other way. "To Nick," Roxy says raising her glass with a smile of relief on her face.

"Speaking of Nick, it looks like he's trying to call me. Excuse me, Roxy. . .Nick, hello, how's your dad?"

"Hi, Kate. He's actually doing much better than I thought he would, but he does need a triple bypass. The good news is the doctor said he caught it in time to limit the damage done to his heart so his outlook is pretty good."

"When's the surgery?"

"He went into pre-op twenty minutes ago so they've probably started. He should be in recovery within a couple hours. I'm going to stay here until I know he's out of the woods and stable."

"Stay as long as you need, Nick. Roxy and I are having dinner, then I'll start the interview. I'm sure we'll be a couple of hours."

"Good, you guys stay put till I get there. I know everybody thinks Bobby is the killer but I'm still not convinced."

"Come on, Nick, don't you think it's time to move on?"

"Maybe, we'll see. I'll call you when I leave the hospital."

The doorbell rings and Roxy goes to answer it with bags of candy in her hands.

"OK, Nick. Got to go, Roxy needs some help."

"All right, Kate, but tell Roxy not to let the bodyguards go until I get there. . . Kate? Kate, you there?" Nick pulls the phone away from his ear. "Shit, she hung up."

Roxy stands in the doorway passing out candy to three little girls in identical, turquoise Elsa costumes holding their bags open and reciting "trick-or-treat" in unison. With no parents in sight, Roxy assumes they must be in the van parked across the street. The girls giggle a "thank you" and run down the sidewalk.

"Such cute kids," Roxy says wistfully. "Sometimes I miss not having a family." Kate nods in understanding and takes another bite of pizza.

The women finish their dinner with only the occasional interruption by ghosts and goblins knocking at the front door. They move into the living room where Kate gets ready to start the interview. She goes through her usual opening questions, getting to know Roxy and making her feel at ease. They talk about Roxy's past and how her transition came about. Kate next asks Roxy if she has any questions she'd like to ask her. Then she moves on to asking Roxy about her views on issues facing the LGBT community.

"Are you OK with everything on the record?" Roxy nods her head approvingly and smiles at Kate.

"Great. What do you think of the new laws being passed in North Carolina and other states that regulate gender issues on public restrooms?"

"I think it's all a smokescreen to take away the civil rights of many of us. I mean, seriously, when was the last time before all this commotion that this was a real issue? There was never a problem until they made it one."

"Do you ever feel discriminated against?"

"Yes and no. Frankly, I'm lucky. I'm what's called a passer. I can pass for a woman almost all the time so I'm not a target for hostility like many of us are."

"And what about the people who aren't as lucky as you are, what sort of problems do they typically face?"

"High unemployment, poverty, no health insurance. In many cases it's difficult to rent a house or apartment, evictions are not unusual. And if you're black you can multiply these problems ten-fold."

"But job and housing discrimination are illegal."

"Yeah, we all know that, but people who want to discriminate and have the power to do so find ways to get around the legal system. They know how to play the game."

"What can be done to alleviate these problems?"

"Hire us. Look, I know it's not always easy for employers but those who have taken the initiative have found there's very little pushback. And we're usually great employees. It would be a big help in making us become more inclusive. And pass laws that protect us from discrimination, not encourage it. Support organizations that fight for our rights and access to resources. I could go on and on." Roxy takes a sip of her wine, then a deep breath.

"Look, when a person begins to recognize that the gender they were born as is not who they are, the change begins slowly after a lot of experiences and often with much trepidation. It takes extraordinary courage for trans-people to live life as truthfully as possible."

"Can I quote you on that?"

"Sure, I'd like that."

Roxy leans back in her chair and picks up her wine glass again. She swirls it gently then takes a healthy drink.

"Excuse me, Roxy, but may I use your restroom?"

"Oh sure, Kate, it's down the hall on the right."

The doorbell rings again and Roxy grabs a bowl of candy. Instead of little kids, this time it's half a dozen teenagers dressed like zombies and acting like them too. Directly behind them is a larger person dressed like Darth Vader who appears to be their chaperone.

After the teenagers have finally stocked up on Reese's Pieces and gummy bears, they shuffle away from the front door and head off down the street. Darth Vader turns to watch them momentarily then steps forward, practically to the threshold.

"Roxy Lynn?" A deep, distorted voice rumbles under the mask.

"Yes, I am. Who are you?" Roxy wonders if this is her crazy neighbor Dave, the one who throws all the wild parties.

"Step back from the door," the tech-modified voice orders as Darth Vader pushes forward through the doorway, a .45 clearly visible under his cape as he spreads his arms to block Roxy's exit. He moves quickly into the apartment and shuts the door behind.

"Don't say a word. Get down on the floor, put your hands behind your back."

Roxy is paralyzed with fear. She couldn't scream if she tried to. Before she can even try to put up a fight, she feels a knee heavy on her back. The intruder then pulls out a roll of duct tape, pressing a strip hard over her mouth then wrapping another piece tightly around her wrists several times.

Just then Kate walks out of the bathroom and down the hall-way. As she turns the corner to enter the living room she sees Darth Vader kneeling over Roxy with duct tape in hand. She screams and surprises him as he jumps towards her and grabs her arm.

"Do that again and I'll put a bullet through her head, understand?"

"Yes, just please don't hurt us."

"Lie down and shut up. Arms behind your back."

Kate carefully moves to the floor, rolling onto her belly. She can feel the heat of his breath through the mask as he duct tapes her mouth and wrists.

"Where the hell did you come from, bitch? I've been watching this place and haven't seen anybody but her. Now I have no choice but to take both of you. Don't either of you move."

He gets up, goes down the hallway and returns quickly with two sheets. He pulls a razor-sharp stiletto from his pocket and slices two eye holes in each sheet.

"Stand up. Happy Halloween, you're going to be ghosts. Quiet, cooperative little ghosts. We're going to walk across the street and get in a van. If either of you try anything I'll stick this shiv in your back."

He takes out the gun and waves it in front of their faces making a threatening sound through his voice changer device, then opens the door and motions toward the street. He stays close behind them giving instructions as they walk to the other side.

As they approach the van, two little boys on the sidewalk yell at him. They're both wearing Star War's costumes and swinging plastic lightsabers wildly in the air.

"Hey, Mr. Darth Vader, we're heroes sent to get you," they shout as they jab their colorful weapons at him.

"Get away from me," he yells just as their mother approaches.

"Hey, buddy, that wasn't very nice, they were just playing." The young mother gathers her little Hans and Luke while shoving a threatening finger at Darth Vader. "You scared them. Come on, boys, let's leave the cranky, old villain alone."

As they walk off, he opens the rear doors of the van and pushes Roxy and Kate inside. He crawls in behind them, closes the door, then tapes their ankles together.

Kate is shaking uncontrollably. Roxy can see the fear in her eyes and wants to fight back but knows it would be futile, or even fatal, at least for now.

Then he takes rope and ties them to the wall of the van so they can't move. He secures his cargo and moves to the front of the van into the driver's seat, pulling a curtain closed behind him to conceal his prisoners. He rifles through Roxy and Kate's handbags that he picked up in the house, making sure he left nothing behind. He finds their cell phones, turns them off and wraps them in aluminum foil. He starts the van and maneuvers it down the street while he replays the scene at the apartment confirming to himself he left no signs of foul play. They won't be considered missing persons for at least 24 hours after a report is filed. By then they'll both be dead and he will be long gone.

I've been in the recovery waiting room for about an hour when the doctor walks in. He has a big smile on his face so I know the operation must have been a success.

"Nick, your father is doing very well and the surgery went just as planned. He should be coming out of the anesthetic soon and you can see him then."

"Thank you, doctor, when do you think he can come home?"

"I'll look in on him tomorrow and make that decision, but I doubt it will be more than two or three days." Dr. Buchanan glances up and past my shoulder. "Oh, here comes the nurse. Looks like you can go in now."

The dimmed hospital lights in dad's room cast everything in a soft, almost peaceful gray except for the neon lights and numbers alternately blinking on the monitor tracking his vitals. The nurse feeding him ice chips turns and smiles at me as I enter the room. Could be the circumstances but she looks like an angel.

"Hi, Dad, it's Nick."

"Hello, son, they tell me I'm going to live." The angel-nurse shoots me a "your dad's a real smart-ass" grin and I nod in agreement.

"That's what I hear, Pop. Doc says you came through with flying colors. How're you feeling?"

"Like a million bucks. Can't feel a thing." The fatigue in his face tells a different story.

"Well, I think some of the drugs are probably still in your system."

"They can keep 'em comin' as long as they want far as I'm concerned." His eyelids fall shut then quickly flutter open.

"Listen, Dad, I'm going to stay for awhile but I have to go see Kate and a friend in a little bit. There is someone else here who wants to see you though."

"Who's that?"

"Your friend I met yesterday at the apartment."

Dad manages a soft smile and opens his eyes wider to look at me.

"Oh, Martha. Did you know she was a nurse?"

"Yeah, your doctor told me that. He also said she may have saved your life."

"God bless her. She's a good woman. . .I know that for sure."

"Well, probably best not to keep a good woman waiting. How about if I have her come in now, would you like that?"

"Send her in, Nick. I need to thank her."

After a few minutes I can tell that my father is a lot more interested in Martha despite his post-op drowsiness than he is in me. I tell him I'll be back first thing in the morning and step outside to call Kate. She must have her cell phone off because it goes straight to voicemail which probably makes sense because I'm sure she is still interviewing Roxy and doesn't want interruptions. I decide to just head over there and join them.

I exit the elevator and step into the hospital lobby, it's a melting pot of the diverse world that makes Vegas, Vegas. The well-worn sofas and armchairs are filled even at this hour with every age, color and social combination that you could possibly think of. As I head toward the exit I look into their faces. Blank stares gaze back, tired and troubled. I can't help but wonder what's it's like to be one of the doctors or nurses that look into those eyes everyday. God bless them.

My T-Bird is now wedged between two, mega-SUV's and I can't see a damn thing as I try to back out. I take a deep breathe and turn on the radio. And, of course, there's Mr. Petty singing about how good it is to be king and have your own way. Spot on.

I slow down when I get to Roxy's street knowing it will be teaming with trick-or-treaters, which it is. I park and walk towards her apartment. As I approach, three little kids walk by me.

"Sorry, mister, nobody's home there, we already tried."

"Thanks. Great costumes, guys. . .have fun."

The kids scatter and I try the bell again. My guess is they aren't answering the door because it's too much of a distraction which is probably wise considering the circumstances. I give the door a hard knock. "Roxy. Kate. It's me, Nick." Still nothing.

I call Kate's phone but there's no answer. I try Roxy's and it's the same thing, straight to voicemail. I'm starting to get a little worried. I knock again harder yet and yell out their names even louder, but nothing. I go around the back and try that door but it's the same thing, no response. I see Kate's car in the lot. That's odd, they probably would have taken her car had they gone somewhere because Roxy doesn't own one.

I look for an office or a manager's apartment but find nothing. Finally in the parking lot I see a sign with the name and phone number of the company that owns the apartments. I call but there's no answer, just a recording asking me to leave a message. I explain that there's an emergency and leave my number. My confidence as to how fast they'll respond is close to zero. It's Halloween and it's a Friday night.

I wait several minutes though they seem like hours. I try to stay calm and think of any scenario that would cause them to leave. Nothing I come up with has a good outcome.

I call Lyle hoping I can talk him into getting the police involved. I know it's a long shot but I have to try.

"Lyle, it's Nick, I have to talk to you, it's important."

"I'm on a date, Nick. Can't it wait till tomorrow?"

"No. Kate and Roxy are missing. They were supposed to be at Roxy's apartment, they're not there and neither of them is answering their phones."

"How long since you've talked to either of them?"

"Probably a couple hours. I just got here a few minutes ago and was supposed to meet them but they're gone."

"Wait. You're telling me it's only been a few hours? You know I can't do anything for at least 24 hours."

"You damn well can if there's foul play involved, Lyle, and you know it."

"And what exactly makes you think there's foul play involved?"

"Look, it's just a hunch but I'm really worried, Lyle. I need to get into the apartment and look around. *Now.*"

"I can't help you there, Nick, but I'll tell you what. You get the super or manager to open it up and I'll send an officer over to look around."

"All right, if that's the best you can do. I'll call you when I get it open."

Then it hits me. Almost everybody I know hides a key somewhere just in case of getting locked out. Like bad guys don't know this. I look around in back but there's nowhere to hide one so I walk around to the front.

I check all the usual places, under the mat, on top of the door frame, but nothing. I'm about to give up when I notice a wooden flower box under the window. I slide my hand under it but no luck. Then I run my finger along the inside edge and—bingo! On a tiny hook in the front corner is a key.

My nerves on edge and stomach churning, I walk to the front door and slide the key into the lock. It opens. I enter slowly, not knowing what to expect and trying not disturb or touch anything. I want everything just as it until the cops arrive.

Lyle picks up the phone on the first ring. "Hey, I'm in," I whisper into my phone as I cautiously move around Roxy's living room.

"That was fast. You didn't break in, did you, Nicky?"

"No, I found a key. Kate and Roxy aren't here, but Kate's car is. How soon can you get your boys over here?"

"I'll call it in now. They should be there in about fifteen minutes."

"Thanks, Lyle, I owe you one."

I can't wait for the police, I need to take a look around. A cold chill runs down my spine, I've got a bad feeling about this. Nothing out of the ordinary catches my eye with the possible exception of some pizza sitting out in the kitchen. Wouldn't they have put it away if they had planned to leave? Everything else looks normal. No signs of foul play that I can see but looks can be deceiving.

Hopefully my gut is wrong and I'm over reacting. Kate and Roxy could come walking in any minute. But with no evidence of foul play, if someone did kidnap them the cops won't get involved in a missing persons case for at least 24 hours. That could be too late. I have to get a search started whatever it takes.

Ten damn long minutes later there's a knock at the door. When I open the door Cagney and Lacey are standing in front of me. The two female officers introduce themselves, ask my name, then explain why they were sent. I give them a brief explanation of what has happened and why I'm so concerned. They both listen to what I say while one of officers takes notes. She looks up at me when she's done, her steely eyes staring at me a couple seconds too long to be comfortable. She turns to her partner and mumbles something I can't hear. She takes out a camera and fiddles with it while her partner prepares the equipment they need. They both take a quick look around, then begin to work their way through each room of the apartment slowly and methodically, taking pictures of everything. They wear gloves and booties as they move from room to room, only an occasional word between them. I was told to stay put and not touch anything and that's what I'm doing.

After about thirty minutes the one I'm calling Cagney walks back into the living room where I'm waiting. She takes off her gloves, booties and hairnet, wipes the sweat off her forehead and turns to me in a business-like manner.

"Sir, we can't find anything that would suggest foul play. At this time we can not consider this a crime scene so CSI will not be investigating unless more evidence is found. You can file a missing persons report tomorrow if you wish, but until then there's nothing we can do."

I listen to what the she's saying and understand it's the company line but it is simply unacceptable to me.

"I understand, Officer, but the circumstances here are very much out of the ordinary. The police need to be involved right away."

She looks at me with those steely eyes again and I can see some compassion, but I do know that rules are rules. "Sorry, sir, that's all we are allowed to do. If you would like to call our division here's the number."

I reject the card putting my hands up. "That's okay. I know the number. Thanks for coming out."

As soon as they leave I call Lyle.

CHAPTER 38

MISSING PERSONS

Kate and Roxy can barely move but their eyes frantically scan the van's dark interior, then lock on each other's face with undeniable fear. Roxy grunts with a tremble as she stares into Kate's eyes, then Kate hangs her head as a tear rolls down her cheek.

Roxy can tell they've been on the road about an hour or so. Their kidnapper hasn't made any stops so they must be on an Interstate highway. There are no windows in the van but she knows they've been travelling at a good rate of speed.

The van begins to slow down and finally comes to a brief stop. Then it moves again, stops again. This happens several times so Roxy figures they must be in a town.

He makes a sharp turn, throwing Kate and Roxy off balance even while tied up. They come to a complete stop and the engine is turned off. The driver removes his costume gets out and throws on a ball-cap. Roxy and Kate can hear him as he walks to the back of the van, unscrews the gas cap and shoves in the pump nozzle.

Kate looks over at Roxy and nods her head twice toward the outside. Roxy listens and can hear what's going on but the gas hasn't started pumping. He must be going in to pay first. Roxy looks at Kate and moves her head like she's saying yes. Then she blinks her eyes, leans her head back against the wall of the van and taps it lightly a few times. She waits a few seconds looks back over at Kate and nods her head yes again.

Suddenly she snaps her head backward into the wall of the van. The pain shoots through her skull, her jaw, her eyes and her spine. It's their only chance. She repeats it four or five more times as Kate joins her, eyes squeezed shut as if to brace against a throbbing anguish.

An elderly man filling his car at the next pump hears the pounding and looks around to see where it's coming from. When he hears it a second time he can tell it's coming from the van.

Roxy tries to hit her head up against the metal wall even harder but this time she hits too hard and knocks herself out. She drops limp. Kate tries to continue but she's feeling weak and dizzy.

As he comes back from paying for the gas, the man who heard the banging confronts him. "Hey, mister, what do you have in there? Something's banging up against the wall of your van like crazy."

"It's nothing," he says turning away from the man.

"Well, maybe you ought to check and see if everything is OK."

"It's none of your business," he says and starts to fill the gas tank.

The man finishes pumping his gas, then goes to get in his car. "Wow, what an asshole. Bet he don't live around here. Probably one of those Vegas pricks."

Kate sees that Roxy's eyes are beginning to flutter. She now knows that she just heard the voice of the man who wants to kill them. She tries to swallow the bile pushing up into her throat as her terror deepens.

After the van's back on the highway he turns toward the curtain and warns, Roxy. "If you and your nosy little friend try another stunt like that, I'll slit your throat and make her watch you bleed to death."

⅄

"Lyle, it's Nick again."

"Did they finish going through the apartment?"

"Yes, but they said there's nothing they can do because there's no sign of foul play."

Lyle sighs. "Well, you know the law, Nick."

"Yeah, I know the law but there's more to this than them simply being gone. I think they've been abducted and they both could be killed."

"What the hell are you talking about?"

"Look, I need to talk to you, Lyle. There are some things you need to know. Right away."

"Can't it wait, Nick? I told you I'm on a date."

"*No, it can't,*" Nick says voice raising. "Please, Lyle."

"OK, we're finishing dinner up now. Meet us at O'Connell's in half an hour."

I check around Roxy's some more looking for clues but come up empty. I call each of their cell phones again hoping for a miracle. I leave a note on the table for Kate and Roxy on my way out: "Call me immediately when you get back!"

I'm tired and on edge when I walk into O'Connell's. This is the place I had my last slip, the one that landed me in the desert fending for my life. The good news is, I haven't wanted a drink since.

I look around and spot Lyle at a table sitting with a woman who has her back to me. As I walk toward them I hear a familiar voice.

"Alice?" I say trying to ratchet down my surprise. "You're Lyle's date?"

"Well, don't be so shocked, Nick. Lyle's been chasing me for a long time," Alice says with a little wink. "I finally just gave in."

More annoyed than embarrassed, Lyle rubs his thumb and finger over his ear lobe, picks up his Jack and Coke and stirs the ice in circles. "Have a seat, Nick, and tell me what's so damn important."

"There are some things I didn't tell you about a case I'm on that has to do with the Mavis Rodgers investigation."

"Well, I'm all ears."

"Why don't you boys talk while I go powder my nose." Alice squeezes Lyle's arm, then gets up and leaves the table.

I watch her walk away then turn back to Lyle. "Roxy Lynn hired me to investigate letters she's received in the last couple weeks alleging she'd be killed on Halloween. They were exactly the same type of letters the other victims of Leviticus received before they were murdered."

"So why the hell didn't you come to me then, Nick?"

"I couldn't, Lyle. I promised Roxy. She has some legal issues in her past that could land her in jail if the authorities found out her true identity."

"So you withheld evidence?"

"I was doing my job, Lyle, call it what you want."

"What did she do?"

"Her crazy half-brother asked her to take him and a friend by a bank so they could cash their checks from work. She waited in the car while they went in and didn't know anything about their plan to rob it until they came running out and jumped back in the car. She's innocent, Lyle, but who's going to believe her? That's why she ran."

"So what do you want me to do, Nick?"

"Well, you have the evidence you need to support the idea that someone may have taken her to do harm. Kate just happened to be with her so they took her too. You can start a full investigation and get a statewide search started."

"That's great, buddy, but you seem to forget that Leviticus is dead."

"I don't believe Bobby was the killer, Lyle. There's too much that just doesn't add up."

"OK, that's great. I'll tell that to my boss and see what he has to say when I want to launch a man hunt for a guy we've already caught."

"I know what you're saying but Kate and Roxy wouldn't have left knowing I was coming over without telling me. They also wouldn't have left Kate's car behind or turned off their cell phones so they couldn't be reached. Damn it something is wrong, Lyle, and they're in a lot of danger. I just know it and we need to act fast."

"I'll do what I can, Nick, but I can't promise you anything."

"That's all I'm asking, Lyle, thanks. I'm heading back to Roxy's and then to my office. You two enjoy yourselves."

"Wait!" Alice shouts as I'm walking out. "I'm coming with you. Sorry, Lyle, I need to do this. We can get together again soon, I promise."

Lyle stands to give her a hug. "Go ahead, Alice, I understand. I'll go get started on whatever I can do."

On the way back to Roxy's we're both deep into our own thoughts. I look over at Alice and she gives me a sympathetic smile then pats me on the shoulder. I turn on the radio. Perfect timing, Petty's belting out "Free Fallin". Yep, that's about right.

I turn on to Roxy's street and slow down to a crawl. The trick-or-treaters are still out in force. I find a spot and pullover. As Alice and I walk up to the door a woman accompanied by two little boys waving lightsabers calls to us from the street.

"Excuse me, sir, but I saw police here a little while ago. Is everything all right?"

"We don't know for sure yet. The woman who lives here might have met with foul play. The police are investigating."

"Oh my, I hope it didn't have anything to do with that nasty man in the van we saw earlier. He looked like maybe he came out of this apartment."

"You saw someone leave this apartment?" I ask, moving to the curb.

"Well, no, but they were crossing the street directly in front of it. I don't know where else they may have come from."

"You said 'they'. How many others were there?"

"He was with two people dressed like ghosts."

"Could they have been women?"

"Maybe, they were both about my size. Yeah, they probably were women."

"Did they say anything? Did you get the license plate of the van?"

"No, sorry. Didn't hear anything and didn't think about getting the plate number at the time. I just thought the man was really rude for yelling at my two boys."

"Would you be willing to talk to the police about this?"

"Come on mommy, can we go? I'm tired," whines the smaller boy tugging at her leg.

"Sure, I'd be glad to," replies the woman as she takes both boys by the hand.

Alice takes down her name and number while I go inside Roxy's apartment to look around one more time. Still no obvious signs of trouble. As soon as Alice steps inside the expression on her face changes from worry to a look of horror. She wraps her arms around herself and shudders.

"Something happened here, Nick, I can feel it."

"I know, Alice, I can feel it too but there's no evidence of a struggle."

Despite my nagging worry, I decide we should head for the office. On the way there Alice calls Lyle and updates him about the woman who saw the people leaving from what she thought may have been Roxy's apartment. Lyle promises to contact her for an interview but not to count on that being enough to start a search. He does give Alice some good news though. It seems that the LAPD interviewed Julio due to the insistence of one Stella Jo Vance. They have since issued a warrant for Wesley Kootz and the Sheriff of Clark County Nevada has dispatched deputies to pick him up.

As the sun goes down the Strip lights up. Tourists are out in droves, some of them still in their Halloween costumes. The threat of a serial killer being on the loose has been squashed by the nightly news running headlines about the capture and shooting of Bobby Westbrook and people are ready to party.

At the office Alice dives right into all the files we have on Roxy's case. We divvy them up and grab legal pads. An hour later we finally take a break and start comparing notes.

I read everything I've written down to Alice to see if anything strikes her as odd or new, but nothing stands out. Then Alice reads everything she's made notes on to me. She rattles through a lot of facts then finally starts on Tucker. Only child, father murdered, mother deceased. Something hits me and I stop her.

"Would you read that again?"

"Sure, only child, father murdered, mother deceased."

"Holy shit, that son of a bitch lied. Tucker said he was flying back to Kentucky to visit his sick mother. Why would he lie if he wasn't trying to cover up something?"

"Want me to get Lyle on the phone?" Alice asks, her fingers ready to punch Lyle's number.

"No, not yet, I know what he'll say. People make up excuses all the time because they don't want others to know what they're really doing. Nobody questions the sick parent story."

"So what should we do, Nick?" Alice scoops up the file folders with a nervous energy not attributable to caffeine.

"Let's focus on Tucker, they're already after Kootz. Wait a minute. Kootz is from Kentucky too. How old is he, Alice?"

"Let me see, " she says, red nails flying over the page. "He's 48."

"And where did he grow up?"

"Shelbyville."

"Holy shit. Same age as Tucker. They grew up in the same town."

CHAPTER 39

My Mountain Retreat

Roxy and Kate can feel the van slowing down and turning. Finally they come to a stop. They hear him get out but there's no sound to indicate he's getting gas again.

He enters the Quickie Mart looking for something to eat. He fills up a soda, grabs a sandwich and some chips, then walks back out to the van. When he opens the door this time Roxy and Kate can feel a blast of cool, clean air. They must be in the mountains.

He sits in the driver's seat eating his sandwich when Roxy starts grunting as loud as she can. He peaks through the curtain with one eye so they can't see him.

"What the hell's wrong with you? What do you want?" he growls, annoyed and angry.

Roxy grunts again and leans her head down toward her crotch.

"You have to take a piss?"

Roxy shakes her head yes.

"If you got to go, just go but you're not getting out, we're almost there so just hold it."

He finishes his sandwich then takes the wrappers and throws them in the bag with the rest of the trash. He picks up the two foil-covered cell phones and tosses them in too. He gets out of the van, walks over to the dumpster and throws away the bag.

After being back on the road for a short time, Roxy can feel the van starting to slow and then turn. She can hear gravel hitting against the wheel wells as it moves over an obviously rutted road. Every dip and bounce, makes Kate's nausea more intense. The pounding she is taking is beginning to take its toll. She knows if she starts throwing up she could choke to death on her own vomit. She tries to convey this to Roxy but her eyes alone can only do so much. Trying to get his attention now would be impossible with all the road noise and the scanner he's listening to.

Roxy lifts her head to look at Kate and notices she's looking very pale. There are beads of sweat on her forehead and her eyelids keep opening and closing as if she's ready to pass out. Roxy tries to nudge her but she can't get close enough.

Kate starts to gag. Her body is gyrating back and forth and instead of being pale she's turning red. Roxy tries everything to free herself so she can help Kate but it's impossible.

Just then the van stops. Roxy can faintly hear the rustling of fabric. Within seconds, the back doors of the van open and there stands their kidnapper in his Darth Vader costume, reeking of sweat. "We're here," he announces.

Roxy starts motioning her head towards Kate and making the loudest sounds she can. He looks over and sees Kate's eyes bulging and her face bright red. He leans into the van and rips the tape off her mouth. Kate heaves and spews brown liquid across the van. She gags again and starts gasping for air. Finally she's able to take several deep breathes and begins coughing and crying.

He pulls out a knife and slices through the tape on Kate's ankles. "I ought to make you clean that up, bitch. Now come with me."

Kate feels so weak she can barely walk. When her legs start to buckle he grabs her by the shoulder and pulls her up on to the dilapidated wooden porch of a rustic old cabin.

Set far off the road on the approach to the Spring Mountains, the boarded-up cabin sits alone in a stand of juniper and pinyon pine. The front porch is barricaded with faded yellow tape pulled across it that reads: "Do not cross, seized property of the U.S. Government". The one-time popular hunting cabin fallen victim to a meth dealer who got busted by the Feds.

He opens the door, drags Kate inside and shoves her toward the bathroom. Much to her amazement there's actually running water supplied by a nearby spring. He pulls out his gun and stands by the open door as she reluctantly relieves herself. She tries to clean herself up from the vomiting when he taps her on the shoulder from behind. "Let's go" he says still using his voice changer. Kate hurriedly cups her hands and scoops two big gulps of water to her mouth.

He grabs her arm, pulls her into a bedroom and pushes her to sit in a large wooden chair. He grabs some tape and rope lying on the floor and binds Kate to the chair's arms and legs. This time he does not gag her. Kate squeezes her eyes closed and looks away holding back a scream.

He then heads back to the van gets Roxy and goes through the same routine. As Roxy enters the bathroom she turns to close the door. He slams it back in her face and snarls at her.

"It stays open!"

Roxy snaps right back. "I'm closing the door, so if you're going to shoot me, go ahead, but the door will be closed."

As soon as Roxy comes out of the bathroom he grabs her arm and takes her to the room where Kate is. He pushes her into a chair a few feet away from Kate and ties her up with tape and rope but like Kate, he doesn't gag her.

"If you two want to scream, have at it, nobody will hear you. But if you start getting on my nerves I'll gag both of you. And I'll give you something to really scream about." He laughs as he closes the door.

He picks up a mop and bucket from a closet, throws off the cape and mask, removes the voice changer and walks back out to the van. He picks up his phone and sends a text: *There are two of them.*

⅄

Wesley Kootz is driving through the desert on highway 163 outside of Laughlin when he sees three Sheriff's cruisers pass him by in the opposite direction. He keeps an eye on them for as long as he can in his rearview mirror until they fade out of sight. He's not particularly worried about being tracked down in the truck he's driving. He borrowed it from an employee who makes his home in Utah but who also flies under the radar as being "legally" employed by Kootz. He hears his phone ping and reads the text he just received. He pounds his fist on the top of the steering wheel. *Who's the other one?* he texts back.

A second later he gets his answer. Reporter with the *Vegas Sun*. Kootz looks toward the heavens with a demanding stare. The moon and the stars are shining brightly, illuminating the immense desert landscape. He continues to stare off into the distance looking for a sign, but all he sees is a desolate landscape.

The Sheriff's deputies pull up to the tent of The Original Church of God in Jesus' Name. There are no cars, no lights. No one seems to be around. The place looks deserted. Four of them make their way into the tent as the other two walk around the perimeter. The place seems to be abandoned until they come to Kootz's land yacht, a 40ft. luxury motorhome with a mural painted on the side of Kootz staring up at the heavens. There is a small light visible through a window so they pound on the door.

Max jumps up at the unexpected knock. Who could it be at this time of night? He stops the video he's watching and hits ESCAPE simultaneously pulling on his jeans and zipping them up. Nervously he heads to the door.

They knock again. "Clark County Sheriff's Department, open up."

Max opens the door and is confronted by four officers each with flashlights pointing at him. "Yes, sir, officers, how can I help you?" he says squinting and running his hands through his hair.

"Step outside please, and tell us your name."

"Yes, sir. My name is Max, Max Holliday, sir."

"Where's Wesley Kootz?"

"I don't know. Everybody's gone. I'm the only one here."

"Did the Reverend happen to say where he was going?"

"He did say something about going fishing in Idaho."

"When did he leave and what was he driving?"

"I, ah. . .I have no idea," Max stutters and looks nervously back over his shoulder.

"Did he say when he was coming back?"

"He gave everybody a week off, so I guess he'll be back then."

"Did you know a young man named Julio Hernandez who worked here?"

Max immediately begins to sweat and feels a nervous cough itching at the back of his throat. He never knew exactly what Julio's relationship was with Kootz but he always thought something about it was odd.

"Yes, sir, I knew him. He was a good kid, is he OK? He up and left a few days ago with some pretty strange people. One of them hit me over the head."

"We need to search this vehicle but you're free to go. However, if you hear from Kootz or he shows up, we expect you to contact us immediately. We have a warrant for his arrest."

Max sputters out "What did he do?" between coughs.

"Human trafficking and sex with a minor."

"No, not Reverend Kootz. He'd never do anything like that, I know he wouldn't."

"If you hear from him or about him, call us, Max. Otherwise you could get in a lot of trouble for harboring a fugitive. Got it?"

"Yes sir, got it. Yes, sir." Max steps back into the motorhome and nervously heads for the bathroom.

A few minutes after the deputies finally leave Max sends a text: *Cops looking for you. Have a warrant for your arrest.*

CHAPTER 40

Our Cabin in the Woods

"Kate?. . .Kate? Are you all right?" whispers Roxy.

Both women are tied and bound to wooden chairs sitting in the middle of a small room in the musty cabin. A pungent odor hangs in the air that Roxy can't quite identify.

"Kate, talk to me."

"I'm not feeling well, Roxy. What's that smell? It's putrid."

"I don't know, it's very strange." Roxy looks down past her feet at the wooden floor. Blotches of dark, uneven stains run across the planks then stop a few feet away.

"Where do you think we are?" murmurs Kate.

"Somewhere in the mountains outside Vegas is my guess."

"Who the hell is this guy and what does he want with us?"

"I don't know, Kate. Maybe Nick was right. I hope not. Now I hope Bobby was the killer."

"What do you mean? You think this guy is Leviticus?"

"I don't know but we better pray he isn't."

"Shit, I'm scared, Roxy," says Kate, voice trembling.

"Me too, Kate."

"No, you don't understand. I'm scared I may lose my baby. I'm having pains."

"Oh my God. You're pregnant?"

"Yes, but I've been having some problems. I don't want to lose this baby, can't even stand to think about it and Nick would be devastated."

"Nick?. . .Nick's the father? I mean. . .sorry, that's none of my business."

"No, no, it's OK. Yes, Nick's the father."

"You need to tell this jerk what's going on right away. He has to let you go. You haven't seen his face yet so maybe it's not too late."

"You really think he'll believe me? I mean, I'm not even showing yet."

"I don't know but we have to try. Let's get him in here."

Roxy starts yelling for him to come in. Even outside in the van he can hear her hollering. Irritated, he throws on Darth Vader again and trudges to the cabin to see what all the commotion is about.

He storms straight into the room where they're being held. "Shut up! What the hell do you want? Stop that damn yelling."

Roxy speaks up, clear and strong, taking a gamble that he won't immediately slit her throat. "Listen. Do you know who she is? She's Kate Simon, a reporter with the *Vegas Sun*."

"I don't care if she's Princess Leah."

Roxy rolls the dice. "She's pregnant. She's going to have a baby. You have to let her go."

"Why the hell should I believe you?" he growls. "She doesn't look pregnant."

"You just need to believe me. Besides, you don't want her, you were after me, right?"

"Maybe, but it's her bad luck. Real bad luck."

"Please let me go." Kate chokes out the words through her tears and sobs. "Please. I don't know who you are so I can't hurt you. I won't say a word to anybody. I promise."

"Fuck you, sweetheart. You think I'm some kind of idiot?"

"Just let her go," Roxy begs. "Drive her back to the convenience store and at least give her a chance. You don't want to kill an innocent woman and her unborn child do you?" Roxy plays her trump card. "What would God think about that?"

Now he's angry. He spits in Roxy's face and backhands her, sending her head rebounding hard off the back of the wooden chair and falling forward. Roxy wails as her eyes roll and she passes out. "So, now you're religious, are you? Maybe I should just nail you to a cross? That can be arranged. Now both of you shut up or you'll be sucking on duct tape again."

He stomps out of the room, locks the door behind him and enters the front room. He immediately notices lights coming up the road. Soon he sees a pick-up truck approaching the cabin and readies his gun. The truck stops and out steps Wesley Kootz. He puts away the gun.

⚘

Every night around 10:30 when the Quickie Mart closes Crazy George makes his way to the dumpster on the side of the building. Crazy George is a homeless vet who did two tours of duty in Iraq, but the last several years he's been a fixture around Cold Creek. During his last tour his unit got pinned down by sniper fire. Six of the eight men were killed and the other two wounded. George was one of the wounded. After spending two years in a hospital and enduring multiple surgeries, he finally got released. The bad news was he had nowhere to go.

For years after getting stateside he tried to find his way back into society. He looked for work and tried to make friends, but it was hard, not like the military where he knew exactly who he was and what he was expected to do. One job after another always wound up the same. He would quit in frustration or get fired for his temper. Finally he gave up and took to the road which eventually led him to Cold Creek, a small town just an hour or so from Vegas in the foothills of the Spring Mountains.

He likes the weather here even though it can get awfully cold in the winter. Most of all he likes the solitude. The locals tolerate him and a few have been very kind to him.

He rifles through the dumpster, carefully picking out bits of thrown-away sandwiches and chip bags with a few crumbs left. He can almost always find a half-full bottle of water or cup of Coke.

Tonight while he's foraging for dinner, he sees two, hand-size objects wrapped in aluminum foil. He pulls them from the dumpster and sets them aside. With all the necessities for his evening meal retrieved from the slop and grime of the garbage, he takes the objects and pulls away the foil. He smiles and slowly shakes his head as he unwraps the two cell phones. Might be worth some money if they work, he thinks. He searches for each phone's ON button and much to his surprise they both come alive. Crazy George feels like he's won the lottery.

He puts the phones in his backpack along with some leftovers and starts walking down the shoulder of the highway. He watches the waning October moon rise over the nearby mountains. The evening is cool, the air is crisp and clean and he's at peace. About a mile later he turns off the highway and follows a barely noticeable path into the woods. He comes to a simple lean-to in a clearing. He's home after a long day, a good day. He crawls into his sleeping bag and begins dreaming of the war one more time.

⚑

Alice and I have been poring over files for hours anxious for more clues. It's approaching midnight and both of us are feeling the emotion of the day. Finally I take my legal pad and flip it over.

"Time to go home, Alice. We've come up with a lot but we aren't going to accomplish any more when we're this tired. Let's get a fresh start early tomorrow morning."

"You're right, Nick. Can you drop me at my apartment?"

I give Alice a ride to her place then I head home to my apartment. I can only think of Kate. Kate, who is under doctor's orders to rest. Kate, who almost lost the baby and Kate, who maybe in the hands of a serial killer.

I struggle to get to sleep thinking about all the horrible possibilities Kate and Roxy may be facing. I say a prayer. Then take out my phone and call Kate one more time. The phone starts to ring and just as I expect it to go to voice mail, it doesn't. I'm hoping and praying she answers. Then a sleepy male voice says, "Hello?"

"Hello, who is this? Let me speak to Kate."

"Who?"

"Kate, I'm calling Kate Simon. You have her phone. Where is she?"

"Don't know no Kate. Found the phone at the Quickie Mart."

"Who are you and where are you?" I ask, trying to dial down the panic in my voice.

"I'm here and I'm goin' back to sleep, mister."

"No . . .No! Who are you? Where are you? I need your help."

"Cold Creek, good-bye."

The line goes dead. I frantically try to call again but this time the phone's been turned off. I leave a message with my phone number for whoever it was that answered Kate's phone. I make it clear that I will pay a reward for the phone if he contacts me. I beg for his help.

Now I'm wide awake with thoughts racing through my mind like wild fire. I call Lyle but no answer so I leave a message. The same happens when I try to call Alice.

I contemplate going downtown and telling the cops what's happening in the hope they might start an investigation, but it's one o'clock in the morning and I know how slowly things move in the middle of the night. I can't stay here and wait. I throw some things in a duffle bag and grab my keys, then I realize I don't have my gun. I had to leave it with Jo at the airport and she hasn't sent it back yet. I have no choice. I have to go and I have to go now. I'll get a jump on things by being at Cold Creek in the morning. Then I'll call Lyle and get things rolling.

CHAPTER 41

To Sleep is to Dream

Kootz walks over to the van where he hears the static monotone chatter of the police scanner.

"You picking up anything?"

"No, nothing yet. So far no search underway."

"Good. Now what are we going to do about that reporter?"

"I don't know. She says she's pregnant."

"Oh that's just great. You believe her?"

"Maybe, she did throw up in the van."

"Have they seen your face yet?"

"No, I thought I'd better keep it hidden until we decided what we were going to do."

"What do you think?"

"I say kill them both. No loose ends." He kicks at the ground with his boot as if to punctuate his comment.

"You have a point, but maybe. . .maybe this is an blessed opportunity. Maybe we could use the reporter to tell our story of

God's plan. We get our point of view in the news by a credible reporter who we let live to talk about it." Kootz raises both arms in the air like he's onstage.

"Knock it off, Kootz. This isn't a revival and I'm not your stupid audience. Besides, what makes you think she'll cooperate with us to spread the word? She might just turn to the cops. I say no, kill them. That's what God wants, that's what Scripture tells us. "

"No, listen, she'll do whatever we say because there's a story in it and reporters love a good story. Plus, if she really is pregnant. . .well, that would give us some leverage."

"Son of a bitch. Don't you think it'd be better if they were both found dead. That would spread the Word and strike fear into all of them."

"Let me at least talk to her."

"Fine, but wear the Vader suit. It's better if they think there's only one of us."

"Good point. Let's get some sleep. I need to think this through and ask God for guidance. We need to be sure we understand what He wants known about the coming revelations." Kootz looks up at the stars with a serious stare then closes his eyes.

"OK, let's pray. Why don't you take the cabin. I'll sleep in the van."

▲

Roxy is still awake, adrenalin keeping her on high alert as if she's guarding precious cargo. Kate has nodded off into a fitful sleep, her face twitching in unconscious grimaces of pain.

Roxy's high begins to fade as she struggles to stay awake, fearing the worst for the both of them if she falls asleep. She tries hard to keep her eyes open but finally falls into a deep, but turbulent sleep and begins to dream.

Roxy is sitting in a courtroom next to the lawyer who is representing her. She looks across the room and sees the prosecuting attorney. Sitting next to him is her former self, Raymond Tisdale. She grabs her lawyer's arm and pulls him close as she leans in.

"What is going on? Why am I here?" Roxy demands.

"You're on trial, dear," replies the attorney.

"On trial for what?"

The attorney huffs. "For stealing Raymond Tisdale's soul and banishing him from life."

"What are you talking about? This is crazy."

"Yes, yes," says the lawyer matter-off-factly. "I hear that a lot, but Raymond petitioned God from the Well of Souls and received the right to know his Judgment Day."

"What in the hell does that mean?"

"It means that if Raymond wins this trial he will return to life as if nothing ever happened. You will never have existed and will take his place in the Well of Souls where you will await your own Judgment Day."

"I can't believe this. I'm leaving." Roxy leans forward to rise from her chair.

"Sorry, dear, but your legs have been removed until the trial is over."

The bailiff, who is dressed all in black with a white tie and white gloves, walks to the center of the room. "Hear ye, hear ye, this court is now in session. All those with legs please rise for the honorable Judge Lucifer Hyde presiding."

The judge walks in wearing a long, red robe. His thick, black, horn-rimmed glasses practically eliminate his eyes. His wispy, white hair seems to float on the top of his oddly squared head.

"*Please be seated. Bailiff, what's on the docket?*"

"*We have Raymond Tisdale vs. Roxy Lynn, Your Honor, a case of soul-stealing.*"

"*Will the defendants please rise if you can.*" *The judge looks them both over, squinting hard when he looks at Roxy.* "*Oh God, is this another one of those shemale cases?*"

Roxy grabs her lawyer. "*Hey, he can't say that, it's not fair.*"

"*Shhhsh, be quiet, you'll piss him off.*"

The judge looks up, adjusts his glasses and says, "*You're up first, Mr. Prosecutor. Make your case.*"

"*Thank you, Your Honor. It's a pleasure to be in your courtroom. This is an outright case of soul-stealing your honor. The defendant took advantage of Mr. Tisdale when he was very vulnerable. She stole his soul, became a woman and then abandoned Mr. Tisdale for eternity.*"

"*Thank you, Mr. Prosecutor. Now, how about the defense, what do you have?*"

"*Nothing at this time, Your Honor.*"

Roxy spins around and glares at her lawyer. She can't believe what he just said. "*What do you mean nothing at this time? Defend me, you moron.*"

The judge bangs his gavel. "*Tell your client to hush up, Defense, or I'll have her gagged.*"

"*Yes, Your Honor.*"

"*I'm ready to give my verdict. Will the defendant please rise? Oh, never mind. . .I find the defendant guilty of soul-stealing in the first degree and sentence her to eternity in the Well of Souls. The plaintiff may now assume his former life.*"

"*Thank you, Your Honor,*" *the prosecutor says as he bows before the judge.*

Roxy shakes her head in disbelief. "What the hell is going on here? This wasn't a trial it was a lynching."

The judge peers over his glasses down at Roxy and shakes his head. "Defense council, you need to explain the law to your client. Court is adjourned."

"What the hell is he talking about and what's your name anyhow? I'm damn sure it isn't Atticus Finch."

"God's law is very precise about this kind of thing. Duality is a mortal sin. It will not and can not be tolerated. Only one person can inhabit the soul and since Raymond Tisdale had it first, it's being returned to him."

"But I am Raymond Tisdale, he is part of me. I didn't abandon him."

"Sorry, Miss Lynn, but God is very clear about this. Only one person can inhabit a soul. His kingdom could not exist in a dual universe."

"Then maybe it shouldn't. What's going to happen to me now?"

"Execution is another process. I have no part in that. They will come for you soon."

"Execution?"

A scream startles Roxy awake. She jumps, as her body impulsively strains against the ropes she nearly falls backward in her chair. As she wakes up she's unsure if she screamed or it was Kate.

"Kate. . .Kate? Are you OK? Did you just scream or did I?"

"I don't know," Kate says with labored breathing. "I just woke up. I'm having some horrible pains."

Exhausted and terrified, Roxy tries to comfort Kate. "Maybe I just dreamt it. Maybe this is all just a bad dream. C'mon, Kate, you can make it. Hang in there."

It's still dark when I pull into Cold Creek. I find a rundown little Quick Shop on the outskirts of town that's not open yet. I pull into their lot, turn off the engine and fall asleep within a few minutes.

The smell of diesel and the metal clunk-and-bang of a delivery truck wakes me. The sun's just rising and the store's now brightly lit inside and out. I hold open the door for a guy with his dolly full of packaged crap snacks and go in to get some coffee and a roll. The bleary-eyed young man behind the counter is busy checking in another vendor and counting all the six packs of beer on his handcart.

The kid rings me up and without a glance says, "That'll be four dollars and thirty cents." I flip him a five and tell him to keep the change. He looks at me with a sincere but shy smile. Shit, what's wrong with this country when someone who comes to work at 5 a.m. is so grateful for a seventy cent tip? I take a sip of coffee and ask about the hunting in these parts.

"Depends on what you're looking for, mister, plenty of deer but not much else."

"Thanks. Say, I'm looking for a friend of mine who owns a cabin up here. He drives a white Ford van. You wouldn't happened to have seen one anytime yesterday, would you?"

"I see a lot of people come and go. I don't pay much attention most of the time."

"He's about my size with dark hair, maybe a little gray in it."

I can see the kid is trying to think hard and help me out. Must be that tip.

"Come to think of it, I did see a white van last night. The man came in and bought a sandwich. He had a cap pulled down over his face so I didn't get a good look at him. I remember though because I thought it was a little weird when he walked all the way across the parking lot to throw away his trash."

"Why's that so strange?"

"Well, 'cause there was a trash can right next to his van. He could have put his stuff in it but instead he walks all the way over to the dumpster. It was like he was trying to get rid of something."

"Do you have security cameras in the store?"

"Yeah, we do. The monitors work but the recorder's been out awhile."

"Did you happen to see which way he drove off?"

"Toward the mountains I think, but ain't sure."

Another vendor walks in and the kid shrugs apologetically, "I gotta get to work, mister."

I thank him and walk out the door. My phone immediately rings. It's Lyle.

"Got your message, Nicky. Where are you?"

"Cold Creek. Just talked to a store clerk who thinks he saw the van last night."

"You stay put, Nicky, until I can get some deputies out there. I'm on my way to the office now so it's going to take a little while."

"Have you run a trace locator on the phones?"

"I've called it in but haven't heard anything back yet. I'll call you as soon as I get something."

"Somebody's got them, Lyle. This isn't good. We need to find them fast."

I disconnect before Lyle can tell me to stay put again. I try calling Kate's phone but it's turned off. Roxy's too, no luck.

Lyle's phone rings right after talking to Nick. He looks at the caller I.D. which only says PRIVATE NUMBER.

"Hello?"

"Lyle, it's Tucker, I'm just checking in. Can you give me an update?"

"Oh, Tucker, it's you. How's your mother doing?"

"My mother's been dead for three years. I went to see my grandmother, I just call her mother."

"Oh. Sorry."

"So what do you have for me, Lyle?"

"Well, there's a warrant out for Wesley Kootz's arrest. It seems a young Latino boy who was working for him was actually kidnapped by a trafficker and sold to Kootz." Lyle sighs with disgust. "Sex and cheap labor."

The phone goes quiet and Lyle can hear a hesitation in Tucker's voice as he tries to speak. He sounds all choked up and unable to talk.

"You OK, Captain?"

"A warrant huh? Yeah, yeah. . .I used to know Kootz. We grew up in the same town. Were friends at one time." Tucker clears his throat again. "OK, got it. Anything else?"

"Yeah, may have a kidnapping on our hands. That showgirl Roxy Lynn and Kate Simon, a reporter from the *Sun* are missing.

Need more evidence but it's looking like foul play so I'm starting a search."

"When did this happen?" Tucker's voice now deliberate and strong.

"Last night. We think they were taken at Roxy's apartment and Kate just happened to be there which certainly puts Bobby Westbrook in doubt as our serial killer. Either that or maybe we have a copycat on our hands."

"Or maybe Westbrook had a partner. Any leads?"

"We do. I'm on my way to the office right now to get things rolling. We have the make and model of a vehicle that may be involved and a possible location in the Cold Creek area."

"Sounds like it's going to be at least a couple of hours before you get things going."

"Probably, but I'll get any deputies in that area started right away." Lyle braces for Tucker's reaction to what he's about to tell him next. "Oh. . .yeah, and Captain? Nick Ross is already there looking for them." Lyle says quietly.

"*What!* What the hell's he doing there?"

"Someone must have dumped Roxy and Kate's cell phones. Nick called them last night and whoever answered told him he was in Cold Creek. Maybe they dumped the phones and somebody found them. Doesn't mean they're in Cold Creek, but it might."

"You get a handle on him, you hear? Restrain him if you have to, dammit."

"I told him to stay put, Captain, that deputies were on the way, but you know Nick."

"Call me when you get up there. I'll text you my number. I want updates."

"Yes, sir." Lyle sighs and shakes his head, glad to get off the phone.

⟁

He turns off the scanner, gets out of the van and stretches. It's a cool, fall morning and a taste of winter is in the air. He looks toward the sky and begins to pray. There's anger in his voice. He now knows about the warrant for Kootz.

Inside the cabin Wesley Kootz wakes up thinking he heard a scream. It's quiet now, maybe he dreamed it. He listens by the bedroom door but hears nothing, so he walks outside to the back of the van where the door is open.

"Good morning," Kootz says. He's immediately startled by the angry reaction he gets. "You OK? Something wrong?"

"I'm fine," comes the irritated response. "Just didn't sleep very well. Think I need some coffee."

"Me too. Anything on the scanner yet?"

"I haven't checked it but I will," he lies, concealing his rage.

"I think I have a plan. After praying last night things began to come together. I'm thinking we tell the reporter that both she and Roxy can live, but only if she follows our instructions." Kootz smiles, confident his plan will be met with approval.

"And what would those instructions be?"

Oblivious to his searing contempt, Kootz continues. "Help us spread the word. I've been writing down what we want to share about God and His will for all of us. I'll give her Scripture to quote and explain what it all means. I'll tell her the reasons behind what's been done in the name of God and tell her why our army must grow."

"You really think we should let both of them go?"

"Look, we tell her we'll hold Roxy hostage until we see if she can get something published. If she can make that happen, help support our cause, then we let her go."

"You think she's going to believe you?" he sneers.

"What choice does she have? If she refuses I'll slit Roxy's throat right in front of her, then hers too."

"We can't let that disgusting shemale go. I want to see her repent. Then I want to see her dead."

"Me too," Kootz smirks. "Kill her as soon as I get the reporter out of here."

"OK, got it, but I think we need a back-up plan just in case something goes wrong. Let's shuttle the pick-up down to the lake. That way we can get out of here on foot if we have to and have transportation waiting for us."

"Amen to that."

⋏

I'm sitting in my car on the lot of the convenience store thinking about what to do next. I've talked to Lyle and I just got off the phone with Alice. I talked to my father earlier and explained the situation to him. Thankfully, it seems that his friend Martha will be staying with him for a few days while he recovers.

I try to imagine what the driver of the van had in mind when he walked over to the dumpster to throw something away. Why wouldn't he have put whatever it was in the trash can right next to the van? I check the dumpster but it's empty. I'm back in the car and about to drive off when my phone rings. It's Lyle again.

"Nick, we've got a location on the phones. I had them put yours in too so we could coordinate. The phones are about a mile from where you are now, just off the highway on your right side."

"Is there anything there, a house or something?"

"We don't see anything. Looks like somebody may have tossed them out. I've got deputies on the way, they should be there in twenty to thirty minutes. Don't leave till they get there."

"Yeah, OK, Lyle. I'll wait." Not happening.

I start my car and leave immediately, checking my odometer so I can clock a mile. As I get closer, I spot a turn-off onto a narrow, nearly-hidden gravel road. I pull in slowly. T-Birds aren't known for their clearance. After about fifty yards the road disappears. I get out, look around and see what seems to be a path leading into the woods.

I start down the trail feeling apprehensive, wishing I had my gun. I follow the path as it cuts through the thick underbrush, and down a small hill. As it curves to the right, I see a grove of pine trees and what looks like a roughly constructed lean-to up ahead. There's a rustle of leaves, then a deep grunt behind me. Before I can turn around I feel the blow to my head, then everything goes dark as I fall to the ground.

CHAPTER 42

CRAZY IN A GOOD WAY

"*Hey! Get in* here. We need help! *Please!*" Roxy hollers again and again as she watches Kate, eyes squeezed shut, try to double over against the pain.

At the van they can hear Roxy's cries for help. "I'll go," he says to Kootz as he puts Darth Vader back on. "You stay out of sight."

He goes into the cabin, unlocks the bedroom door and enters the room. Kate sits in the chair, her face pale and sweaty, her breathing labored and slow.

"She needs help. She needs a doctor. Untie her for God's sake," Roxy pleads.

He walks over to Kate and fumbles with the rope as he tries to untie her. Kate rubs her bruised wrists and looks up at him angrily with tears in her eyes. "I need to go to the bathroom, now."

He's silent as he cuts the tape around her ankles, grabs her by the arm and pulls her out of the room. Once in the bathroom he stands by the open door like a sentinel, watching her.

"Close the goddamn door," Kate screams. " I need some privacy. I'm not going to try anything. I can barely walk. Just close it!"

He slams the door shut and pounds his fist on it. "You got two minutes."

Kate pulls down her jeans and sees the blood-soaked underwear sticking to her body. She quickly takes them off and tries to clean herself with water and a rag that's been left lying on the bathroom floor. The blood won't stop.

She sits on the toilet, each cramp leaving her feeling more faint and lightheaded than the one before. Exhausted, the waves of pain eventually begin to subside. She knows what has just happened.

"What are you doing in there?"

"I need more time. I'm sick. Leave me alone." Kate can barely get the words out.

"What?" he hollers. "I can't hear you."

"I'm sick. Leave me alone," Kate moans.

He takes a chair props it up against the bathroom door, locking her in. Then he pounds on the door again. "I'll be back for you soon. Don't try anything."

He walks outside and sees Kootz sitting in the van, listening to the scanner. "You hear anything yet?"

"Sounds like they've started a search, we better move fast. You didn't hear anything about me on here when you were listening earlier, did you?"

"No, why would I hear something about you?" He lies again as his anger builds.

"Never mind, forget it. Let's shuttle the truck down. You drive the van."

$$\blacktriangle$$

When I wake up my face is smashed into the leaves and dirt. Everything is blurry and my head is throbbing. I start to lift myself off the ground when I hear a voice in front of me.

"What are you doing here, mister? Why'd you sneak up on me?"

I pull myself to my knees and see a bearded man in front of me holding a club. He looks like he's barely out of high school and has an odd smile on his face. His long, matted hair is pulled back in a ponytail and he's wearing a CPO coat and Dodger's cap.

"I'm looking for the phones. Do you have them?" I ask as I struggle to my feet.

"Oh, are you the guy that called last night?"

"Yes, I'm Nick. What's your name?"

"George."

"Did you get the text message I left you about the reward?"

"Yeah, I got it. Sorry I hit you over the head but I spook pretty easy. I'll get 'em for ya."

As my eyes begin to refocus I look around at his place. The lean-to is simple but cleverly designed, situated between two trees that hide it well. The entrance is propped up with weathered 2 x 4's that can close it off when laid flat. The top has camouflage netting draped over the sides making it almost invisible.

"Here you go. This is how I found them, in the foil."

"Thanks, George. Did you see anyone around where you found them? Two women or a man?"

"Nope. Found them in the dumpster at the Quickie Mart after it closed last night. You gonna' give me three hundred for the both, right?"

"Absolutely, that's what I said. Here you go." I pull out three hundred dollar bills from my wallet and hold them out for him to take. He doesn't even look at them, just stuffs them in his pocket.

"So, you lookin' for somebody around here, mister?"

"Yes, I am. There are two women whose lives may be in danger. I care about them a lot. I think they may be with a man who is armed and dangerous."

"And you think they're hidin' out in these parts?"

"That's my best guess but I have no idea where to begin looking."

"I know these hills like the back of my hand. That's what I do, hike all day. Gives me a sense of peace. You know what I mean?" George squints, his eyes sweeping the hills as if already on the hunt.

"Yeah, I guess. You have any idea where somebody might try to hide out around here?"

"Back up on the ridge would be the most likely place. It's pretty deep into the forest. Not many people go up there except hunters."

"Are there any cabins back there that could be broken into?"

"Yeah, there's a few, but you sure wouldn't want to pick one of those hunting cabins. If one of those boys showed up they'd have some fire power, and they don't take kindly to that sort a thing."

"Well, thanks for your help, George. I really appreciate it." I take the phones and start to walk off when he yells at me.

"Hey, know what? I do know a place. About a year ago the Feds busted a guy up there that was runnin' a meth lab. I heard they seized the property and boarded it all up. Nobody would be goin' near that place unless you wanted to hide."

"Can you take me there?"

"Sure, just let me close things up."

He pulls the boards from the entrance of the lean-to and closes it up, then he pulls down the camo-netting over the front. Every man wants to protect what's his. We walk out together in silence until we get to my car. Then he starts laughing.

"What's the matter, something wrong with my car?"

"No, no, it's a great car but it ain't gonna get us where we need to go. You'll bust an axle real quick."

"So, what can we do?"

"Get in. About a half mile up the road make a right turn, I got a friend who might be able to help us out."

My phone rings. It's Lyle again. "Nicky, where are you? Don't you hang up on me."

"What's up, Lyle?"

"There's a chopper on the way and we're setting up roadblocks. I'm on the way too so you need to stay put and rein it in buddy, got it?"

"You're breaking up, Lyle. I can't hear you. I've got a lead I'm following up on. I'll call you if it pans out." Just as I'm hitting

END I can hear Lyle. "I'll have you arrested, Nick. Tucker says I have to. Nick? Nick?"

⅄

He's listening to the scanner while alone in the van on the ride down the hill. The warrant for Wesley Kootz is being broadcast over and over along with new information about a search now forming in the Cold Creek area for a possible kidnapper. He turns off the scanner and disables one of its power cords before Kootz gets in the van for the ride back.

Kootz climbs in and immediately starts writing out the finishing touches to the message he wants Kate to release to the media.

"I'm telling you, once this message gets out to the public we'll have thousands wanting to join our fight."

"You really think so, huh, Reverend?" He's furious that Kootz has betrayed him, betrayed what he believes in. He's done listening to Kootz's blathering, he's made up his mind.

Kootz is oblivious to his sarcasm. "I'm sure of it. What I've written is very powerful. I think it came straight from the mouth of God. You know, like the Ten Commandments," Kootz says smiling proudly.

"Wonderful, but let me talk to them first. Then we can switch."

⅄

Kate's lying on the floor in the bathroom. Her legs and thighs covered with blood. She opens her eyes and realizes she has no idea how long she's been passed out.

She pulls herself up slowly and begins cleaning off once again. She throws her blood-soaked panties in the trash can and stuffs some tissue into her jeans hoping most of the bleeding has stopped. She hears the chair being pulled away across the floor as the bathroom door opens.

"Come with me." She notices a scar on the back of his hand as he takes her by the arm back into the bedroom and ties her to the chair once again.

Roxy can see that Kate is in a bad way. "She needs a doctor. Can't you see that? She needs help, you son of a bitch. . .do something!"

"Both of you shut up and listen to me."

Roxy fires back. "You'd be a hell of a lot easier to listen to if you took off that stupid Darth Vader outfit and that thing you've got on your voice. It's not Halloween anymore, Darth."

He walks over to Roxy, shoves his hand under her chin and yanks back her head as he pulls out his stiletto and runs it sideways over her throat. He looks over to Kate. "This is what I will do to her if you don't follow my instructions."

Kate trembles as she watches the knife move across Roxy's throat. " I understand. What do you want me to do?"

"I want you to publish the information I'm going to give you and explain to your adoring readers how God saved your life in order to help them avoid eternal damnation."

"I'm not sure what that means, but fine," Kate sighs. "I'll do whatever you say. Just let us go."

He steps back, holds the knife to his lips and lets out an evil, sarcastic laugh.

"No, I've changed my mind. I'm going to slit her throat in front of you so you understand what it's like. I want you to see the power of God and witness His works."

"*No! No!*" Kate begs. "Please don't do that. I promise I'll do whatever you want. *Please.*"

"What about you, Roxy Lynn? Do shemales believe in God? You want to live or should I slit your throat right now?"

"You know I want to live but I'm not begging your sorry ass for my life. I'll take my chances on the other side if my time is up."

"Oh, aren't you shemales the defiant ones. God will deal with you and your kind. You can all spend eternity together being defiant in hell."

"She didn't mean it," Kate pleads, voice quivering. "Please let us go."

He paces back and forth across the room several times. Kate sees a new sense of anxiousness about him.

"Look, I'll give you one more reason to do what I say." He pauses and steps closer to her. "I know why your brother was killed. And I know who did it. I'll tell you why now and if you follow my instructions, I'll tell you who later."

Kate can't believe what she's hearing. All these years not knowing who killed her brother or why and now this monster claims to have those answers. She sits in stunned silence until he demands a reply.

"So, no brotherly love, huh? Fine, I can see to it that you join him very soon."

"No, sorry. . .I mean yes, I loved my brother. I'm just in shock and don't feel well. I swear to God I'll do what you say. Please just tell me what happened."

"You know your brother was gay, right?"

"Yes, I knew that. We were very close."

"Did you know he had a lover at the time he was murdered?"

"I knew he was seeing someone but he wouldn't tell me who. I don't think he wanted me to know because it was someone in the department."

"I'm not saying whether his lover was or wasn't in the department, but this I will tell you: your brother had decided to become a woman. He was going to transition even if it cost him his job. His lover was very angry about his decision and felt betrayed. They argued for months and your brother threatened to expose him. His lover had never come out for fear of ruining his career."

Kate hangs her head and closes her eyes, trying to push down her rage about her brother's murder.

"Who killed Mark?" she snaps losing patience. Her head throbs from hitting it on the bathroom floor when she passed out and from the humming drone of his modulated voice.

"The night your brother was killed he was on a stakeout, closing in on some big-time cartel drug dealers. It was supposed to look like they killed him, but actually he was murdered by his lover. Nick Ross was to be killed that night too but he showed up late because he'd been out drinking and passed out."

"Tell me who did it. Please, I need to know. I'll do whatever you say."

"No, not now, but here's what I will do: I'm going to let you both go. Just remember to follow the instructions I give you exactly or I'll come back for Roxy. I did it once and I can do it again. Oh, and if anything should happen to me don't think you can forget about our deal. There's someone else who knows about this and will carry out the orders I have been given. I'll be back."

"I understand. Now please untie us and let us go."

"Not yet. Someone will find you very soon. Remember me in your dreams."

⟁

I turn on to the road that George is pointing at and follow his directions until we arrive at a dense stand of Ponderosa pines. Off to the right, in a small clearing I see a small, dark cabin.

"This is it. The guy lives completely off the grid," says George as he points to the solar panels and the satellite dish on the roof of the cabin. "Pretty cool, huh?"

"Yeah, cool," I reply though not that interested in discussing the lifestyles of survivalists right now. "You want me to come with you, George?"

"No, you wait here. He's a little skittish about strangers, kinda' like me. Only his war was Vietnam."

I wait in the T-Bird and watch as George knocks on the cabin door. After a few minutes, the door cracks open four or five inches and I can see George talking to someone who's holding a Ruger in his hand. Then I see the other hand reach through the open door and give something to George.

George nods, turns away and starts walking toward a large shed. A few minutes go by when suddenly I hear a loud rumbling. The shed door opens and out comes George behind the wheel of a pristine '68 red Ford Bronco with a bikini top. He pulls the rumbling classic up next to me and shouts, "Get in."

He guns the engine and our heads snap backwards as we lunge forward on to the road. The loose rock pings and ricochets off all four wheel wells as we literally take off. George leans over to me and smiles.

"Put your harness on," he hollers. "When we hit the backroads it's going to get rough."

"Why aren't you wearing yours?"

"Restricts me too much, I like freedom."

"Can I ask you a question, George?"

"Sure, what is it?"

"Why do you constantly have that smile on your face?"

"Oh, I have what's called, 'Angelman' syndrome. Makes you smile all the time even when you don't want to."

"That must put you in some awkward situations."

" Yeah, funerals are a bitch."

CHAPTER 43

LOVE AND HATE

He walks out of the bedroom leaving Roxy and Kate still bound to their chairs. Kootz is standing outside with pen and paper finishing up his litany of instructions "straight from the mouth of God."

"I've finished it. Everything is here on these pages that God wants done. Once the reporter makes this information public the war will begin," Kootz proudly exclaims.

"Good. I've talked to them. Now you put the outfit on and go give them your instructions."

Kootz eagerly takes the outfit and begins to put it on.

"You shouldn't have betrayed God," he bellows inches from Kootz's face.

"What? What are you talking about?" Kootz stumbles and drops the mask.

"The boy you bought and used as a sex slave," he pushes his finger into Kootz's chest.

"Now, wait. . .wait a minute, I can, uh. . .explain," Kootz says stuttering nervously.

"You've betrayed God and you've betrayed me."

"No. No, listen to me," Kootz begs.

"No, you listen to me. I trusted you. I believed in you. I changed my life and my aberrant ways to follow you. But you're a liar and a sinner," he says with an eerie calmness.

He pulls out his gun and places the barrel hard against Kootz's throat. Kootz throws his hands in the air and steps back.

"Get down on your hands and knees and start praying, *Reverend.*"

"I will, I will. . .don't kill me. I was weak. I was a sinner, but I've repented. God forgives sinners, remember? Please, I'll do whatever you want."

He takes the gun by the barrel, swings his arm up in the air and comes down on Kootz's head pistol-whipping him. Kootz falls to the ground, bleeding hard but still conscious. He steps up and places a boot on Kootz's neck so he can't move, waits a moment then bears down harder.

"I killed for you in the name of God. I planted evidence for you to convict an innocent man. But I believed in what I did and can be forgiven if I was wrong. But you, you are a trai-tor. What you have done is unforgivable. Now you can face the Almighty and beg for forgiveness because you'll get none from me. Nobody betrays me."

He drives his boot hard into Kootz's neck and in one pow-erful motion forces it downward, snapping the bones like dried twigs. Kootz's body reacts violently, his muscles contracting until he becomes rigid while his head lays still. Then just as quickly the muscles relax and his body collapses into a limp corpse.

He drags the body across the porch then loads it into the van. He grabs the instructions Kootz had written for Kate and walks back into the cabin. He opens the bedroom door slightly and tosses the papers at Kate then barks out his order.

"Here are your directions. Follow them to the letter or else."

Nick is holding on for dear life as George pilots the Bronco through sliding turns and airborne bumps. "How much longer till we get there, George?"

"Just a few minutes. It's over the crest of that hill up ahead."

My question only seems to make George more excited. He guns the Bronco and we go even faster. Then, just as we crest the top of the hill, a white van appears heading right at us. George slams on the brakes and we skid sideways off the road into the brush as the van shoots by.

"That's him! That's who we are looking for," I shout as I turn and watch the van speed off down the road.

George floors it again and the Bronco bounces back up onto the road with the cabin now in sight. "I need to check that cabin, George, and see if anyone's there, if not we'll go after him."

George doesn't let up till we're right on top of the cabin then he hits the brakes and comes to a sliding stop at the front door. I jump out and start yelling Kate and Roxy's names.

"Nick, in here! We're in here!" They're alive and my heart jumps to my throat.

I rip the latch off the bedroom door and see them tied to the chairs, their exhaustion and anguish clearly apparent despite their relieved smiles.

"Oh my God. . .Are you OK? Either of you hurt?"

"We're fine, just get us out of here," says Kate.

"Give me a second. I'll be right back." I race back to the Bronco to let George know.

"George, they're here and they're safe. Come help me."

"I'm going after him." George signals toward the road.

"No, George, don't. I'm calling the police, they'll catch him. He can't get away now."

"I have to, Nick. You take care of the women."

Before I can stop him, George smiles, waves and disappears over the ridge, the Bronco fading away in a cloud of dust. I turn and run back into the cabin.

"OK, ladies, I'm going to get you both untied but I need to call Lyle first and let him know what's going on. Every second counts in nailing this psycho."

"Do it, Nick, we're fine. They need to catch that son of a bitch," Roxy says with more than a hint of revenge in her voice.

I reach for my phone as I bend over to kiss Kate on the forehead. She doesn't look well. "Lyle. I found them, they're alive."

"Nick. Where the hell, are you? What's going on?"

"The kidnapper just left. If you ping my phone you can get the location. We're up on the mountain, somewhere and. . ."

"Nick," Roxy interrupts. "Tell him that Kate needs medical help. She had a miscarriage."

What Roxy just said is like a blow to my gut. I look at Kate but her head is hanging down.

"Kate needs medical attention, Lyle."

"Got it, Nick. I'll have the chopper put down as close to you as possible once we get the coordinates. They'll fly her out."

"Oh, and there's a guy in a red Bronco chasing the van, Lyle. He's on our side."

"Got it. Don't worry, we'll get this son of a bitch. I promise."

George is flying down the mountain at breakneck speeds, sliding through corners and flooring it on the straights. The dangerous section of the road is just beginning when he sees the vehicle he's after up ahead.

Now that he has the van in sight, he punches the Bronco even harder until he's almost on top of it. It's obvious the driver now knows he's being chased.

George's mind has transported him back to the barren and dusty roads of Iraq in pursuit of the enemy. The sensations he would feel during a firefight have returned and he feels fully alive as he drives faster and faster.

The single lane road has little room to pull alongside or pass. George waits for an opening, adrenaline pumping through his veins. He's sure the driver of the van will try to keep him from passing. As they round a corner, George sees a break. He floors the Bronco and swerves to the right, then quickly reverses veering back to the left. He pulls alongside the van, determined to force him over.

The van lunges and tries to run him off the road, but George drops back to avoid getting pushed into the mountain. He guns the Bronco again as the road widens and storms in alongside the van ready to do battle.

This time the window of the van is open and a .45 is pointed straight at George. *Pop, pop, pop.* The first bullet tears through George's jaw spinning his head around. The second just misses shattering the windshield. The third enters George's neck cleanly severing his carotid artery. Blood erupts violently from the wound spraying a deep, pink mist into the air. George slumps over and falls out of the Bronco right before it hits the canyon wall and rolls several times. The van George was pursuing comes to a stop in the middle of a sharp turn that overlooks a 300-foot drop-off. He pulls Kootz's body into the driver's seat and puts the untraceable gun in his hand.

He shoves the gearshift into D, gets out and slams the driver's door with a push forward to start it rolling. He watches as it approaches the edge of the cliff then smiles as it rolls and bounces against the side of the mountain, the sharp red rocks shredding it on the way down. Finally it hits the bottom of the ravine and bursts into flames. He walks away. It's only a short distance down the road to the trail that will lead him to where the pick-up truck is waiting.

▲

I work on untying Kate while I'm talking to Lyle. I can tell she's very weak. My blood is boiling thinking about the asshole who did this to her and Roxy.

"I love you. Everything will be all right," I say hugging her, nuzzling her sweat-soaked hair. "You're safe now."

I feel her shaking as she begins to cry. "It's OK, it's OK, I'm here, Kate. You need to rest. Come with me, you can lie down on the bed until we get help."

I help Kate on to the bed, then set about getting Roxy untied. When she can finally stand up she throws her arms around me. "Oh my God, Nick, you don't know how good it feels to be free. Thank you, thank you."

"Did he hurt you? Are you OK? I was so worried when I couldn't reach either of you on your phones."

"Yeah, Nick, I'm fine. He threatened us repeatedly and slapped me around pretty hard, but I'm alright, at least physically. Not so sure about the psychological part though. I may never get another good night sleep again."

Within minutes, a line of police vehicles descend on the cabin. Lights and sirens pierce the silence as they arrive in a billowing cloud of dust. Lyle steps out alongside several deputies and walks toward me.

"You all right, Nick? Are the girls OK?"

"I'm fine and Roxy seems to be all right. It's Kate I'm worried about. I think she needs to go to the hospital. She just had a miscarriage."

"I'll radio the chopper and have him land as soon as possible. We'll get her out of here and back to Vegas."

"Thanks, Lyle."

"You do know I should arrest you for interfering in police business, but you know I'm not going to, don't you?"

I look at Lyle and realize just how exhausted I am. And grateful. I extend my hand. "Yeah, I know, and I really appreciate it, Lyle." My mind shifts back to the killer. "You catch the van yet?"

"I've got some bad news on that front, Nick. Your buddy who was chasing the van is dead. The chopper spotted the crash site a few minutes ago when they saw the fire."

"What fire? What happened?"

"We think maybe he was trying to run the van off the road when he crashed into the mountain. The van missed a turn, went over the cliff, and caught fire when it hit the bottom of the ravine."

"Son of a bitch, Lyle, that guy gave his life for people he didn't even know. He really was a soldier and every bit an angel."

"I've got deputies arriving at the scene now. We'll see if any shots were fired." Lyle pauses to rub his ear. "Let's get you guys out of here. I'm having the house sealed off until CSI gets here."

"I'll go get Kate and Roxy ready, but please let me know as soon as you find out who was driving that van."

▲

He gets to the pick-up, starts it up and pulls out of the parking area on to the main highway. After a few miles he sees police cars up ahead with lights flashing. Two cars are in front of him and both begin to slow down as they approach the roadblock.

Deputies have both cars in front of him pull over for a search. He approaches slowly and rolls down his window. As a young deputy walks up to the truck, he reaches down, pulls out a shield and flips it open in the deputy's face without a comment. The deputy waves him through.

The lieutenant at the road block wonders why the pick-up wasn't stopped and calls the deputy over to him. "Why wasn't that pick-up searched, deputy?"

"He had a badge, sir, so I let him through."

"Do you know what kind of badge it was?"

"I don't know for sure his hand was blocking part of it. I think it ended with a 'I'."

"You mean like CSI?"

"No, I've seen those they look different."

"Could it have been FBI?"

"It's possible, I just can't say for sure."

CHAPTER 44

DELIVERANCE

As I sit in a waiting room at University Medical Center the events of the past few days fully occupy my thoughts. Kate's going to be all right, thank God. She lost a lot of blood and is severely dehydrated, but the doctor said she will make a full recovery. I just hope a full recovery includes body and soul.

I know this has been hard on her. I can see it in her eyes. The deep heartaches from my own past keep trying to surface but this time it's different. Kate's alive, we have each other and I feel stronger. The last twenty-four hours have changed me in some way. The power that had consumed me and had given me the ability to look beyond the veil has shifted. I felt it when I looked into Kate's eyes at the cabin and knew something was wrong. I still feel a presence, but now it's in my heart.

The nurse walks into the waiting room and taps me on the shoulder. "Mr. Ross, you can see her now but don't be too long, she needs her rest."

I open the door to Kate's room and look in. She's lying there in bed with an IV in her arm and several wires running from electrodes to a monitor bedside. She sees me and looks up with a tender smile.

"Hello, Nick, you miss me?

I'm a real sucker for sweet but smart-ass women. I smile and walk to the bed. "Missing you would be an understatement for what I've felt," I say taking her hand in mine. "How *are* you ?"

"A whole lot better now that I'm not the prisoner of a serial killer."

"I bet there aren't a lot of people who can make that statement, sweetheart." Her grin breaks into a full-fledged but weary smile.

Then she turns serious. "Have they caught him, Nick?" Kate's been out ever since they put her on the helicopter and has no idea what's been happening.

"He's dead, Kate. The van went over a cliff and it burst into flames when it hit the bottom."

Kate sits up grabbing her sheets. "Oh no. . .he said he knew who killed my brother and would tell me if I helped him. Dammit! Who was he, Nick? Have they identified him?"

"What? Your brother? Easy, sweetheart, you still need to rest. When we find out who he was we'll know a lot more. I'm meeting up with Lyle later and he's going to fill me in. I'll let you know what I find out, but right now you just rest."

"I will but I really need to know, it helps. By the way, I guess you're off the hook now."

"What do you mean, off the hook?"

"Well, you know what I mean. You don't have any commitment to me anymore."

"What are you talking about, Kate? I love you, that hasn't changed."

We sit in silence for awhile. Not the uncomfortable kind but the content kind where both people are thinking. Kate looks up first. "How are you doing, Nick. . .really."

I look into Kate's eyes and see a sadness there that only a woman can know. A tear begins its journey down her cheek, as I take her hand and move closer to her on the bed.

"Listen, Kate. You and I both know nobody gets through this life without pain. All we can hope for is at least an equal amount of joy and someone to share it with. The crazy psycho who abducted you will never know happiness or sorrow. In the last two weeks I've learned more about myself and life than in my first 40 years. And this is what I'm absolutely sure of. . .I love you and I want to be with you. We can start over, together."

"I'd like that, Nick. I love you, too."

I take her in my arms as well as I can, maneuvering around wires and tubing. I hold her close and feel her hug back. What a wonderful feeling, I hope it never ever ends.

I hear the door open behind us and Kate's nurse enters the room. "It's getting late, sir, and she needs her rest."

"OK, I'll leave soon, just give us a minute."

"Of course."

"The doctor says you can go home in the morning, sweetheart. I'll be here first thing. Sleep well, love you." I lean forward to kiss her but she's already fallen asleep.

Back in my T-Bird, cruising down the Strip, I'm feeling better than I have in a long time so it doesn't surprise me when Mr. Petty comes on the radio singing about finally feeling good, one special woman and about the pain-in-the-ass waiting it took to get there. I'm almost to O'Connell's to meet Lyle and Alice when my phone rings, it's Roxy.

"Nick, my hero, it's Roxy. How's Kate doing?"

"She's going to be fine, she just needs some rest. How are you? I've been thinking about you and was just going to call."

"Not so good, actually. I'm pretty scared, Nick."

"Now what's wrong, Roxy?"

"I can't help feeling like there was more than one killer. I thought I heard voices when we were tied up at the cabin, but they were so faint and I was so tired, I couldn't be sure."

"Have you told the police? Have they questioned you yet?"

"No, I'm suppose to meet with them in the morning, but that's the other thing, I'm really scared I'll be arrested for that bank robbery. Actually, I don't know if I'm going to show up or not."

"What else can you do, Roxy? What are you thinking?"

"I'm thinking I might just leave town."

"No, don't do it, that won't solve anything. Look. I'm meeting Lyle at O'Connell's in a few minutes, why don't you join us and talk to him. He's a straight shooter and I promise you won't be arrested. Might even be a surprise there for you."

"I don't like surprises. I don't know, Nick. Let me think about it and I'll call you back."

Roxy is shaking as he hangs up from talking to Nick. "I'm not going to prison," she says quietly, then walks into her bedroom and starts packing a bag.

When I get to O'Connell's I see the usual crowd. Just off the end of the bar, Lyle and Alice are sitting cozily at a table having a drink. Alice smiles when she sees me and motions toward the table.

"Nick, over here."

I get to the table and she immediately throws her arms around me and gives me a big hug. Then she backs up and puts a hand on her heart. "Lyle filled me in, Nick. I was so relieved to find out everything turned out OK, but I'm sorry about Kate. Is she going to be all right?"

"Kate's fine, Alice, thanks. She's coming home tomorrow."

Lyle runs his finger around the rim of his Jack and Coke, looks up and smiles at me. "Have a seat, buddy, and I'll fill you in on what we know."

Alice grabs my arm. "How about a drink, Nick? Hey, Jimmy, get Nick a Mississippi highball."

"Sure thing, Alice," says Jimmy from behind the bar. "One ice water comin' right up."

"Thanks, Alice, very creative," I say taking a seat. "So, Lyle, what do you have for me?"

"Well, we identified the body in the van. It was Wesley Kootz. We also found the .45 he used to kill that buddy of yours who was chasing him."

"Not a buddy but definitely a good guy. Any sign of a second person possibly being involved? Roxy thinks there may have been another man at the cabin. She thought she heard voices."

"No evidence that would support that yet, but we're still doing DNA testing."

"Where's this leave the Westbrook case? Any changes?"

"Absolutely not. If anything it reinforces it. Looks like old Kootz and Westbrook were working together. The killings started shortly after Westbrook joined up with Kootz's show. We think Bobby was setting the victims up and Kootz was killing them. Sick sons of bitches."

"So then why would Westbrook run?"

"Who knows. Maybe he got cold feet, or maybe he and Kootz had a falling out. Hard to say."

"What about Tucker? He lied about his mother, there's a lot of evidence that points to him and from what I've seen he's pretty much an asshole. Sorry, Alice."

"No problem, Nick," Alice says sipping her drink. "Big improvement over your typical use of 'fucking asshole'."

Lyle winks at Alice then turns back to me. "I talked to him, Nick. He didn't lie about his mother. He went to visit his grandmother and that's what he calls her—mom All the other evidence is purely speculative."

"I don't know, Lyle, there's something there. I can feel it."

"Well, you won't have to worry about it for awhile. Tucker just got picked to be on the advance security team for the Olympics in Rio. He's heading down there along with that guy McCain from the FBI to work with the local police departments."

"And what about Roxy? Is she going to get picked up for the bank robbery?"

Just as Lyle is getting ready to answer my question, he looks up. "Well, speak of the devil," he says pointing across the room at Roxy who's making her way toward us, maybe not dressed to the nines but looking pretty damn good.

I stand up and pull out a chair for her. "Glad you came, Roxy. You look great. How you feeling? Can I get you something?"

"No, thanks. I'm OK, Nick. I just want to get this over with."

"I was just asking Lyle about the charges when you walked in. So what about them, Lyle?"

Lyle rubs his earlobe with his left index finger and thumb while taking a long drink of his Jack and Coke from the glass in his right hand. With a stoic look on his face he turns to Roxy. "The prosecutor here talked to the District Attorney in L.A. and I'm afraid I'm going to have to place you. . .under the influence of Mr. Jack Daniels. Jimmy! Get the lady a Jack and Coke," Lyle says barely cracking a grin.

"Lyle, you son of a bitch," I say throwing one arm around a stunned Roxy.

Lyle laughs and slaps the table, then turns serious. "The charges have been dropped, Roxy. In light of the circumstances and since you haven't been in any trouble over the last ten years they agreed to abide by the statute of limitations which have run out."

Roxy reaches across the table to hug Lyle. "Oh, my God," she says her eyes filling with tears. "I can't believe it. I'm free. I'm free! Oh, Lyle, I could kiss you."

"A handshake will be just fine, honey."

"I'll take you up on that kiss," a voice says walking up behind Roxy.

Roxy's face lights up and she jumps from her chair. There stands Pence, arms outstretched.

"Oh, my God. . .Pence! What are you doing here?" Pence wraps his arms around Roxy in a warm embrace before uttering a word.

"As soon as I heard about the kidnapping and saw your face all over the news I got on a private jet to Vegas. When I saw Nick's name I remembered he was helping you, so I tracked him down after I landed and gave him a call. Told him I wanted to surprise you. And here I am."

Roxy is beaming. Her nervous and fearful demeanor replaced by a contagious, ear to ear smile.

"Damn, girlfriend, you look beautiful," says Alice. "And very, very happy."

"I can't believe this," says Roxy still hugging Pence. "This might be the best day of my life. I'm a free woman, thanks to all of you. And Pence. . .well, I'm speechless. I just wish Kate was here."

"You'll see her soon," I say. I sit back and take it all in, watching Roxy transform right in front of me. Her release from the past is an exhilarating thing to see and her hope for the future is inspiring. I'm very happy for her and I understand—completely.

Epilogue

Six months later in Rio de Janeiro

Brazilian news organizations are reporting that another transgender woman was found murdered early Friday morning when her mutilated body was discovered in a dumpster in the North Zone of Rio. She is the fifth victim in the past three months and had the same note attached to her as the previous four. The note quotes a bible passage and was signed, *Leviticus.*

ACKNOWLEDGEMENTS

would like to offer my heartfelt gratitude to all those who have helped me get this book started, provided nudging and nagging and support along the way, and then helped me eventually kick it over the goal line.

I want to thank my two writing groups, The Laguna Beach Advanced Writers Group and The Third Street Writers Group, for their encouragement as well as critiques. Additionally, I want to express my appreciation to author, poet and Assistant Professor of Creative Writing at Saddleback College, Brett Garcia Myhren for challenging me and providing a completely fresh perspective on my writing.

A very special thank you to former Orange County Police Crime Lab Director Larry Ragle and his wife Nina for their early read and support of my book as well as some critical feedback and direction.

I want to acknowledge the great assistance given to me by my writing friends and personal friends who generously were willing to read first drafts, second drafts, final drafts and final-final drafts. My thanks to: Amy Dechary, Sally Eastwood, Susan Jacobs, Victoria Kertz, Sandra Monahan, Rina Palumbo, Tom Saltbush, Ed Shaw, Vana Vernon and Amy Yoder. Also thanks to my novelist friends Suzanne Redfearn and Kim Barnes for your professional perspective both on writing and the business of writing. And to Christine Fugate, journalist, author and teacher, who pushed me to turn her writing class short story assignment into a book

A special thanks to lifelong friend, poet Robert Wrigley.

Finally, thanks to all the various journalists whose reporting on the cruel and illegal discrimination of the transgender community caught my eye and to those in that community who so graciously answered my questions and helped raise my own awareness.

"Be who you are and say what you feel, because those who mind don't matter and those who matter don't mind."

- Dr. Seuss

A Note to the Reader

I hope that you enjoyed reading Duality. There is no greater honor for a writer than to know that his or her work was enjoyed by the reader. And if you enjoyed Duality, please tell others and consider posting a review online, for there is no greater support you can give a debut author than your word-of-mouth recommendation.

Please visit me on Facebook as Dennis Lockwood.

About the Author

D. M. Lockwood has been a musician, business executive, counselor, financial consultant, songwriter and lawn bowler.

He grew up in a small town in southern Illinois and now lives in Laguna Beach, California with his wife, Pat. His novel *Duality* is the first in a series of Nick Ross crime stories. His next thriller is expected out in late 2017.

www.ingramcontent.com/pod-product-compliance
Lightning Source LLC
Chambersburg PA
CBHW020528110726
47899CB00004B/1299